DARK MAFIA HEIR

ENEMIES TO LOVERS FORCED MARRIAGE ROMANCE

MAFIA VOWS
BOOK 3

KAYLA MASON

Copyright © 2025 by Kayla Mason

All rights reserved.

No part of this book may be reproduced in any form or by any electronic or mechanical means, including information storage and retrieval systems, without written permission from the author, except for the use of brief quotations in a book review.

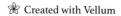 Created with Vellum

1

VIVIENNE

The man sitting across the club has his dark eyes pinned on me. He's swirling a glass of whiskey in one hand while giving me a predatory smile that sends a shiver down my spine.

I'm celebrating my twenty-first birthday with my sister at De Angelo, one of the biggest Italian clubs in New York. My papa said today is the day I transition into full adulthood, which could mean a lot of things.

For girls outside the mafia, it might mean they've finally grown up to earn their freedom. But it's different for girls in my world. For us, becoming twenty-one only means we're way past the age to be traded off like breeding mares.

The man's smile turns into a smirk as he signals for me to come closer.

I cringe, almost rolling my eyes. Does he think I am a stripper or something? Whatever, I don't care. He gives me the ick.

I turn around to face my little sister, who's vibrating with the music and flipping her hair. Honestly, I can't tell if she's excited or just drunk from all the drinks she's had—which is only a few shots, by the way.

Harper is nothing like me. I'm a party animal, and my sister is the ladylike one—the one with good grades who makes our father proud. And she's pretty, just like our mother.

The only thing we have in common is our father's emerald eyes. I look more like our mother with my straight red hair.

I poke my sister's ribs to get her attention, and she shudders. "Are you okay?"

She stops flipping her hair and raises her head to look at me. Her emerald eyes crinkle under flickering neon lights, and she has the wildest smile plastered on her face. "I am. This is so fun."

I chuckle as I hold her hand and join in her dance. The bass thumps through my veins, syncing with the pounding in my ears as I let the music take over. I'm not thinking about anything except the rhythm, how it moves through my body, the way it makes me feel alive.

But more than the music, I am glad Harper is having some fun at last. "Come on, Harp! Don't hold back!" I shout over the music, grabbing her hand and pulling her closer to the center of the dance floor.

We're both so lost in the noise around us that I don't notice the man from earlier striding toward me until he wraps his arm around my waist.

I jerk, repulsed by his touch, as I turn around to face him with a frown.

The asshole has the nerve to smile. "I see you girls are having fun," he says. "I want in, and maybe we can go somewhere else from here."

I tuck Harper behind me and square my shoulders. We

snuck out tonight and there's no bodyguard here with us. A stupid decision I made in the heat of the moment—a decision I'm now regretting. Papa will be so mad if he finds out I put Harper in danger.

"The only place you'll be going from here is your grave if you lay your hands on me again." I tilt my chin, looking at him straight in the eyes, and ignoring the way my heart is pounding against my ribcage with fear.

"Feisty." He pulls on his lower lip, eyes glinting with irritating lust under the flashing strobe lights. "I like it. I like you."

I give him a once-over, at least making a feeble effort to assess him. His short, dark hair is in an unattractive mess, his nails have dirt under them, like he works on engines at a car shop, and, worse, he smells bad.

Imitating Papa's intimidating glare, I stand my ground and square my chin, hoping this loser gets the hint. "But I don't like you. Scram, Jerkface. I'm sure you'll find someone else to have fun with."

The wry smile melts off his face like heated wax rolling down a candle, and the real ugliness inside him is unmasked. Jerkface grabs my wrist, his fingers curling around my skin so tight, I know it'll leave a mark as bright as a ruby bracelet. Snarling, he yanks me forward, momentarily cutting the breath from my lungs. I stagger. I didn't see that one coming.

"Vi!"

"Stay back, Harper." I wave her away, not wanting her even an inch close to this madman. I *am* scared, terrified, in fact. My heart is running a marathon inside my chest, and my head is pounding.

But I'd rather fight until I draw my last breath than allow this man even to touch a hair on my sister's head. She's staring at me, lips quivering, fingers fidgeting helplessly, and eyes tearing up quickly. And I know, if I don't do something soon, Harper will call Papa. And then all hell would truly break loose.

"I'm warning you for the last time: Let me go, or else—"

"Or else what?"

When his dirty finger touches my lips, my skin crawls, and a wave of nausea hits me at once. I want to puke and scrub off every trace of this man's hand on my skin.

The world around us is still in crazy motion. It's ridiculously loud. Neon and stage lights blink in rhythm to the ongoing beat while they jump, dance, and sing in unison to "Be My Lover."

The DJ cranks up the vocals, and the energy spikes to the roof. Jerkface pulls me closer, snaking his lean arm around my waist, while he peers into my eyes like he wants to steal my soul.

"Thinking of different ways you could scream, baby doll?" I hold my breath while his finger goes down my neck. His breath smells like citrus and rum, and it stirs the queasiness in my belly. "No one's going to hear you."

He is right, except I manage to release a supersonic scream; the party animals in this hall are most likely deaf. In a flash, an idea hits me, a sneaky strategy I'd seen Papa's men use during sparring sessions. All I have to do is distract him and make a run for it with Harper.

"Fine." His brow twitches, saying he doesn't understand. "Let me go, and I'll go with you wherever you want without making a fuss."

A frown crosses his lips. "That easily? All of a sudden, after you asked me to leave?"

I try to keep my expression neutral and my tone resigned to make him believe I sincerely agree with him.

"Yes, because I am not stupid. I can see you are right; struggling is going to do no good in this noisy environment. So, let me go, and I'll go with you."

Doubtfully, he looks at me, and I hold my breath, praying this tactic works—that he actually falls for it and releases his hand from my waist, giving me the opportunity I need.

Five seconds pass—*because my brain can't stop counting how long it'll take until freedom finally comes*—and, after watching me closely like a hungry predator, he finally shrugs and drops his arm.

Perfect.

Elation and adrenaline had to be the best combination of emotion and energy that a human could experience, because that powerful combo flows through my veins, fueling my burning desire to put a fist in the man's face, like dried sticks feeding a fire.

I don't hesitate. I don't pause. I curl my fist as tightly as I learned from Dabi, one of Papa's men, and swing my arm, aiming directly at Jerkface's jaw.

Screaming, Jerkface falls to the floor on his side, cursing, whimpering, and holding the side of his face.

But I am startled because my fist still hangs in the air. I didn't touch him.

"That was a friendly warning."

The rich, smooth, resonant baritone from beside me ignites a fire in my core, its vibrations coursing through me, spreading molten heat that tingles all the way down to my toes, and I turn around, only to be blown away by a sight too surreal to be true—like a perfect stranger from one of Alisha Rai's novels.

To top it off, he checks off all the other boxes: tall, dark-haired, and stunningly handsome. The type of handsome that makes you forget to look out for other characteristics of their personality. The type of handsome that makes a woman *feel* like a woman. She just wants to be in his arms, touch the hard lines of his muscles, and sleep on his chest. That type of handsome is this stranger standing beside me, glaring at Jerkface with cold, dark eyes that hold promises of death.

He slides his hand—the same one that sent the madman crumpling to the ground—into one of his black dress pants pockets and raises a brow.

"What are you waiting for? Get out."

Jerkface doesn't waste another second. Without another word, he hops to his feet, clutching his bleeding mouth as he scurries away without looking back.

My hand drops to my side as Harper and I stare at this *hero* in awe. Even though I am the only one between us who appears grateful to the stranger for literally swooping in to save the day. Harper looks terrified, probably still deciding whether to call Papa.

Slowly, I muster a small smile at the stranger, who still has his eyes trained on the shadow of my harasser.

"Thank you..." My words hang in the air while I sweep my gaze over this man's striking features. Firm, bow-shaped mouth, chiseled jawline, eyes that don't just look but see, and a classic fifties pompadour haircut. The stranger appears young, but his aura, the way his shoulders stand stiff, the swiftness of his punch, the hard lines at the corners of his eyes... everything about him oozes years of experience navigating this crazy world.

Regardless, I am not deterred. Older man or not, he rescued me from the snares of that idiot. So, he deserves my gratitude. I try again.

"Thank you, sir."

That startles him. A deep, *sexy* chuckle rumbles at the back of his throat, and with a smoothness that makes me fall even harder, he turns and faces me with a dazzling smile. Dark eyes, the color of molten chocolate, lock onto mine, assessing every inch of my body, from my bare shoulders to the length of my mini pink slip dress, sending a tingle across my skin. I am feeling light-headed, and I'm not sure if it's because of the few drinks I had or the effect of this man not-so-subtly checking me out.

My knees wobble, and I clear my throat. *Damn.*

"Sir?"

I didn't take note of it before, but now, as I listen keenly, I hear an accent. And the best way I can describe it is as a tempting roll of the tongue—reminiscent of olive oil drizzled over fresh bread, with his words stretching long and smooth, like melted mozzarella. My ears itch to hear more of it. I beam back, easily forgetting what brought him here in the first place.

"Is it strange to be called that?"

A playful glint crosses his eyes, like it's fun to indulge me.

"No." He shakes his head, still giving me that dark, delicious, intense look that swallows up the noise around us and makes me feel like I'm the only one in the room. "I'd prefer if you called me by my name."

I suddenly remember that I'm not the only one in the room—Harper is here, too. My eyes find hers, and I try to snap out of whatever spell this man has me in.

"I'm sorry, but we have to go."

He looks over his shoulder and smiles at Harper. "Don't you think I should buy your sister a drink? That man tried to ruin your night, but I can make up for it."

Harper does not look too convinced. Her eyes tell me

she is uncomfortable and wants to leave, but his charm seems to have worked on her, too, because she rubs her arm and nods. "Sure. You did help us, so I guess one drink is not too much to ask for."

"*Grazie.*" *Thank you.*

And my stomach drops with a warm sensation, as if everything suddenly clicked into place. It makes so much sense, that poise, the insane level of unearthly beauty, and the accent.

He's Italian.

By the time I snap back to the present moment, he's telling Harper something about taking me to the bar across the street because the drinks there taste better. He extends the invite, but Harper doesn't want to join in. He directs her to stay in his VIP section because it's safer there and advises her to keep her phone close.

He's a stranger, and we should not trust strangers, but I can't help the tug in my chest as I watch their interaction and his gentleness with my sister.

Harper gives me a cautionary glance, one with a message: *Don't hesitate to scream or call if you have to.*

I nod. Message received and sent back.

Satisfied, she clutches her purse and walks away with a bodyguard we hadn't even noticed before, leaving me and the perfect stranger alone.

"She's safe, don't worry." He turns back to me and extends his arm. "Shall we?"

The music pounds through my chest, a deep bass that makes the floor vibrate beneath my feet, although I think my heart is beating for some other reason.

Shyly, I blush and hook my arm through his, allowing him to lead us through the sea of gyrating bodies and smooching partners. His tall frame, standing out like a six-foot-three athlete, cuts through the masses like a knife, and I follow close behind, my fingers slipping into his without thinking.

We move toward the back of the club, away from the pulsing lights and sweat-slick air, to the back door with the neon exit sign gleaming atop. The heavy door creaks as he shoves it open, and a rush of cool night air hits me, sharp and refreshing against my flushed skin.

I laugh quietly when he closes the door, blocking the thrum of the club, and ushers us into the narrow alley, dimly lit by flickering streetlamps at the far end. It's quieter out here, but my heart's still racing, the adrenaline from the night pumping through my veins.

I brush my hair behind my ears. "This is crazy." I smile up at him. "I don't even know your name, and we're in an alley."

Mirth flashes through his eyes, but he just stands there in all his intimidating glory, with his hands tucked into his pockets. He looks sharper than a knife, wearing a black button-down tailored to his broad chest.

"Antonio." His shoulders nudge toward the bar at the other end of the street. "And I really did bring you out to get a drink across the street."

Something crackles in the air between us, thick and suffocating, like static before a storm, and it pulses between us with every glance, every breath. It's a heat that crawls across my skin, shrinking the space between us, until it's just the two of us, locked in this silent, unspoken thing.

I swallow to find my voice. "But?"

There's a dark, sharp flicker behind his eyes, somehow daring me to look away, but drawing me in at the same time. When he takes steps toward me, I take a step back.

He moves again, and I move back, slamming into a wall

behind me. My pulse quickens, a steady thrum in my chest that echoes this tension cracking between us.

The corner of his lips curves upwards, and I can tell he's enjoying this. I square my chin, narrowing my eyes with a feigned defiance. "The bar is across the street. Why aren't we moving?"

He's too close, not close enough, and every nerve in my body screams for more, for less, for something to break.

"Because, what's crazy is that I don't even know your name, and I feel a crazy urge to kiss you senseless, until one of us gasps for air."

Damn. That didn't just leave his mouth. Did it?

My breathing falters as the heat flares higher, the tension pulling tighter like a thin rope about to snap, and I know he feels it, too. It's in the way he's standing, just barely holding himself back, as if one wrong word, one wrong move, and we'd be crossing a line we can't come back from.

Nervously and on impulse, I blurt, "Vivienne. And it's my birthday today."

Hearing that seems to snap something inside him because his hands leave his pockets and find solace on my cheek, like he needed the slightest excuse to touch me. They are big and warm; I can't help but lean in.

"I should give you a gift then."

Gently, his fingers trace the curve of my mouth, and the loud thrashing of my heart in my ears makes it hard to think or breathe. I should say no. I should turn on my heels and head back inside, grab my sister, and leave without looking back at this handsome Italian stranger.

This is escalating very fast, but I can't bring myself to move from this spot. My body calls to his own; a wild, irrational yearning to feel the weight of the man on me, to know what it feels like to be suffocated by his strength. I want—

no, crave—every inch of him. Every muscle, every taste of him.

He lowers his lips to mine, and my heart flutters when the dim streetlight casts a warm glow on his olive skin.

"*Buon Compleanno*, Vivienne." *Happy Birthday.*

When his mouth closes on mine, fireworks explode in my head. I grip his shirt, my fingers curling into the crisp fabric to steady myself. He cradles my face and moves against me like he fears I'll break. I moan into his hot mouth, tugging on his shirt. I don't want the restraint. I want him to unleash. For a moment, it's just us, lost in a bubble of wild passion with no cares or worries.

Then, a crack splits the air.

I recognize the sound too well.

Gunshot.

I freeze, breaking our kiss as I pull away from him, the sound ringing in my ears. Panic replaces passion, fast and hot, and my mind snaps back to reality.

My sister is inside.

"Harper!"

2

ANTONIO

Vivienne falls to her knees once we get to my VIP section, pulling her sister, who crouches low by the table, into a hug.

"Harper," she whimpers behind me. "Are you okay? Any injuries? I'm sorry I left you alone."

"None, Vi. I'm fine. I'm glad you didn't get hurt, either."

My breath steadies, knowing her sister is not hurt, and my hand moves instinctively to my side, gripping the cold steel of my gun. The sisters huddle close to me, and Vivienne's eyes flicker from the weapon between my belt and back to my face. Her eyes grow wide but are trusting, knowing I won't let anything happen to them.

"Ready?" I ask, and she nods.

The club is in chaos. Lights flash in red and blue, pulsing with a beat no one seems to hear anymore. People are screaming, pushing, shoving to get out. Gunfire cracks through the air—sharp, fucking loud, and cutting through everything else. I don't flinch. They fall behind me, and I keep moving, fast but calm. I shove someone out of our way, then pull the sisters even closer to me. Vivienne's breathing is rapid. I glance at her once. Her eyes are teary, but she nods. They're good.

A bullet whizzes past, shattering glass, and people scream louder. In one swift motion, I pull out my gun, aim, not wasting a second, and fire back at the masked attacker. Harper shrieks beside me as the shot rips through the chaos. I push forward, cutting through the panicked crowd. The front exit is just ahead. I can see the throng of people pushing out.

"Stay close," I growl.

When we get close, I lift my gun in the air and fire. People shriek, clearing a path for us until the cool night air hits our faces. Safety. Glancing around, I scan for my car. I see it parked a few steps away, as well as a dozen men surrounding the perimeter. I spot Luca's broad back and shiny buzzcut, and we keep moving until we get close enough.

"Where's Lorenzo?"

Luca's eyes narrow suspiciously at the girls while he responds. "The boss wants to know who's involved. He sent him to catch one of these fleabags. So, he's coming."

"*Portali a casa.*" I guide them forward. *Take them home.*

Luca's eyes hold questions, but he doesn't say a word. He opens the door, and they scramble in with not enough speed.

"*Adesso.*"

He needs to move, now. I keep my stance firm, my eyes trained on every person trooping out from the club. The driver's door slams, the engine revs, and headlights flash. Luca tips his forehead with two fingers before driving off, but my eyes stay on Vivienne until they're out of sight.

"Nio!"

I turn around to see Lorenzo emerging from the back of the alley. With his hair hanging loosely from the bun on his head, the younger man lazily drags an unmasked man across the dirty pavement.

We need answers, and maybe this man will be able to provide us with one.

When he gets close, he flashes a cocky smirk, and the man gasps as Lorenzo hauls him forward. Blood smeared across his jaw, the panic is evident in his eyes now. He's struggling, but Lorenzo keeps his grip firm. He knows what's coming. He should.

"Is this the fleabag?"

"*Si.*" Yes. "I caught him trying to escape with a few others. Turns out, this one can't run very fast."

"You put two fucking bullets in my leg, you psycho!" The man's screams echo in the now almost empty road. Police sirens wail from a far distance, but I know we'll be out of here before they arrive.

"Count yourself lucky that the big boss wants you alive —otherwise, you'd have more than two bullets in your fucking leg, *stronzo*."

I step closer, my shadow falling over the man like a storm cloud. If I allow their banter to prolong for a minute more, Lorenzo is more likely to lose his shit and beat the crap out of him, regardless of Dante's request. He's always been the one with the shortest fuse between himself and Luca.

Gently, I nudge the man's feet with my shoes to get his attention. Blazing, panicked eyes snap to mine.

"What's your name?"

Angrily, he glares, hissing through gritted teeth. "Fuck you!"

Lorenzo lunges, twisting his body, and the heel of his shoes slams into the man's head. His bun falls loose, and all the hair on his head flies when he attacks. "How fucking dare you? *Bastardo...*" He kicks him. "*Puttana... testa di merda...*" Scoundrel... shithead.

Cursing, he kicks him again and again. And again.

"Lorenzo!"

He swears and brushes his hair behind his ears, blinking back the bloodlust rage in his eyes before backing away from the battered man.

More blood stains the pavement, and the man curls into a fetal position, muttering incoherently to himself.

"Let's try again, shall we? What's your name?"

Lorenzo picks him up by the shoulder, lifting him to a kneeling position to face me. "Speak."

Giving Lorenzo a sidelong glare, he spits thick, bloody saliva onto the pavement. "Hayes."

Shaking his head, he walks up to me with a bitter chuckle and shrugs doubtfully. "That's the vaguest shit I've ever heard."

"It's just his name. He'll tell us more." I smile at the man and point my gun at his temple. "Won't you, Hayes?"

"You're wasting your time on me, Antonio Mancini. Tell your boss I'm not saying shit."

Before another word escapes my lips, Hayes twists to the side—quick, too quick. His hand darts to his pocket, and in an instant, there's a flash of green: a leaf—small, thin, but unmistakable even in this dim light. Poison.

Lorenzo and I lunge at the same time, but it's too late. His jaw snaps shut, crushing the leaf between his teeth, and he swallows. His eyes lock onto mine, defiant and desperate all at once.

No scream. No curses. No plea. Just silence as his body

begins to seize, the toxin working fast. Then, he drops to the floor, the light dead in his eyes.

"I should have just killed him." Disgusted, Lorenzo spits and kicks the corpse in annoyance. "Shit. He proved to be useless, after all."

I roll my eyes, and we start walking toward his car parked on the curb. "I blame your fucking temper. Maybe if you'd invited him out to dinner instead of putting two bullets in his legs, he'd have told you everything you needed to know and offered even more?"

He laughs, running his fingers through his hair, before we hop in. "I'm sorry. Next time, I'll think of asking a fleeing culprit out to dinner, before putting bullets in his legs to stop him from escaping."

Narrowing my eyes at him, I face the road ahead when the engine starts. Everyone knows Lorenzo can be a thorn in the side, but his rash, irrational methods always work. That is, until today.

It doesn't matter. Hayes' death won't hinder us from finding out who launched the attack. Dante always gets what he wants, when he wants it.

My phone vibrates, and I take it out of my suit and put it on speaker.

"What?"

"Nio?" I glance at the screen again. The caller ID says Dario, but it's not Dario's voice. "Giovanni? Where the fuck is Dario? Why are you with his phone?"

There is only one reason someone else would handle Dario's phone, and that was during emergencies.

Giovanni's voice is quiet and hard, but I feel the weight of his words sink down on my shoulders like a ton of bricks after he says, "Dante's dead. Dario is with Doctor Matteo, trying to sort shit out."

Lorenzo's fingers freeze on the wheel, and he hastily swerves to a corner, stepping on the brakes.

Dante's dead.

The big boss himself is dead, and I sure as hell know he didn't have a fucking accident or fall ill overnight. Blinding rage hits me hard, and my lungs constrict until the air in them burns.

"What the fuck happened and when?"

"Almost an hour ago, right after we got a call about the attack on the club. It was a direct hit. He was lured out to a bay and shot. Six times."

The air in my lungs turned to flames, threatening to consume everything in its path until I find the person responsible.

Dante wasn't the best person. His heart was as dark as the evil that plagued the world, and he had many sins he was yet to atone for. Still, he took me in when nobody else did, trained me, made me the man I am today. He taught me all I know now, and for the longest time, I was indebted to him.

Without Dante, there'd be no Antonio Mancini.

No Lorenzo.

No Luca.

I clutch the phone with a death grip, gritting my teeth while blood pounds in my ears. "Are there any leads?"

"The last person he was in contact with was Peter Cole."

Just then, my phone screen lights up with a text message from Luca. I assume he's telling me what I already know about Dante being dead, so I ignore it. Giovanni is still talking about Dante's communication with Peter occurring about two hours before the hit, when another text comes in.

"Hold on, Giovanni."

Hastily, I open the messages to type a quick response,

and my heart sinks to the bottom of my chest when I read the last one.

Luca: Nio...

Luca: Fuck, Nio, this is urgent.

Luca: Those girls... the sisters... they're Peter Cole's daughters.

3

VIVIENNE

Papa's study is eerily quiet, as it usually is. The air is thick and smells like polished wood and old books. But, otherwise, everything else is properly organized, and the surfaces are spick and span. Just the way he likes it.

He is sitting across the desk, his head bowed and his face buried deep in the pages of an encyclopedia. Deep down, I know he did not summon me to share knowledge.

Uncomfortably, I drag the frayed hem of my skirt and fiddle with my fingers as he flips through yet another page, wondering when he'll finally break the silence.

After a few more minutes, more pages rustle before he clears his throat and slams the book shut with an unnecessarily loud thud. He brings his head up, and I see the white strands lined neatly between his chestnut-brown hair.

"Vivienne."

I drag the hem of my skirt again, suddenly feeling the nerves wrack. He called me by my full name. Not Vivi or the stubborn one. Just Vivienne. Knowing Papa, that means serious business.

He raises a brow as he waits for a response.

"Yes, sir."

"You turned twenty-one yesterday, did you not?"

The nerves are rattling now, causing sudden panic to spread through my entire being, because I know what this is… this moment between Papa and me.

Turning twenty-one means I have come of age. And like every other girl in this cursed mafia, I am now expected to fulfill my duty to our family.

"Did you not, Vivienne?"

Sometimes, in times like this, I hate how unnaturally calm Papa poses to be. I have seen him in action, angry and throwing all the things around him. But now, it is just him, in his brown Armani suit, with a faraway look he always has in his eyes when he talks to me, like he can't stand looking at me.

"I did, Papa."

"Good." He smiles for a brief moment and caresses the edges of his encyclopedia. "Then, you know you have come of age to do greater things, yes?"

"Greater things for whom?" I blurt before I can stop myself. But since it's out, I don't bother stopping the flow.

He doesn't answer my question; he just shakes his head with that annoying smile and drums his finger on the desk.

"Always the stubborn one, Vivienne. Soon enough, you'll understand that this is the life you've been born into, and there is no escaping it."

I want to scream at his smug face that I am well aware that I was born into a life of bondage, where everyone else gets to dictate what happens in my life, except me. But I don't scream. If I do, he might smack me across the face with that big book—just to force his knowledge upon me. Instead, I keep quiet.

That's always the best action with him, anyway. Allow him to say all he wants to, nod, and then leave.

After he doesn't say another word, I know he's done planting the seed. He'll just schedule another meeting to water it, until the seed grows into a tree.

I nod, stand up, and then leave.

"But he didn't say anything."

"He didn't have to." I cut a piece of buttered croissant and put it in my mouth. The butter melts in my mouth, but I don't taste it. "The meaning was clearly there. He's preparing my mind for the idea of marriage. Alyssa was sold off—married to that weirdo, Milano—when she turned twenty-one."

Harper laughs and takes a bite of her muffin. "Papa's not going to sell you off—or marry you off to a weirdo."

Rolling my eyes, I huff. Like father, like daughter, sort of. It's like they were joined at the hip. He always takes it easy with her, and she always stands up for him.

"Doesn't mean I won't end up getting married against my wishes."

She shrugs, and we continue eating in silence.

The café is warm, the scent of coffee and baked bread wrapping around me like a blanket. Harper, who's seated across from me, stirs her cappuccino, her spoon clinking against the ceramic mug in a steady rhythm. She starts talking about something—probably something related to Papa—but my mind keeps drifting back to last night.

The moment before the gunshot.

Antonio.

I can still feel his lips against mine, the gentle but hard

way he kissed, like he was pulling something out of me. There was something electric about it, something that lingered long after that unsmiling man drove us away from the chaos.

"You're not listening, are you?" Harper's voice snaps me back, and I blink at her, realizing my hand hangs mid-air with a piece of croissant partly bitten off.

My chest flutters, and I drop the croissant, gingerly dusting off my fingers.

"Sorry," I mumble, glancing around before leaning in a little closer. "I was thinking about last night... the guy."

Her eyebrows shoot up. "The savior?" she asks. That was what we nicknamed him last night.

I nod and reply, "Him. Antonio."

Just saying his name out loud gives me the shivers. Smiling, I touch my lips.

Harper shakes her head. She doesn't agree. "Vi, come on. He looked dangerous."

I didn't expect her to, but seeing her express it makes me want to keep my excitement to myself. "How? To me, he looked like every normal millennial man. He had good composure, great character, and—"

"He pulled out a gun from thin air," she interrupts with wide eyes.

"Correction: He pulled the gun out from between his belt. Not thin air. And so what? Papa has a room full of guns and some other things we don't even know."

"That's all the more reason you should be careful. Any man who has a gun tucked between his clothes should not be trusted."

It stings when she says that, and I don't hesitate to release that bitterness. "But you trust Papa with your life."

She stops stirring her cappuccino, and her shoulders

sag. I don't have to look at her to know she's looking at me soberly. "Vi, you know what I mean."

I don't want us to dwell much on Papa, so I shrug, swirling the foam in my coffee with a half-smile. "I don't know; there was something about him. But it's not like I'll see him again."

"Don't rule out the possibility of running into him again. The way he showed up yesterday, he could be out there, positioned to show up out of the blue again to come to your rescue. If he does, just remember that he looks like the kind that shows up, messes with your head, and then disappears."

Her tone is sharp, protective. Most times, she's always like this, trying to save me from bad decisions. I appreciate it, but sometimes, I just want to live a little.

I open my mouth to defend him—though I'm not even sure what I'd say—when I suddenly get this feeling. It creeps up my spine like a shiver, only colder and heavier. My eyes flick around the room, scanning the faces. The couple in the corner, the guy at the counter ordering a pastry, the barista cleaning up... everything looks normal, but that sense of being watched clings to me.

"Vi?" Harper notices my shift. "What's wrong?"

I don't answer right away, still looking, still feeling it. I might be paranoid, but...

"I don't know," I whisper, pulling my bag onto my shoulder. "Come on, I think we should go."

4

ANTONIO

Vivienne knows I'm watching her. She can't see me, but I'm sure she can feel me staring at her from the driveway across the café. It's obvious from the way she keeps looking around anxiously.

I wonder if her pulse is racing as she scans the place, or if her blood is whooshing in her ears from nerves. It's not a good feeling to know someone is watching you, and it's even worse when you have no idea who it is.

A smile tugs at my lips—Peter Cole doesn't know what's coming. I can't wait to savor his shock when he learns I'm hunting his precious daughter.

"Nio, I don't think it's a good idea for us to mess with Peter Cole's daughter," Luca says, his face marred with concern. "This could start a war."

He's right. Messing with Vivienne could start a war, but I don't give a shit. Not when Dante is about to become food for bugs underground. Not when my mentor was taken from me in such a cruel way.

I'll start a war... Scratch that! I'll turn the whole fucking world upside down if it gets me the answers I need—and the only way to do that is through Peter Cole.

Vivienne picks up her bag and stands. She urges her sister to do the same, and as she rummages through her bag, her red hair cascades over her face. She leans over the table, and my dick twitches at the shape of her ass.

Fuck, that girl is hot in a way that can make a man beg on his knees. I've been with a lot of women, but something about her makes her irresistible. It's not just her beauty, but her fierceness and protectiveness.

If she weren't Peter Cole's daughter, she could have meant something more to me—someone dear. Not that I'd fall in love with her, but I'd keep her all to myself.

Even now, despite knowing who she is, I'm tempted to make her mine. Besides my thirst for revenge, it'll be fun to see Peter's face when he discovers that his little girl warms my bed and sucks my cock.

"Dante wouldn't have wanted this," Luca says. Those words are enough to make me snap my head in his direction.

"Dante is dead. What he would've wanted does not matter." My insides flare with rage. "What matters is that I punish those who stole his life from him. Do you understand?"

Luca hesitates, but he finally nods. "How are we going to do that? Dante won't just talk because you want him to."

I smirk as Vivienne and her sister walk out of the café. Vivienne suddenly stops walking and turns around.

Her emerald eyes meet mine, sparkling under the afternoon sun with so much life that I almost want to drain them of every drop, slowly, until only darkness remains.

For a moment, I want to think she's seen me, but the

tinted windows do not give me the chance to be that delusional.

She stares at my car for a moment longer before her sister, Harper, grabs her hand and pulls her along with her.

"Oh, trust me—there's a way to make him talk," I drawl with amusement.

Luca shakes his head. "Please tell me it is not what I'm thinking, Nio."

I chuckle sardonically at the surprise on his face. For someone who tortures men to death while smiling in their faces, Luca is such a soft guy.

He'd be better off selling cotton candy at Disney or wearing Barney costumes if he wasn't so good at shooting a gun.

It's not that he's a good guy. For most of us, women and children are where we draw the line. While I would like to continue being that perfect gentleman who wouldn't drag a woman into mafia business, I've gone past the point of giving a shit.

My phone buzzes, and my alarm goes off—it's almost time for Dante's funeral. My chest tightens with an ache I haven't felt since I lost my family.

It's the feeling of losing someone you care about, and it fuels me with so much hate and rage that nothing else matters.

The car roars beneath me as I turn on the engine and flash a mirthless smile at Luca. "If what you're thinking is as dark and twisted as the voices in my head, then you're right."

I've always hated funerals. The gloomy faces and red-rimmed eyes are something that makes me uncomfortable.

And there is a little bit of jealousy at the fact that people get to bury their loved ones—something I never had the chance to do since I became homeless after my parents and younger brother were murdered.

I was just seventeen then. Too young and afraid to protect my family. I'd run the night they were killed, and I lived on the streets for a while before Dante found me and brought me home.

He taught me everything I know, from how to shoot a gun to how to be ruthless and cold-blooded.

The only thing he'd not taught me was how to move on when he was no longer here. He was the last family I had left, and they took him from me.

Dry leaves rustle under my feet as I walk toward the group of people gathered in one part of the cemetery. From a distance, I can see Dante's white coffin waiting to be lowered to the ground.

I've killed more people than I can count, but this hits different in a way that makes my chest hurt. I still can't believe I won't get his annoying calls or hear him nag when I drink his favorite whiskey.

It feels surreal.

I stop before the priest and bow my head as he prays for Dante's soul. Birds chirp in the distance, and any ordinary person might cherish the scent of flowers and earth.

But not me. All I can smell is the stench of formaldehyde and rotten corpses. This place reeks of death, and it makes me nauseous.

The prayers are over after what feels like an eternity, and Dante is lowered to the ground. I take a fistful of sand and toss it into the grave, vowing to exact revenge on whoever is responsible for his death.

My mind drifts back to Vivienne. She'll be the perfect tool for my revenge. I'll use her while breaking her bit by bit until Peter goes on his knees to beg me to return his little girl.

After the funeral, we retreat to Dante's house, and I go upstairs to greet his wife, Mariana.

She's sitting on the dresser in her room, and my jaw clenches when I see the bitter smile on her face and the tears trailing down her cheeks.

Mariana looks like she's aged twenty years in just two days. Her fair skin is now pale, her eyes deep in their sockets, and she looks so much thinner.

Dante and Mariana didn't have any children together, but they raised me like I was theirs. Everything I have now, I owe it to them.

I knock gently on the door so as not to startle her.

She flinches, quickly wiping away her tears and turning to face me with a forced smile. "Antonio." Her voice is shaky. "You're here."

"*Si.*" Yes. I enter, walk inside the room, and lean against the vanity table. "You weren't at the funeral."

She nods. "I couldn't bear to see them put him in that cold ground. My husband hated the cold—" She chokes on her words and trails off. More tears run down her cheeks despite her struggle to fight them. "I'm sorry."

A numbness creeps through my limbs, as if the weight of the world is weighing me down. I hate to see Mariana this way. Her tears hurt me even more than Dante's death.

I get on one knee in front of her and take her hand, brushing it softly with my thumb. "I will find who did this, and I swear to God, I will avenge Dante. I promise."

She cups my face with trembling hands. "I know you will, child. But you must be careful. I cannot afford to lose you, too."

"You won't. I will come to you the moment it is done." I take the back of her hand and press it to the top of my head. "You must be strong for me, Mariana. I cannot face Dante in heaven if I can't keep you happy."

"I won't die until every one of those bastards does," she assures me. "I won't rest until all our enemies are in their graves."

I turn my head to the door as the sound of footsteps draws nearer.

Lorenzo appears in front of the door, greeting Mariana before shifting his attention to me. "The men are waiting for you, Nio."

I nod and return my attention to Mariana. "I have some things to take care of. We'll have dinner after I finish."

She bobs her head.

I rise to my feet and follow Lorenzo to the living room, where some of the members of the Cosa Nostra are waiting. Dante was the head. Now that he is dead, someone will have to fill his spot.

Rafaelle Vitale is the first to speak. "We have to move on from this, but we must first appoint someone to take Dante's place. I think we all know who it must be."

Luigi Santoro speaks up next. "Dante had no children. There is no one to take his place."

He glares at me, and I glare right back at him. Luigi is like a green snake in a field of green grass. Cunning and conniving with his own selfish interests. His greed will be the death of him soon enough.

"He had a foster son who he wanted to take his place,"

Rafaelle says. "Antonio will be the next leader. There's no better person to take the position."

Some of the members agree with a nod; some don't react at all. Luigi is seething, though. I want to gouge his eyes out and feed them to him for daring to glare at me in that way.

"So, a boy of unknown origins becomes the head of the Cosa Nostra?" Luigi chuckles sardonically. "That won't happen, not while I am alive."

As much as I would like to watch the drama unfold, I have a plan to kickstart it. I don't have the time to stay here and listen to Luigi's nonsense.

"If it can't happen while you're alive, then die," I say, my voice cold and emotionless.

"How old are you, boy?" His chest heaves with anger. "You don't deserve that position, you're—"

Before he can finish, I pull my gun from the holster strapped to my chest and fire twice. The first bullet slams into his chest; the second drives a hole between his eyes. Blood splatters as his body collapses with a thud.

Panic erupts in the room, and the tension reaches a palpable level.

Still holding my gun, I stand and scan the room, daring any of them to speak. "Does anyone else have a problem with me leading the Cosa Nostra?"

No one says a word, but they all shake their heads.

A maniacal smile splits my lips. "Good. Now, let's get to business, shall we?"

5

VIVIENNE

I pull up to the mansion as the steady drum of rain on the windshield drowns out the engine's purr. The wrought-iron gates swing open, as if they'd been waiting for me.

My father's estate looms ahead, bathed in the faint glow of the exterior lights. Normally, the sight of that tall, white building would bring me comfort, but not since that last meeting with my father.

A voice in the back of my mind tells me to accept whatever fate I'm dealt, but I can't accept the idea of being sold off like a commodity.

Harper believes Papa won't trade me off—but she's naïve, trusting him far too much. Papa will do anything for power, even sell us off like property.

The rain intensifies as I step out of the car. Cold droplets soak my hair and run down my cheeks, mingling with the floral perfume I sprayed before leaving school.

I clutch my coat tighter around me, my heels sinking into the gravel with every hurried step to make it inside before I'm completely drenched in the rain.

The mansion stands before me, imposing as ever, but the unfamiliar cars parked in front make my stomach churn with unease. Cars with plate numbers I haven't seen before, and men who look like they would burn the house down in a heartbeat if it came to it. I can sense something is wrong.

I halt midway up the steps. It's too quiet—there aren't any guards in sight.

Papa likes a quiet house, so I don't expect it to be buzzing at this hour, but there should be maids running around and guards doing their thing. Why is there no sign of life aside from the guards outside?

The rain keeps pouring, and the sound now feels ominous, like a warning I can't quite decipher. My hand hovers over the doorknob, and I hesitate, heart racing in my chest for no reason I can explain.

Then I hear it—gunshots. Three rapid, muffled shots from deep inside the house.

My breath catches—I freeze, hand still on the doorknob, as the sound seems to vibrate through me, making my legs buckle. I should run. I should scream. I should call someone, anyone. But I'm frozen with fear.

I swallow hard, my head pounding as adrenaline floods my veins. I force a sharp breath—I can't run. This is my home, and I must ensure that Harper and Papa are okay.

My hand shakes as I push the door open into a dimly lit foyer. The marble floors gleam and the chandelier sways gently in the draft from the open door—but the air inside feels unusually heavy.

Something isn't right. The silence, the gunshot. Something's terribly wrong.

I can't hear anything now. Just the sound of my blood whooshing in my ears, louder than the rain outside. I step forward, my shoes making soft, wet sounds against the polished floor. My father's study is down the hall, where the shots came from.

I don't want to go there. I'm afraid of what I'll find. But I must know what's happening.

I take another step.

The scent of rain mixes with something else. Something coppery.

My stomach twists as nausea creeps up my throat. My instincts are kicking against me, taking another step toward the study, but I force myself to keep moving, one foot in front of the other. I just need to see my papa. To know he's okay. That everyone's okay.

As I approach the study, the door is slightly ajar, light spilling out into the dark hallway. I reach for the handle, my fingers trembling, and push it open.

What I see makes my heart stop.

I see two bodies on the floor—no, not just bodies. Two of Papa's men lie lifeless in a pool of their own blood, their heads riddled with holes. One man's cold brown eyes stare at me, as if trying to see through the void.

My blood turns cold instantly, and a gasp leaves me when I see the gun pressed to my papa's head.

All heads turn on me, but it's only one that catches my attention because I recognize those dark brown eyes instantly. I would recognize that handsome face and sharp jawline even in my dreams.

Standing in front of my father with a gun pressed to his head is the handsome stranger from the club the other night. The same man I considered my hero. The one who'd kept me and Harper safe.

His eyes glint with amusement as they meet mine. "Look who we have here," he muses. "It's darling Vivienne."

"You're..."

"We meet again," he says calmly.

I stagger backward, too stunned for rational thought or words. *He knew who I was*—that phrase plays on a loop in my head.

He's not surprised to see me, which means he knew who I was. He approached me on purpose, and... my eyes sting with tears.

"Vivienne," Papa whispers my name. "Leave this place. Leave. Now."

"Why, Peter? You don't want your precious daughter to witness your execution?" The man laughs manically. He's nothing like the gentleman from the club that night.

It all makes sense now. Him pulling out a gun and all. Harper was right about him, but I'd been too horny to think straight. Even now, as I look at him, all I can think of is the way he kissed me that night.

Damn, I've lost my mind. I'm sick!

"Vivienne, leave!" Papa yells this time.

"The girl stays," the man insists. "I'll put on a good show for her."

My gaze bounces between him and my papa, and a storm of anger rages inside me—one that takes over my entire body and pushes me to do something extremely stupid.

Before I can stop myself, I'm halfway across the room, pounding him repeatedly and screaming, "Leave my father alone, you sick bastard!" My fists slam into his back, chest, and arms—but he doesn't even flinch. It's almost as if I'm hitting him with a tiny feather.

He catches my hand and forces me against the desk, lowering his face to mine. His breath warms my skin as he presses a finger under my jaw—a touch that burns deep, making my body betray me. Even as I rage, I feel my core tighten and my nipples harden.

I close my eyes, begging my body not to act so foolishly. Who gets turned on in front of a dangerous man, with two dead bodies on the floor and her father being held at gunpoint? I really need to see a therapist.

"Open your eyes, *gattina*," he whispers, his voice so dark and husky. His breath is so hot against my skin.

I open my eyes and glare at him, silently willing him to see my loathing. "Don't call me that!" I spit out, "I'm not your kitten, *bastardo*."

He tilts my face to meet his, bringing his lips so dangerously close to mine. "But you will be soon enough."

I try to kick him, but he moves in time, catching my leg and holding it up. He leans in and whispers in my ear, "Easy now, *gattina*. You don't want Daddy dearest to find out what you've been up to, do you?"

I'm boiling with fury, but I know better than to act rashly. The fact that he is even playing these games with me means I won't die, at least not today. But my papa, I don't want him to get hurt. "Don't kill my papa, please."

He snorts in derision. "Don't worry, *gattina*. Your papa won't die today. He won't die until he gives me all the information I need."

He tosses me away like I'm a pile of trash and shifts his focus back to my father. "You have two weeks to tell me who killed Dante and why."

My father lets out a shaky breath, but that is as much as he can react to threats. I've never seen him show fear, regret, or remorse in all the twenty-one years I've been alive. "Antonio—"

"Play games with me, and I'll wipe your entire family off the face of the earth," Antonio warns. "I'll start with your daughters—watch as I tear them limb from limb until nothing remains."

My father's throat moves as he swallows.

Antonio's gaze meets mine, and he grins a lopsided smile at me. "We'll be meeting again, *gattina*. Take care of yourself until then."

I want to yell that I hope we never meet again, but I don't. He's about to leave, and I don't want to give him a reason to stay longer.

I don't realize I'm holding my breath until he and his men leave. I turn to face Papa, who appears so calm, as if two of his men aren't dead, and he didn't have a gun pressed to his head just moments earlier.

"What the hell is happening, Papa? What do those men want?"

"When did I have to start explaining myself to you, Vivienne?" he asks in a condescending tone that makes anger swell in my guts.

"You've put my life—and Harper's—in danger. What if Harper had been home to see all this?" Thank goodness she's in the dorms; she'd have passed out by now. "I know those men wouldn't have come if you hadn't done something wrong. Who the hell is Dante, and what do you know about him?"

"Since we're giving each other explanations," he starts, his voice laced with annoyance. "How about you start by explaining where and how you met Antonio Mancini?"

I swallow to push down the lump in my throat.

"You can't tell me, can you?" he sighs. "Rather than asking questions that won't change anything, think of ways to help."

"Help?" I scoff. "You created this mess, Papa. How is it my job to help you fix it?"

He slams his hand on the desk and shoots up to his feet. "Because our entire family depends on this, Vivienne. You, your sister, and I, all our lives are at stake here."

The atmosphere crackles with tension.

As much as I'd like to nag him to death, he's right. I can't bear the thought of Harper getting hurt in the midst of all this. I have to figure a way out. Antonio is a psychopath. He'll really hurt us if we don't give him what he wants.

"How do I help?" I ask.

Papa draws in a breath and sits down on his chair. He steeples his fingers in front of him as he thinks. "An alliance is the only way out of this mess. We need strong allies to back us up."

I feel a rush of urgency coursing through me. "How do we secure an alliance?"

"Through marriage." My father gives me a sober look. "You'll have to get married."

I take a step back, a wry smile creeping on my face, disbelief lurking beneath the surface. "You're joking."

My father frowns. "I don't have time to crack jokes with you, Vivienne."

I shake my head as tears blur my vision. "I can't get married. I have to finish school, get a job, and then live a normal life. That was the plan. You can't take that away from me."

"You don't have a choice. Neither of us does. It's either that or we're food for worms and crows," he says without a hint of remorse. "Think about yourself and your sister."

The first streak of tears rolls down my face. Right, Harper. I can endure anything, but not Harper getting hurt. I'll walk through fire to keep her safe if I have to. "When do I get married?"

"I'll make plans for that," Papa answers. "I'll find a good match for you."

I laugh. "Should I be grateful?"

My father lowers his head and heaves a sigh. "I'm sorry I failed you."

"I'm not surprised, Papa. You've always failed me since I was a little girl. I don't expect much from you." I start to leave, stepping over the puddle of blood and the dead bodies I'd forgotten were still there. "Get someone to clean this mess before Harper comes home," I say over my shoulder as I walk out the door.

There's so much to unpack—so much to cry over and lose sleep on—but one thought brings me to my knees, and it isn't about a sudden marriage. It's Antonio. What the hell did he mean by "we'll be meeting again"?

6

ANTONIO

Vivienne is like a ghost, haunting me even in this moment.

No matter how hard I try, it's a losing battle not to think of her. She's like an itch beneath my skin, driving me insane in the most intoxicating way.

I close my eyes, trying to push her out, but the memory of her laughter and the way her emerald-green eyes spark with mischief keeps resurfacing.

I force myself to focus on the woman kneeling in front of me and sucking my cock, but every time I do, I'm reminded not only of the curve of Vivienne's smile—the way it lights up her entire face—but also of her delicate body pressed against mine.

The way the swell of her breasts heaves when she breathes, her curvy hips and heart-shaped ass. That girl is a fucking goddess, I swear. She's not the kind of woman anyone easily forgets—she leaves footprints wherever she goes.

She has a mouth that is too smart for her, and she's so

fierce. No woman has ever challenged me the way she did last night.

I could see the fear in her eyes. Despite that, she managed to hold her own against me even in the face of death.

I have a feeling she's about to become the object of my obsession, and I plan to put her to good use.

The woman in front of me starts to pump, licking the tip of my cock like it's a blow pop. Nothing she does moves me the way thinking of Vivienne does, so I close my eyes and pretend it's Vivienne kneeling in front of me.

I imagine her taking me in so deep that I can feel the back of her throat and her small hands wrapped around my cock.

Fuck, thinking of it is pure ecstasy. I want her so badly.

With each stroke, I lose myself deeper in the thought of her—her soft skin against mine, her voice, filled with that intoxicating mix of sass and kindness.

I can almost feel her warmth enveloping me, igniting something primal and raw. It's nothing like I've ever felt before.

But just as I'm about to lose myself completely, the door swings open with a loud creak. Lorenzo, Luca, and Dario enter, their boisterous laughter shattering the fragile moment like glass.

I groan in annoyance, and the woman scrambles for pieces of her clothing, flushing in embarrassment. She's a stripper I met at the club last week. Our first sex was good, the second even better.

But it hasn't been the same since I met Vivienne. I don't want anyone else but her.

"What the hell?" I growl, irritation clawing at me as I snap my eyes open. I quickly push away the image of Vivienne from my thoughts and glower at the three guys. "Have you guys ever heard about the thing called knocking and waiting for permission to come in? You should try it."

Lorenzo raises an eyebrow, a smirk playing on his lips. "Didn't mean to interrupt your... *private time*, Nio."

"Yeah, really," Dario chimes in, laughter bubbling in his throat. "What were you thinking? You're usually more discreet. Imagine I walked in with my wife?"

"Enough!" I bark, heating up with embarrassment as I tuck my cock inside my pants. "Sick bastards."

The woman, now fully dressed, casts a wary glance at me before slipping out of the room. The door clicks shut behind her, leaving me alone with these three assholes and the frustration simmering just beneath the surface.

I let out a frustrated sigh. I'd been so close to getting the release I'd been wanting for so long.

"He's been acting strange ever since he met the Cole girl," Luca says. "If I didn't know better, I'd say she has something on him."

"Sounds like an obsession to me," Lorenzo jokes. "Who'd have thought a day like this would come? The almighty Antonio Mancini, obsessed with a woman."

"Let's just get to business," I snap, trying to redirect the conversation. "We have more important things to discuss than my personal life. What do you want?"

Dario grabs one of the mesh chairs across from mine and sits on it. "How did your meeting with Peter go?"

I groan at the mention of that asshole's name. "He refused to give out anything useful. The old fucker said he didn't have a clue who was responsible, but I have an idea on how to make him talk."

Lorenzo settles into the chair next to Dario while Luca keeps standing. "How? Kidnapping his daughter?"

I nod. "It's the only way. Knowing that asshole, he's probably thinking of a way to get rid of me."

"He'll need to ally himself with someone powerful to do so," Luca says. "And we know the only way he can truly do that is by giving away one of his daughters. It sure as hell won't be the youngest."

"I know." I'd given it a lot of thought, and there was a straightforward solution to that. "It won't happen."

"You intend to stop the marriage?" Dario asks.

"I do." But I don't tell him it's not just because of my revenge. I can't bear the thought of someone touching Vivienne despite my hate for her and her father. She has to be mine so I can torment and break her however I like.

No one else can have her before I do, and even after that.

I GRIT my teeth so hard my jaw aches.

I thought Peter was an asshole, but it turns out he's worse than that. The asshole is willing to marry off his daughter to someone three times her age just to keep himself safe.

Sure, I'd expected him to do something stupid out of desperation, but I'd tried to hold on to the hope that he would love his daughters enough not to do something idiotic.

Turns out I'm the stupid one for thinking that.

Luca and Lorenzo just came home after a long day of secretly following Peter around the city to find out what he is up to. Safe to say they did not come bearing good news.

"You've been pacing the entire house ever since we got back," Luca says, his eyes following my every movement. "You have to calm down—it's just a wedding."

"Don't fucking tell me what to do. Do you think I only care about Vivienne getting married? It'll be harder to get a confession out of him if he has a powerful ally backing him up." I stop pacing and shift my weight to one leg. "Dante is lying cold in the ground, and that bastard is more concerned about marrying off his daughter to that old geezer."

"If he's willing to go that far, then whoever is behind Dante's death must be someone powerful," Lorenzo says. "He fears that person more than he fears you."

"Underestimating me will be his ruin." I sit down, but my feet relentlessly tap the floor. I'm restless as fuck. "When is the wedding?"

"They haven't fixed a date yet," Luca answers. "But the proposal dinner is next Friday. The wedding should be soon after."

"Next Friday," I echo. It's Saturday, so that will be less than a week from today. Peter's really in a hurry to secure this new alliance. Unfortunately for him, I'll make sure it doesn't go through. "Did you find out where he plans to host the engagement party?"

Luca bobs his head. "I'll email the address over to you."

"We have to get the men ready—we make our move next Friday," I say. "We're taking the bride with us."

Luca and Lorenzo exchange a stunned look.

"The bride?" Lorenzo asks.

"Do you have a better idea on how to stop the alliance?" I return. "Should we just walk in and shoot everyone? It's quicker if you ask me."

Luca rests back in his chair. "What are we going to do with her?"

"We'll hold her hostage. If Peter wants his daughter back, he'll have to give us the information we need."

Lorenzo scratches the back of his head, clearly not comfortable with this insane plan of mine. "And if he insists on not saying a thing?"

Peter is a narcissistic asshole, but I doubt he'll gamble with his daughter's life. Men like him are usually possessive over what they feel is their property.

"Let's hope he doesn't because I'll be forced to kill her." My head is a mess, so I walk to the wine bar in the corner of the living room and grab a bottle of tequila with a shot glass.

I return to my seat and pour myself a shot. I drink in, wincing as the drink trails down my throat and settles in my stomach, as if I just swallowed a hot piece of metal.

"Mariana won't like this idea," Lorenzo points out. "You know how she feels about holding women hostage."

"She won't know unless either of you runs your mouths," I tell him. I promised her I would get revenge for Dante. What I didn't promise her, though, was that I would seek revenge in a holy way.

Revenge is messy; she knows that much. And honestly, all she needs to know is the basics, not the details.

I have a plan, and it's going to be perfect if my men follow my instructions. "We need to make sure we can get out of there without a hitch. You all know what to do. Lorenzo, you'll take care of the security and scout the place. Luca, you'll help with the arrangements. I want this to be seamless. No mistakes."

My gaze drifts off as I think about my Plan A, Plan B, and Plan C, just in case. This won't be easy, but it will be worth it. I can feel the heat of revenge burning within me, fueling my every move.

"Peter will be expecting you at the wedding," Luca says. "What do we do if he has already made plans of his own?"

"Have some of our men keep an eye on him. Bug his car, his office. Do whatever needs to be done."

I refill my glass and down another shot of tequila, a smug smile curling my lips as I think of Vivienne. I can already picture the shock on her face when I ruin her little wedding. I can't wait to see the way she'll glare at me with those big, beautiful eyes—the fierceness and defiance I'll find in them.

I hope she enjoys whatever time she has now, because her life will change forever in a couple of days.

7

VIVIENNE

It's been a week since Antonio held a gun to my papa's temple. Thankfully, Harper didn't come home until the next day, so she has no idea what happened that night.

But I haven't forgotten—it still haunts my dreams. I can't forget the dead bodies lying in their pools of blood or the crazed look in Antonio's eyes as he threatened my papa. It still feels like I am stuck in a nightmare.

"We'll be meeting again, gattina."

I haven't forgotten his promise—not for a single second. I could brush it off as him just trying to scare me, but I know he wasn't bluffing when he said that. Antonio is simply not the type of man to make promises he won't keep.

A shiver runs down my spine at the thought of getting entangled in whatever business he has with my father. It doesn't help my case that I attacked him, either.

Goddammit, I'm in the mix already.

I flinch as something warm and rough glides down my thighs—and that's when I remember where I am.

I'm at a dinner with my papa and the man I'm supposed

to marry—a man three times my age and a disgusting piece of shit.

I pull my legs away from his reach and frown at him, but the bastard doesn't take the hint that I am disgusted by his touch. Either that, or he doesn't just give a shit about respecting boundaries.

He smiles, his gray eyes gleaming with a sick amusement that makes bile rise in my throat. I can't believe this is who my papa expects me to marry.

My stomach churns as a wave of anxiety surges through me. My papa's eyes lock with mine—and for a moment, I hope he sees how much I hate being here. But he ignores me, shifting his gaze to Enzo.

"We need to hasten things before Antonio figures out our plan," Papa says, his brows creasing slightly. "We don't have much time."

Enzo chuckles darkly. "You're a fool if you think he hasn't figured it out by now. He is no fool."

"I don't care if he has. What matters is that we make our move before he does."

"Then we must move the wedding forward—set it for a month from today," Enzo decides.

My chest tightens when my father interjects, "A week." He glances at me as if he's daring me to protest. "There is no time to waste."

I gulp down my water to stifle the rage churning in my gut. I dislike how my father is treating marrying me off as if I am nothing more than one of his prized possessions.

No one here cares about me or what I want. The only relief I'm getting in all of this is that I'm the one in this situation, not Harper. She doesn't even know about this yet, but I can imagine how angry she will be when she finds out. Perhaps Papa will listen to her and call off this engagement, but I doubt he will. Not with how desperate he is to get Antonio off his back.

When the glass door to the restaurant opens, I almost consider running away—escaping to a far-off country where no one knows my name.

I could find a job, get married to a regular guy, and live a normal life.

Papa's men will probably find me before I even board a flight, but there is a chance they won't. The only thing holding me back is Harper. She'll have to go through this torture if I'm not here, and I can't allow that to happen.

Like me, my sister has dreams—she's damn smart. She deserves to spread her wings, not be caged by some old geezer like Enzo.

There's a long silence between them, and the tension in the air is palpable.

"I can't get married in a week," I blurt out, my mind racing—clearly losing it—as even my father's death stare fails to stop me. "Heck, I don't want to get married at all."

"Vivienne," Papa growls quietly.

"You did what you did to Antonio—so why should I pay the price?" I growl, my fists clenching with the rage I've harbored since I arrived. "If you need a marriage alliance, why don't you get married yourself?"

Enzo scoffs, his gray eyes narrowing on me. "You do not speak when we're speaking, child."

I shoot him a glare. "So you do know I'm just a child compared to you," I retort.

Through the corner of my eyes, I see the way my papa is staring at me, as if he is barely holding back from flying across the table to shut me up.

"I won't warn you again, Vivienne. Sit!" he says, this time his voice is louder than before.

I finally face him, unable or unwilling to hide the hate and disgust burning in me. At this point, I don't give a shit—even if the world were to collapse, I'd watch it burn.

"Or what?" I yell back. "You'll tie me up and send me off with him?"

There's a flicker of something in my father's eyes, but I know it is not remorse or recognition that he is wrong. No, my father is incapable of feeling such emotions. Whatever it is, I can't wrap my fingers around it, and it doesn't last long.

"If I need to, then I will," he says indifferently. "You know what's at stake."

"No, I don't," I shoot back. "The only thing at stake here is my entire life. Why am I paying for something you did wrong? It makes no sense."

"We've already talked about this, Vivienne. There is only one other option," my father says in that calm voice of his.

My blood curdles as my eyes twitch with rage. He's at it again—threatening me with Harper as if she weren't his daughter or his responsibility. "Don't you dare mention her. I'll deliver you to Antonio myself if you even think of it."

We stare at each other long and intensely enough to rupture a volcano.

It's the first time I've dared not only to talk back to my father but also to threaten him. And it's not just empty threats—I'd do anything for Harper, even betray our father.

And I think he knows. He recognizes my rage for what it is.

Enzo silently watches us with a slight curl of his lips. The asshole is having fun. Unfortunately for him, I do not run a circus, so he can entertain himself somewhere else.

I stand up to my feet without taking my eyes off my father for even a moment. "If you'll excuse me, I need a moment to myself."

My heart is pounding in my chest, and there's a knot in my throat that makes it hard for me to breathe. I'll pass out if I have to stay here for an extra second.

My father doesn't nod to permit me to leave, but I start for the bathroom anyway. I feel the weight of his gaze boring straight into the back of my head, and my legs threaten to give out with each step I take toward the black door of the women's toilet.

But it's not just my father's gaze that makes my scalp prickle and my pulse start racing. It's something else... someone. Someone is watching me; I can feel it.

I whip my head around, trying to find who it is, but there's no one. Not even a single person is staring in my direction now, including my papa. He's gone back to his conversation with Enzo, probably telling him to ignore my protest and that my opinion doesn't matter.

Turning around, I briskly walk into the bathroom, away from whoever is watching me. Maybe there's no one there, and I am just being paranoid because of Antonio's threat.

I rest against one of the sinks and stare at my reflection in the mirror. My smoky makeup is flawless; I styled my hair in a neat bun, and the silky black dress I'm wearing does a good job of showcasing my cleavage.

Papa said I needed to wear something like this. He said it's good to give a sample of what I would be offering to entice the buyer.

A mirthless smile spreads on my lips. He doesn't consider me human at all. To him, I am nothing short of an asset he can flaunt and buy allies with.

My gaze darts to the window, and for a second, I imagine what would happen if I jumped from it. We're on the first floor, so the most I'd get is a broken leg, but I could run away and be free from all of this.

No.

I can't do it because I know what that would mean for my sister. Tears well in my eyes, but I blink them away before they can roll down my face. My makeup is flawless tonight, and I won't ruin it over a situation I have no control over.

I refuse to be the mafia princess who is a victim. I'll be strong, and who knows, Enzo could die in a year or two, and I'll get my freedom back—that is, if I don't put a pillow over his face on our wedding night.

My skin crawls at the thought of his rough, wrinkly hands on my body.

The bathroom door opens, but I'm too lost in thought to check who it is.

Repeating the words of affirmation to myself, I sniffle and start to wash my hands. I'm about to pull out a tissue from a box in front of me when I notice someone in a dark hood standing behind me.

I whirl around to see who it is—but in a flash, he throws a bag over my head and shoves me against the counter.

Fuck. Fuck. Fuck.

My blood turns to ice, and a cold sweat breaks out on my skin. Who the hell is he? Is he going to kill me? I know I wanted to escape from my father, but not like this—not as a corpse.

Shit. *I should have taken my combat classes seriously*, is all I can think of as I clench my fist and throw it at him. He catches my hand mid-air and flips me so my back is pressed against his chest.

I catch a whiff of his cologne, and it smells oddly familiar. I'm sure I've inhaled that musk and sandalwood scent before, but my mind is spinning too much to remember where.

I throw my feet back to kick him, but he pulls away, evading my kick before he wraps his strong arms around my throat and hauls me closer.

"Who the hell are you?" I scream, panting from my efforts to free myself and the adrenaline pumping through my veins. "My papa is outside. Let me go, or he'll kill you."

There's a deep chuckle behind me, and the warmth from his breath heats my neck. My nipples harden, and there's a rush of heat in my stomach. I think I've lost my damn mind. No way I felt that over a stranger who's most likely here to kill me.

"Is that you showing concern for me, *gattina*?" he asks, his voice low and dangerous.

My eyes widen, and my heart rate triples as realization dawns on me. "Antonio."

"We meet again, darling," he says, his voice laced with amusement.

I feel something prick the skin around my neck, and the world spins into darkness.

8

ANTONIO

"She'll wake up soon," I say to Lorenzo, who's been staring at me nonstop since I carried Vivienne's unconscious body to the car an hour ago.

The fucker's not even trying to hide his concern for her, and while I do not normally explain myself to anyone, Lorenzo and I are more like brothers than master and worker.

He's one of those people I know who will gladly lay down his life for me if the need arises. I trust him with my damn life.

He sighs and shifts his gaze back to the road. "Peter must've found out she's missing by now."

Luca nods from the passenger seat. "I bet the old bastard is going crazy looking for his precious daughter. Too bad he won't be seeing her for a while."

I glance at Vivienne sleeping peacefully on my legs. Her long lashes flutter in her sleep, and her lips are pouty. She's so beautiful that it's a struggle for me not to trail a finger over her lips or her perfectly arched brows.

Luca is right. Peter will probably go insane looking for

her, but not because she is his precious daughter. He'll go insane because he just lost a valuable pawn on his chessboard.

Men like Peter are all the same. Their greed runs deeper than any love for anyone. He wouldn't have put a price tag on her if he valued her. Scratch that. He wouldn't have let that old asshole lay his disgusting fingers on her despite her visible discomfort.

I'd been watching them from the moment they entered the restaurant, and it took all the restraint in me to not walk over to their table and knock Enzo's teeth out of his fucking mouth.

My chest constricts with the need to protect this woman I should hate. I should want to punish her and rip her apart layer by layer until there's nothing left, but the thought of having her all to myself arouses me more.

Lorenzo reels the car through the intricate white gate of one of my mansions at the outskirts of the city. I bought the house under a fake name, so Peter will never be able to trace her here, no matter how hard he tries.

I had some staff clean the place up and assigned some of my men to watch the mansion. Not even a ghost can penetrate the area, given its high level of security.

Lorenzo pulls over in front of a white monstrosity and turns his head to face me. "We're here, boss."

"I have eyes," I tell him, narrowing my eyes on Vivienne.

Her lashes flutter again, and for the first time, she stirs in her sleep. Looks like I'll have to carry her to her prison in bridal style. My lips curl with a smile as I imagine how pissed she'd be at that.

Luca gets out of the car and opens the back door for me. I slide out and lean over to carry Vivienne. I manage to get her out of the car, but her eyes suddenly open as I'm about to lift her into my arms.

She squints from what I assume is the brightness of consciousness and closes them back. When she opens her eyes again, she's taking in her environment and the faces surrounding her.

"Where am I?" she asks almost inaudibly. Before I can reply, there's a flash of fear in her eyes, and she pulls away from my reach. "Why am I here?"

I take one slow step after another toward her, my lips twitching. "What is it, *gattina*? Don't like your new home?"

"Home?" She looks around, still confused. "This is not my home. You... kidnapped me from the restaurant."

"*Si*. I did take you from the restaurant," I say with a nod. "Would you have preferred to marry that old bastard?"

Her eyes sparkle with tears. "Take me back, now!"

I stop walking toward her and lift my brow. "Or what, you'll scream?"

Her throat bobs as she swallows. "Try me."

A chuckle rips from my throat. I don't blame her; her mind is fogged, so she's a little confused. There is no way she'd think anyone in this world can save her from me, because no one can. Not Peter, not Enzo, and not even the police.

I take one last step toward her, so close that our clothes rub together and her delicious, flowery scent invades my nose. "Scream, Vivienne. I dare you."

She's feral and fierce, so I expect her to scream, but she doesn't. She just stands there, staring at me for a heartbeat.

I lower my head, bringing my face to hers. "Cat got your tongue, *gattina*? Scream."

Her chest heaves, and her face turns red.

I smile. "Are you giving up already? It won't be fun playing with you if you give in so easily."

"Go play with yourself, you son of a bitch!"

I barely have time to register her glare before Vivienne's fingers jab into my eyes. Pain sears through me—white-hot and blinding. I curse, instinctively reaching for my face, but before I can react, her forehead slams into my nose with a sickening crunch.

Agony explodes through me. My vision blurs as a sharp, piercing pain shoots through my face.

Blood. I can taste it already, metallic and bitter, filling the back of my throat as it streams down from my nose.

For a second, I'm disoriented, stunned by the pain, and that's all she needs. Through my hazy vision, I see her darting away, her red hair flashing as she bolts for the gate.

Rage ignites through the haze. She thinks she can just run? Not a chance.

I wipe the blood from my face, my breath ragged, the fire in my chest stronger than the pain in my nose. She's fast, but she doesn't know who she's running from.

"Vivienne!" I growl, running after her like a predator after its prey. If she wants to play it this way, then I guess I'll have to make it even more fun for her.

She looks back as she runs, and her green eyes widen at how close I am to catching up with her. She runs faster, but she's no match for me as I grab her wrist from behind and pull her toward me.

"Let go of me!" she screams, trying to fight me off.

I tighten my grip on her. "All that screaming and running won't save you from me, *gattina*. Save your strength."

She tries to jab her fingers into my eyes again, but I'm faster this time, evading her attack. But the sharp pain that jolts down my arm proves she's smarter than I thought, because fucking bit me hard enough to bleed.

Anger flares through me. I've had enough of her drama. Holding her two hands together, I throw her over my shoulder and start for the mansion.

She screams, biting and scratching as she hits my back. All of that is for nothing. I've had bullets pierce through me. Her punches are barely enough to inflict any serious injuries on me.

I toss her on the floor in front of Luca, and she scrambles up to her feet. She's glaring at me with so much hate.

"Take her inside," I order.

Luca nods. He reaches for her arm, but she shrugs away from his touch. "Why me? What did I do wrong?"

"Nothing," I reply, tilting my head. "You're paying for your father's crime."

"What did he do to make me pay the price?" Her voice trembles. "You could have taken or killed him if you wanted. Why me?"

An image of Dante's lifeless body flashes before my eyes. The bullet wound to his chest and head, his lifeless eyes. A new wave of rage fills me.

I wrap my hand around Vivienne's neck—channeling all my hatred for Peter—and hiss, "Someone very important to me died because of your father."

My voice is colder and harsher than I intend, but I don't care. I want her to feel whatever rage and fear Dante felt in his final moments. "I lost money because of him, too. You'll never be free from me until your papa pays for everything he's done."

Tears roll down her cheeks, but she laughs sardonically. "You're a fool, Antonio. My papa will not risk his life to save me. You'll never get what you're looking for."

I lean into her, bringing my lips to her ear. "You better pray he does, or you'll never leave this place alive."

She tenses. "Kill me now."

I pull away and smile at her. "There's no need to rush it; you'll die if I don't get what I need. For now, I'll have to settle for marrying you."

Her eyes widen, and her mouth falls open. "Marry me? What does that mean?"

I snort in derision. The look she's giving me makes it seem she would rather marry Enzo than me. It fuels my rage even more. "You'll be my wife soon enough, *gattina*." I push a lock of red hair from her face. "And don't even try to run. You'll be shot dead before you even make it to that gate."

She spits at my foot, her eyes burning with hate and defiance. "I'll never marry you. I'd rather hang from a tree than marry you."

A lopsided grin forms on my face. "We'll see about that."

"Animal," she barks. "You're a fucking pig. I hope you die. I hate you."

"You'll soon have a valid reason for all of those negative emotions, darling." I nod to Luca, and he starts to drag her away, toward the main building.

Vivienne doesn't fight him, but she keeps raining curses at me.

She's a fierce one. I'm amazed by how she managed to stand her ground despite the obvious fear in her eyes and despite knowing I could easily kill her if I wanted. She makes me want to taunt her more.

"We both know you won't kill that girl," Lorenzo says, stepping beside me.

I smirk. "I won't kill her, but that doesn't mean I won't break her if I need to."

"What if Peter retaliates before we have the chance to get

what we need from him?" he asks. "She's his daughter. He won't just sit back."

"I know." I shove my hands inside the pockets of my slacks and lean against the car. "I have to marry her as soon as possible so we can focus on finding out who is behind Dante's death."

Lorenzo narrows his eyes at me. "Are you marrying her to get back at Peter, or just because you want to own her?" He gives me a more serious look. "You like that girl, don't you?"

I frown, detesting the accusation in his tone. "Find me a priest, and stop talking shit. I'd rather chop off my cock than like one of Peter Cole's spawns."

I'm getting defensive. It's never a good sign when I get defensive about anything. It's a fact that I'm unusually drawn to the girl. But I can't decide if that is because I see her as a challenge or if I am genuinely intrigued by her.

It doesn't matter either way; she'll be mine soon, and I'll get to the bottom of Dante's death. I can discard her after I am done with her.

Lorenzo stares at me intently for a moment, then he sighs. "Yes, boss. How soon do you want the wedding to be?"

I don't give it much thought. The quicker I lay my claim over her, the better. It'll send a message to the other mafia families not to get involved in my business. I will also be inviting a few of my trusted allies to the wedding. I need them to spread the word about my marriage to Peter Cole's eldest daughter.

"Tomorrow night," I say. "I'll make her mine tomorrow night."

9

VIVIENNE

I've been pacing the dark room Luca locked me in, thinking of a way to escape from Antonio and whatever this place is.

I still can't believe that man had the nerve to kidnap me from my own engagement dinner and bring me here. And what was that he said about us getting married?

No. There's no way he meant that. He was just bluffing; he had to be.

My shoulders sag, and my legs grow weak, almost giving out from the weight of everything that's happening. It's all too much for me to process.

I lower myself onto the queen-sized bed and clutch the sheets as though my very life depends on them. My thoughts drift to my father and sister, wondering if Papa is desperately searching for me or if he believes I ran off to avoid marrying Enzo. And Harper... what will she think when she finds out? She'll be shattered, and she'll resent Papa for putting me through this.

I startle as the door unlocks from outside. Expecting

Antonio or one of his men, I instead see an older woman enter. Most of her once-black hair is now gray, and deepening wrinkles betray her age, although she looks no older than fifty, perhaps in her mid-fifties.

"Good evening, child," she says as she walks to the vanity table across from the bed with a tray of food. "It's been hours since you arrived, and I thought you might be hungry, so I brought you some food."

I rise to my feet and stare at the plate filled with spaghetti and meatballs. It smells so delicious that my stomach rumbles with hunger. I haven't eaten anything for a day now.

I'd been so anxious about my engagement to Enzo that I lost my appetite a day before I even met him.

It's not the mouthwatering dish that has my attention, but the shiny knife sparkling under the overhead light. It whispers to me, filling my head with stupid ideas.

"I squeezed some fresh oranges for you," the old lady says gently. "Eat—I'm sure you'll like it."

She seems like a nice person, and nothing like Antonio. That's why I turn to her and give her an apologetic look before letting my impulsive thought take over.

I quickly grab the knife from the plate and hold it to her throat. "I'm sorry," I say to her, and I mean it. "This is the only way I can get out of here alive."

For someone who has a knife pressed to her throat, she is oddly calm. "You can't escape from here, child. Not even as a corpse."

I can't tell if she's on Antonio's side or if she's just being pessimistic, but I don't let it deter me as I glance at the wide-open door. That door, this woman, and the knife in my hand are my ticket out. "We'll see about that. Move."

She huffs out a breath as if I'm a fly who has perched on her arm merely to bother her. "You can't escape from here. The boss won't let you."

"That is not for you to decide." I press the knife hard enough to her throat so she doesn't think of anything stupid as I lead her out of the room and down the hallway.

The dim lighting barely reveals the old portraits lining the walls, casting shadows that stretch and warp, adding to the eerie atmosphere of the mansion.

It's way too quiet here, and I can hear the old lady's soft breaths as she follows me without putting up a fight. It's unnerving how she's acting as if this is all a minor inconvenience, nothing to worry about.

We reach the end of the hallway, and I glance at the stairs stretching out to my right and left. I'd been a bit out of it when Luca dragged me up here, and now I have no idea which way to go. "Left or right?"

She glances left before giving me a faint, almost condescending smile. "Right," she says, her voice smooth and unbothered.

I don't know whether to trust her, but I can't afford to hesitate. Each second is a gamble, and Antonio or one of his men could show up at any moment.

My fingers tremble slightly against the knife's hilt, but I force myself to keep moving, pressing it a little more firmly against her throat to maintain control. That is when I realize I knew nothing about this woman.

I don't know her name or why she's here. She could be a victim of Antonio's madness, just like me.

My pulse races as I start to climb down the stairs, my gaze bouncing to the foyer and back up to the hallway just in case someone comes in.

"Who are you?" I ask the woman, partly out of curiosity

and also to keep the churning in my stomach under control. "Why are you working for someone like Antonio, and why does he want to marry me?"

The woman chuckles softly. "I don't think you should be asking a question like that with a knife pressed against my throat, child. As for why he wants to marry you, I think you'll figure it out soon enough."

"Figure what out?" I snap, feeling a surge of frustration at the fact that I will always be a pawn in this game. Whether it's my papa or a man who kidnapped me. "Just tell me, why does he want to marry me? I'm sure he can still achieve whatever it is he wants, whether he marries me or not."

Her eyes twinkle with a mix of pity and amusement as she replies, "I don't think Antonio himself realizes why he wants you. You'll both figure it out when it's time."

I grit my teeth, fighting the urge to scream at her.

My head is too much of a mess, and I don't need cryptic nonsense right now. I need answers and a way to get out of here.

We reach the bottom of the stairs, and the foyer stretches ahead of me, lined with more doors. It feels endless, and the weight of walking through that door and making it out of here alive weighs down on me like a physical force.

Still, I sigh in relief when I see there's no sign of Antonio or his men anywhere. It would be a hassle getting through the door if they were here.

"Which one leads out?" I ask, scanning the doors for any sign of escape.

"The main door is at the end of the hallway," she replies calmly. "But you won't make it."

Her confidence sends a chill down my spine, but I can't

let her words get to me. I have to keep going. Each step is a fight against the voice in my head telling me this might be hopeless. There's no way escaping from this place would be this easy.

Suddenly, I hear slow and steady footsteps behind me. My heart leaps into my throat, and my hands start to tremble with fear. It's all over if Antonio or anyone else comes in here.

No time to think—I shove the woman aside and bolt down the hallway, sprinting for the door at the far end.

Still clenched in my hand, the knife feels slippery with sweat, but I don't let it go. I'm feral, and I'll attack anyone who tries to stop me, no matter who it is.

"Stop!" a deep voice booms from behind, and I know without looking that it's one of Antonio's men. It doesn't sound like the one who dragged me upstairs, so it must be the other one, Lorenzo.

I don't stop. I can't. The door is so close now. Just a few more steps—

A strong arm wraps around my waist from behind, yanking me backward with such force that the air is knocked out of my lungs. When I look back to see who it is, I see that it's not one of the men from earlier. I haven't met this one before. He's as tall as a mountain with one very white eye and the other blue. He's not ugly, but the icy expression on his face makes him look like a monster from my nightmare when I was a child.

The knife flies from my hand, clattering uselessly on the marble floor. I struggle, kicking and writhing in the man's grip, but he's too strong. I am too weak.

Panic surges through me as he drags me back, my feet barely touching the ground.

"Enough!" Antonio's voice cuts through the chaos like a whip, commanding and unyielding.

The man holding me stops, loosening his grip just enough for me to breathe, but I'm still trapped.

My eyes dart around, searching for any possible way out, but there's nothing.

Antonio steps into view—his dark eyes locking onto mine—and his cold, calculated expression sends a wave of dread crashing over me.

"I told you, *gattina*," he intones, deceptively calm. "There's no escaping me. We're getting married, whether you like it or not."

My heart hammers in my chest. For a moment, I lose my voice—then I manage to choke out, "You're insane if you think I'll ever marry you."

Antonio steps closer, his gaze fixed on mine. "Insane? Perhaps. But you belong to me—completely. Do you know what that means?"

I scowl at him, my nostrils flaring with rage. But God, he's also so dangerously close and smells so good that I find myself a little distracted.

Focus, Vivienne. You hate this man.

I'm definitely not attracted to that fifties pompadour haircut or the black suit he wears like a fucking devil. I hate him—I *should* hate him.

He nods to the man holding me.

The man nods back and releases me instantly.

I stumble slightly but catch myself, glaring at Antonio as I back away from the man. "I'll never be yours," I spit with as much disdain as I can. "I won't marry you. I'd rather die than marry a pig like you."

Antonio smirks, a dark gleam in his eyes. "I didn't ask if you will, Vivienne. You don't have a choice."

The truth stabs me like a knife in the chest: For the first time since being brought here, I realize how truly trapped I am. Antonio's word is law in this place, and I'll only leave here if he lets me.

My ego will not allow me to beg him, but I can negotiate with him. I can make him see how fucked up this is, so I try. "I'm sorry you lost someone dear to you because of my father, but you have to let me go. I promise I'll force him to give you the answers you need."

Antonio cocks his brow.

I have no idea if that's a sign that my words are getting to him, but I try to take advantage of it. "No, I'll find out whatever he knows and bring the information to you myself, please."

His lips twitch with a half-smile. "Are you trying to strike a deal with me, *gattina*?"

I square my shoulders and nod. "I am. I will do whatever it takes to leave this place. Just let me go?"

His half-smile turns into a full, lopsided grin. "That doesn't sound like you're begging me. It sounds like you're giving me orders."

"I won't beg if that's what you want."

He inches closer to me, the heat from his body warming me up. Placing a finger under my chin, he tilts my face so my eyes meet his. "I saved you from marrying that old bastard. If anything, you should be thanking me."

"I would be thanking you if you didn't kidnap me like some animal. I would be on my knees thanking you if you weren't forcing me to marry you."

His thumb trails my jawline, and his touch ignites a flame on my skin. "I don't need you down on your knees thanking me, *gattina*. There are plenty of other things I would rather you do if you're desperate to go on your knees."

"And what—" I trail off when I realize the perverted thoughts behind those words. My cheeks flush, and there's a flutter in my stomach. "Pig!"

He chuckles softly. "I've been called worse."

Pulling away from me, he claps once. The front door opens, and two women enter, pushing a rack of wedding gowns in various designs and shades of white.

My jaw falls open, and I gape at Antonio, unable to muster any words.

He does a perfect job at reading my expression and explains before I even ask. "Pick a dress you like. We're getting married tomorrow evening."

I scoff. "Like hell I will. You'll have to kill me first."

I turn around and start to leave, but he grabs my wrist and hauls back, pushing me against the wall and pressing his body against mine.

Damn. He's so strong… and I must be losing my mind, because why the hell am I getting turned on?

"Leave," he growls.

Everyone else in the hallway takes the nearest exit outside.

"Don't provoke me, Vivienne," he warns. "Be a good girl and do as you're told."

I don't want to do as I'm told. I want to provoke him and push against his limits until he has none left. Maybe he'll let me go then, or punish me. "What will you do if I don't? Kill me?"

He leans in, and his hot breath caresses my earlobe as he whispers, "I won't kill you, but I'll punish you."

His words seep through my skin like poison, simmering

in my stomach and awakening a throb between my legs. "Punish me."

I need to see how far he'll go to prove his dominance over me. I need to know how my body will react to his torture.

His tongue grazes my throat, and a soft moan slips from my lips, the unexpectedness of it sending a shiver down my spine.

The sensation is overwhelming, pleasure mingling with the heat of his touch. "Since you're so eager to be punished," he murmurs against my skin, his voice low and dangerous, "make sure you don't regret it."

His lips follow with a trail of scorching kisses, each one igniting a fire beneath my skin as he moves along my neck, claiming me with every breath.

My heart is pounding as he speaks, and my body is trembling with anticipation. I don't know what comes over me, but I suddenly feel like I'm in a game of chicken, daring him to go too far, daring myself to break under his touch.

He pins my hands above my head, and I don't bother to fight him. "You asked for it," he growls, sliding down the arm of my dress and exposing my breasts.

My nipples are taut and aching, the cool air and his gaze making them even more sensitive. A wave of goosebumps races across my skin as I catch the raw, hungry desire flickering in his eyes, his stare devouring every inch of my exposed body.

The intensity of his lust sends a pulse of heat through me, making me hyperaware of just how vulnerable and bare I am before him.

I try to keep my eyes locked on his, but the current of desire surging through me makes it hard to remain in control.

He's right; I did ask for it. But in this moment, with his hands on me and his lips burning a trail up my neck, all I can think is that I'm not sure I want him to stop.

"Please," I whisper, my voice barely audible. I want to tell him to stop, but I can't bring myself to say the words because I want him. I'm attracted to this man as much as I hate him, which is confusing.

Antonio's eyes flash with a predatory gleam.

He never breaks eye contact as he uses one hand to gently pinch my nipple before bringing his other hand down to brush against my clit. A wave of heat floods my body, and a low moan escapes from deep within me.

His eyes flare with excitement at the sound, and he grips the waistband of my dress, pulling it down over my hips and discarding it onto the floor. "*Mio Dio,*" he purrs. "You're beautiful, *gattina.*"

My heart flutters, a delicious ache settling low in my core, making me crave his next move.

He glides a hand up my thighs and growls at the pool of wetness between my legs. "I see you're hungry for me, *gattina,*" he whispers. "How long have you been thinking of me doing this to you?"

"I..." I let out a raspy breath as he presses a thumb against my clitoris and starts to rub it. "I haven't been thinking of you."

He flashes a wicked smile at me and pushes a finger inside me. "Liar," he whispers against my ear. "You're dripping with need, and you still lie to me."

I open my mouth to argue, but a deep, needy moan is the only sound that comes out.

Antonio's eyes darken with desire as he watches me lose control. His lips curl into a smirk as he continues to touch me, probing me further with his fingers and rubbing against my most sensitive spots.

I arch my back and whimper at the pleasurable sensation that courses through my body. My mind is a jumble of conflicting emotions: anger at being trapped by this man, desire for his touch, and a strange sense of longing for something more.

A slow, burning pressure coils deep in my core, tightening with each thrust of his finger in and out of me. It threatens to unravel me completely.

I wrap my arms around his neck, my fingers digging into his flesh as I allow the sweet sensation to cocoon me completely.

Antonio pushes another finger inside me, curling it all the way to my G-spot, and that is all it takes for my orgasm to explode through me.

I cry out with pleasure, my eyes and head rolling back and my legs trembling.

He holds me up, rubbing my clitoris harder and faster as I come on his fingers.

It takes minutes for me to recover from the intensity of the best orgasm I've ever had in my life—the only orgasm I've ever had because my father wouldn't let me date anyone. He'd threatened to kill whoever laid a finger on me, and I couldn't stand the thought of anyone getting hurt because of me.

My first and only kiss was in high school, and the boy's father had mysteriously been involved in an accident the following day. That was enough warning for me not to try anything stupid again.

Antonio releases me and thrusts his fingers full of my juices into my mouth. I lick myself off him desperately, wanting to feel more of what he has to offer.

But he doesn't give me more. He smiles cruelly. "Choose a dress, *gattina*. We're getting married tomorrow, and I won't ask again."

He slides his fingers out of my mouth and starts to walk away.

I slide down the wall, and a wave of shame washes over me. Shame that I gave in so easily to this man who I hate, and I enjoyed every bit of it.

10

ANTONIO

"It's not too late to call the wedding off," Dario says, his brows knitted with concern. "She's Peter Cole's daughter. She could end up betraying you."

My lips curl with a smile. "It's my wedding evening, Dario. Of course, it is too late to call off the wedding," I muse. "Besides, I'll need to trust her for her to betray me. She's a prisoner here, nothing more."

There's a moment of silence in the room as I put on my suit in front of the tall mirror in my closet. When I turn around, I notice that all of them have their eyes on me and their brows raised.

"Is that what you tell yourself? That she is nothing more than a prisoner to you?" Dario asks, still wearing the same confused expression on his face. "No man marries a woman just because she is his prisoner, Nio. You like her."

I spin around to face him with a frown. I can feel the anger bubbling up inside me. "Careful, brother. Dante is dead because of her father. It will be a snowy day in hell before I fall in love with that girl."

"You sound like you're in denial. Does Mariana know about this?"

I start to fix my cufflinks—Dante bought me these cufflinks on my thirty-sixth birthday. They're silver, and the first letter of my name is carved in italics right in the middle.

I'd never worn them because they're not my style, but now I regret that he never got the chance to see me wear them. It's my way of carrying him with me—my way of letting him know his death was not in vain because I'll be sending his killers to hell soon.

"Mariana knows." I couldn't risk her hearing about it from someone else. Despite her grief, I knew she'd try to stop me, so I only sent her a text.

"And she's okay with this?" Dario asks, his brows furrowing with confusion.

"I don't know if she is, and it won't matter if she isn't."

Dario opens his mouth to argue, but I raise my hand to mark the end of the conversation. My revenge starts tonight, and I don't want to waste any more of my energy arguing over something irrelevant.

There's a knock on the door before it's pushed open, and Luca saunters inside. "The priest is waiting, boss," he says.

"And my bride?" I ask.

"She's waiting, too. You have to be at the altar first," Luca tells me.

I nod, my lips curling with a smile as I imagine my bride in one of the wedding gowns I picked out for her. I'd also booked a hairstylist and a makeup artist. What is a wedding if she doesn't look perfect?

Turning to Dario, my brow arches. "Are you coming, or will you stand there and nag me about my choices?"

He sighs. "Let's go. Ginny's waiting, too."

I narrow my eyes at him, surprised that he would bring his wife along despite the occasion. "Ginny?"

"Yeah. I told her about it, and she insisted," he answers, looking a bit disappointed himself that she is here.

"Looks like I have a lot of women who'll try to kill me on my wedding day," I muse.

Dario shakes his head with pity. "Just in case any of them confront you, I advised you not to do this."

I chuckle and shove him aside. "You advised me to do this."

His grumbling follows me as I leave the room and start down the stairs leading to the patio, and then his footsteps follow.

The patio is decorated with pink and white flowers and ribbons. The aisle is lined with chairs covered in ribbons on both sides, and out of the corner of my eye, I catch a glimpse of someone who shouldn't be here.

Salvatore Russo, head of the Camorra. We'd been in a cold war for years since Dante became the capo, and neither of our families bothered to form an alliance or even cross each other's territories now.

"Which one of you invited that old bastard to my wedding?" I ask, my gaze bouncing from Luca and Lorenzo to Dario.

None of them answers.

I've tried to keep this wedding a secret from those outside my alliance group. If Salvatore is here, it means one of my men snitched, and I have to find out who it was before the rat gives out more information to my enemies.

Lorenzo leans in. "I can ask him to leave."

I shake my head. "That won't be necessary."

While I am certain Peter and Salvatore are far from

allies, I cannot poke Salvatore in the wrong rib. I can't risk him running to Peter to run his mouth.

The fact that he dared to come here means he wants something, my attention or perhaps a deal.

Whichever one it is, I have to hear him out first and weigh my options.

Salvatore smiles and waves at me from where he stands across the patio.

I walk over to him, wearing the fakest smile I can find. "Well, well, if it isn't the devil himself."

He scoffs, taking me in with so much arrogance in his gaze.

I clench my fist, fighting the urge to gouge those ugly eyes of his out.

"For someone who kidnapped a girl from her engagement dinner and is forcing said girl to marry him," Salvatore says, "you're more of a devil than I'll ever be."

I snort. Sick bastard. "Why are you here?"

"Let me see." He taps his thin, wrinkled lips and pretends to think. "I wonder what Peter's reaction will be when he finds out about this little wedding of yours."

I stare him down, cursing at the way he gets on my last nerves with such little effort. I drop the façade of a smile and wear my cold mask. "It is not a wise choice to threaten me in my own home, Salvatore."

"Threaten you?" He tsks. "I wouldn't dare. I am here to offer a proposal."

I spot Mariana standing with Dario and Ginny. It's a struggle not to let my attention drift to them. "This proposal of yours better be worth my time."

Salvatore chuckles. "I'm sure you've heard about the ongoing war between the Bratva and the Irish Mob."

"What about it?"

His brows shoot up to his receding hairline. "You may not be aware, but Malachy encroached on my territory eight years ago. There's no better time for me to get back at him than now."

I heave a sigh as disgust creeps up my throat. The bastard may not notice, but I'm bored with this conversation. "How do I come into the mix?"

He smiles. "Good question. You're closer to the Irish territories than I am. I need you to help me take it."

My horselaugh escapes from my throat. "Me? I didn't realize we'd established the type of relationship where we help each other, Salvatore. That's impressive!"

"Think of everything we could have," he urges in a near whisper. "We could run this world together, Antonio. We could find Dante's killer as quickly as we could snap our fingers. Everything will be ours, you and me."

My nostrils flare at the mention of Dante's name from his filthy mouth. "Don't ever mention his name again. Dante would be turning in his grave if he knew this stupid plan of yours."

"Watch it, boy—"

"No. You fucking watch it!" I growl. I don't give a fuck if all eyes are on us now. "Don't forget whose ground you stand on. I am not Dante; I can make you vanish with just a snap of my fingers."

As much as I respected Dante, he was weak and reluctant to shed blood. He trusted easily and could hardly recognize a viper smiling at him. That became his undoing.

I am different, though, because I won't hesitate to shed blood or start a war if that is what I'll need to achieve whatever the fuck I want.

Salvatore's eyes are red with rage, but he knows better than to act on it. "Careful, you might regret this."

"Regret does not exist in my books, old man." I point my right index finger at him. "And let me warn you: You're a dead man if word of what is happening here gets to Peter Cole."

His throat moves as he swallows, his chest heaving so hard I can almost hear the pounding of his heart. So this is what a mix of false bravery, rage, and fear looks like?

I hear light footsteps as someone walks up and stands behind me. "She's coming down in a couple of minutes," Lorenzo says.

"Now, if you don't mind, I'd like to excuse myself. Enjoy the wedding." I grin cockily at Salvatore.

I feel the scorch of his glare burning through the back of my head as I head to the altar.

"What does he want?" Lorenzo asks.

"He wants to take over the Irish territories, and he needs my alliance to do it," I reply.

Lorenzo is silent for a moment. "What did you tell him?"

"I turned down the madness, Lorenzo. What was I supposed to do? Jump at the offer and become his ally?" I know Salvatore's nature better than I know my own shadow. Only a fool will fall for his sweet words about alliance and whatnot. That fucker will kill me and try to take over my territory the moment he gets what he wants.

The door leading to the foyer opens, and everyone turns their attention to it as someone announces the bride's entrance. Suddenly, everywhere is quiet as anticipation hangs in the air.

My chest flutters at the thought of how beautiful Vivienne would be in whatever gown she put on, which is strange because I have never felt that sort of sensation before.

She steps into view, and it's like the whole world narrows down to just her.

Her dress is this perfect white, the kind of white that makes everything else look dull in comparison. It flows around her as she walks, hugging her body in all the right places, yet falling so gracefully that she almost seems to glide down the aisle.

The lace on her sleeves and the skirt encrusted with diamonds catch the light, delicate and intricate, just like her.

Her hair is pinned up, a few loose curls framing her face, and her veil trails behind her, soft and sheer, like something out of a dream.

She's beautiful in a way that stops me cold. It's like she's looking right at me, and she isn't even smiling, yet my chest tightens with the weight of it all, the beauty, the realization that this woman is mine.

I may not have her fully—*yet*—still, she is mine.

Her eyes lock onto mine, and there's this moment—just us in the middle of everything.

The crowd, the music, the decorations, it all fades away. All I can see is her, moving toward me, step by step. She looks perfect. No, not just perfect. She looks like she was meant to be here with me in this moment.

Every second feels like it stretches forever, and yet it's over too fast. She's closer now, only a few steps away, and I don't think I've ever wanted anything more than I want her in this moment.

Dario's words start to ring in my head.

"You like her."

Maybe he wasn't wrong, and I really do like her. But in the mix of it all, there is deep, seething hatred and resentment.

I hate her for being Peter's daughter, and she hates me

for stealing her away and forcing her into this marriage. She'll kill me if she has a chance, yet I can't stop looking at her and wishing all of this was real.

She reaches where I'm standing, and I extend a hand to her.

Vivienne stares down at my hand, and then she glares at me before reluctantly taking my hand and following me to the altar.

"You're beautiful in that dress," I whisper to her.

She snorts with derision and rolls her eyes. "You'll be beautiful with a knife in your heart," she whispers back.

We both face the priest, and the old man smiles at us before he begins his sermon.

"That's not a nice thing to say to your husband," I tease. "We'll be married in a couple of minutes. You should learn to be nice."

She huffs out a sigh, and her teeth dig into her lower lip. "Stealing women and forcing them to marry you is not nice, but here we are, husband."

I chuckle at the meanness in her tone as she drags out the word *husband*. I'm glad to see her fierce spirit hasn't died down yet. She's not the type to give up even when she's been defeated.

"Women? You're the only woman I've ever stolen, *gattina*," I say, inching closer to her. She smells so good, and something inside me is itching to inhale her scent.

"You sound proud of yourself."

"I am," I agree. "Taking you away from that restaurant is one of the best things I've done. I don't regret it."

She hisses, "That's a weird thing to be proud of, but I'm sure you'll regret it soon."

I'm about to reply when the priest calls for our rings.

Luca steps forward with them.

We exchange our vows, and though I expect Vivienne to be hesitant, she doesn't even stutter as she says hers.

To anyone watching from the outside, they'd think she's just accepted her fate. But I know her too well to think so. She's probably planning a million ways to kill me, and I'm boiling with excitement as I anticipate what her methods will be.

The guests start to clap when the priest pronounces us husband and wife, and says, "You may kiss your bride."

11

VIVIENNE

My heart throbs against my ribcage, but not with fear. It's something darker, something I hate admitting even to myself.

The man standing in front of me—my enemy and my husband—makes my breath hitch. He looks absolutely dashing in his black suit and that fifties pompadour.

He's watching me, his gaze never once leaving mine, like he owns me. And that's the part that makes my blood boil. He *thinks* he does. The vows are said, but they feel hollow, nothing but a farce.

A lie we're forced to tell in front of everyone here.

This is wrong. Every second of this day has been wrong. He kidnapped me, forced me into this dress, into this marriage. He stole my freedom, made me his prisoner.

But despite the hatred coiling in my stomach, I can't ignore the way my body reacts when he's near. The tension crackles in the air between us, and I despise it almost as much as I despise him.

The priest steps back, and it's time. Time for the kiss in

front of everyone that will mark me as his forever—until he is dead, that is.

The room fades into a blur of faces, but all I see is him, standing so tall, so composed, like he's already won. My fists curl at my sides, my nails biting into my palms.

How dare he?

He leans in, so close I can feel his breath on my lips. My heart stutters, and I curse myself for it. Then, in a voice only I can hear, he whispers, his words sliding over me like silk, yet sharp as a knife.

"You're mine now, *gattina*," he says, his warm breath glazing over my neck like the tempting whisper of sin. "You're mine forever. Let another man touch you, and you'll realize how truly ruthless I can be."

The possessiveness in his voice sends a shiver down my spine, and I hate that my body reacts to it.

His eyes are dark and unyielding as they lock onto mine, daring me to defy him.

For a split second, I consider it, but I know I won't. I can't. Because as much as I want to push him away, as much as I should hate every part of this, there's a part of me that craves him.

The pull between us is so intense that it is driving me insane.

Before I can catch my breath, his lips crash against mine, firm and demanding. The kiss is fierce, controlling, and yet... my traitorous body responds.

I hate him, but God help me. I want him, too. His hand slides to the small of my back, pulling me closer, and I feel myself melting into the kiss, even as my mind screams at me to stop.

This is what he wants. For me to surrender. To give in to him completely.

And damn it, part of me already has. But I can't let him see it. I'd rather die than give him the pleasure of knowing how much he's gotten to me.

"Congratulations on getting married," a voice says behind me.

We quickly pull away from each other, and I spin around to find a woman who looks to be around her early sixties.

Regardless of the wrinkles and her pale skin, she's stunning. It's honestly not hard to know she was a beauty when she was younger.

I chew my lip and glance at Antonio. I don't know this woman, and I'm struggling to muster a reply.

"This is my foster mother, Mariana," Antonio says. He cups the small of my back. "She and Dante raised me after my family was murdered when I was seventeen."

I blink at Antonio, completely stunned. "Your family was what?"

He smiles and ignores my question. "I'm glad you ladies have met."

I sense that he doesn't want to discuss his family with me. I mean, I wouldn't share details about my family with him either.

Still, I feel my chest squeeze with pity for him. I understand grief well enough since I lost my mama when I was just seventeen.

I can't imagine how hard it must've been for him. God, I can't even begin to think of all the anger and pain burning inside him.

Staring at him, I notice the way his smile doesn't meet his eyes and how soulless and cold his dark brown eyes are. I wonder if that experience helped to shape him into the cold person he is now. It must've played a part, that I know.

"And me? Why am I being excluded from this special

meeting?" another woman asks as she joins us. She's beautiful, with dark hair and blue eyes that sparkle under the sunlight.

"No one excluded you, Ginny," Antonio says. He shifts his attention to me. "Ginny, this is my wife, Vivienne. Vivienne, Ginny, Dario's wife."

Ginny's smile grows wider as she steps forward and hugs me. "It's so nice to meet you, Vivienne. You're so beautiful."

I don't know whether to hug her back or not, considering this is not a happy wedding, and I really do not want to get attached to anyone in Antonio's life. I don't want to be rude, though, so I don't pull away. "You're beautiful, too."

She pulls back, her smile dropping, and she pouts. "I'm so sorry about all of this. I know you didn't want to end up in this situation."

I glare at Antonio, who winks at me. I hate the way his eyes crinkle and the way my stomach flutters at it. "At least someone understands me."

"Of course. I'll always come around, so you won't be too bored. I bet living with Antonio won't be all that fun," Ginny says.

I want to tell her that I would rather she sneak me out of here and back to my own home, but I don't. I can't trust anyone here, no matter how bright and genuine their smiles appear. "That would be nice."

I mean it. If I'm in hell, I'd rather have company than be all on my own and depressed. Plus, I can form a friendship with Ginny and use it to my advantage.

A sigh catches my attention. Mariana is staring at me like I'm an alien who just fell to Earth from another planet. I guess she's trying to decipher me. She wants to read my thoughts and intentions for agreeing to this marriage so easily.

Unfortunately for her, I plan to fool everyone completely from now on. I'm in the land of wolves waiting to rip me apart, and wearing fangs is the only way I can survive.

Smiling to their faces and conniving against their backs until I am out of here is something I must do.

But that look on Mariana's face tells me she's already solved me like an easy puzzle. I shudder at the thought that she can read me better than anyone could read an open book. The feeling is unsettling, and one thing is certain: I do not like being around her.

Clearing my throat, I say, "I'd like to excuse myself. I'm hungry and exhausted."

Antonio nods. "Get Agatha to make you something to eat."

I flash a fake smile at him. "Will do." My grin grows wider as I turn to Ginny. "Please, make sure to visit. I'd love to know you better."

She bops her head with so much happiness that I feel bad for lying to her. "Certainly."

IT'S BEEN two hours since I officially became Mrs. Mancini, and I can't stop staring at the huge rock on my finger with disbelief.

I took a shower after I came up, and Agatha brought me dinner. Antonio is still somewhere around the house, and I assume some of the guests have already left by now.

The room is quiet, save for the soft ticking of the clock on the wall, but all I can focus on is the ring. The diamond catches the dim light, scattering fragments of brilliance across the walls, like tiny stars dancing in the shadows. I twist it slowly around my finger, feeling its weight.

Although I never gave much thought to getting married, I never imagined this is how I'd end up wearing a wedding ring.

The diamond is flawless. It's huge, too.

Anyone looking at it would think it's a token of his love for me. But I know this is just a symbol of the power he now has over me. A reminder that I now belong to him.

My thumb brushes over the band, smooth and polished, and I can't help but wonder if this is how my life will be from now on—beautiful on the surface, but hard and cold underneath. Trapped in something I never asked for but can't escape.

I try to ignore the way my pulse quickens just thinking about him.

He's not here, but I feel him. The ring is proof. A part of him wrapped around me, always reminding me of the vows we exchanged—if you can even call them vows. He said the words with such control, such certainty, while I could barely breathe.

And yet, there's this pull. A strange, unshakable draw that keeps me captivated, even now. There's this overwhelming urge to dive into Antonio's world and see who he really is. A stupid hope that underneath his cold and cruel exterior, there's a teenage boy who's just angry at the world for the way he lost his family.

The ring sparkles again, and I hate that a part of me finds it beautiful. I hate that deep down, I don't know if I'd take it off, even if I could.

But the feeling is brief as my thought drifts to Harper. She must be frantic right now, thinking of me and hoping I am safe wherever I am. I do not really care about my father, but my little sister needs me, and I can't just be Antonio's prisoner wife.

No, I need to find a way out of here.

I think for a moment. While I intend to put up a show for Antonio and his family, any attempt to just run away could put my life at risk. Gaining his trust and making him believe I like it here is the only way out.

And to get that, I must give him everything I have to offer. My virginity.

My heart rate picks up at the idea of giving my body to Antonio just to gain his trust, but my core throbs because I know that is not the only reason. As much as I want to deny it, I'm attracted to Antonio.

Every fiber of my being aches for him, and I would rather give it to him than that slimy old man my father wanted to sell me off to.

I hear voices downstairs—Antonio's voice and someone else's.

This is my chance.

I strip off the white robe Agatha brought for me to wear, and I'm only left in my panties. I can't make Antonio see that I want him, but I can make him angry enough to want me, too.

Drawing a breath, I leave the room and start for the patio with my bare breasts exposed and my nipples hard from the thought of him touching them.

Luca is the first to see me, and he quickly looks away. Lorenzo does the same when he sees me.

Antonio has his back to me, but he catches on and quickly spins around.

There's a flicker of rage and desire in his eyes when he sees me. "What the hell do you think you're doing?" he asks gruffly.

I wrap my fingers around my throat and pretend I'm doing nothing wrong. "Oh, I'm thirsty. Don't mind me. I'll go grab a glass of water in the kitchen." I turn toward the kitchen.

"Stop right there!" Antonio orders, his voice thick with authority.

I stop walking, and a smug smile curls on my lips. I have him right where I want him, jealous and possessive.

His shoes clink against the marble floor as he stalks toward me. Shrugging off his suit jacket, he covers me with it.

I expect him to nag me; instead, he throws me over his shoulder and marches up the stairs. I hit his back and kick against the air, pretending to fight him, but he doesn't even budge.

We reach the room, and he lets me down gently. His thick brows furrow, and his eyes narrow on me. "What was that about?"

My brow quirks. "What was what about?"

He towers over me as he inches closer, and I instinctively pace backward until I clash against the cold brick walls. "Don't play games with me, *gattina*."

"I am not playing games with you, Antonio. I was thirsty, and I—"

"Thirsty for my cock?" He presses his body against mine, and I gasp when I feel his dick poking against my thigh.

He's hard, and I can feel the wetness dripping between my legs. We're both crazy for each other right now, hungry to kiss and fuck each other.

"You wish. I wanted water," I lie, despite the ache between my legs and the racing of my heart. "I want... water."

"So, you went downstairs and flaunted your breasts in front of my men because you're thirsty?" he asks, his voice deep and husky, filled with more desire than my brain can handle.

I nod. "Yes. I—" I trail off as his fingers glide between my breasts.

He cups one of them and twists the hard nipple on it. A blend of pain and pleasure waltzes through me, and my breath hitches. "Do I have to remind you that you're mine now, *gattina*?"

I don't answer, so he twists my nipple again. Fuck, I love the wicked intentions behind his punishment. I love how possessive he is, and that's the problem, because I know I shouldn't.

"Answer me, *gattina*," he purrs, bringing his face dangerously close to my neck.

"I don't…" Shit, I know the words he wants to hear, but I don't say them. I need him to punish me and claim me. I want to push him to the edge and see how far he goes with his torment. "I am not yours."

"Wrong answer."

A moan escapes my throat when he leans in and bites my neck softly. I grab his shirt, pulling him closer, and inhaling his citrus and woodsy scent. I want to warm myself up with his heat, and God, I'm losing my mind from how much I need him to punish me.

He cups the back of my head and sucks the life out of me as he kisses my neck.

I'm moaning, holding his shirt tighter and pressing my bare breasts to his chest. The organ between my legs throbs with need. Every single nerve in my body tingles with a hunger only Antonio can satiate.

He kisses his way down to my chest and, taking one of

my breasts in his mouth, he sucks the nipple while teasing the other with his hand.

"Antonio," I moan as my head falls back and my eyes roll in. I'm cocooned with pleasure as liquid flames seep into my veins.

He parts my thighs and slides a finger between my legs. He groans, and a dark smile stalks his expression. "You're wet, *gattina*. Let me take care of you."

Before I can register what is happening, he drops to one knee in front of me and presses a firm finger to my clit. I shudder as the sweetest sensation rushes through me.

"Relax," he whispers. "You're going to like it."

I'm panting with anticipation, grinding against his finger. That is how desperate I am. There's so much tension building inside me, and I'm afraid I'll explode if I don't find an outlet soon.

He positions his head between my legs, and that is when I feel the flicker of his tongue on me.

I let out a primal groan and clutch his hair. I want—*need*—more of that.

He does it again, licking me like I'm a sweet chocolate bar, and all I can do is rest back, relishing how good it feels as he sticks his tongue inside me and fucks me with it.

12

ANTONIO

The taste of Vivienne on the tip of my tongue is divine. She's delicious in an intoxicating way, and I can't get enough of her.

Her nails dig into my flesh, and her legs curl around me. She pushes herself up against me, bucking her hips and spreading her legs wider. Her moans are soft and sensual, and my dick twitches almost painfully to every sound that she makes.

Sliding my tongue out of her and gliding it over her clitoris, I push a finger inside her and watch in amusement as her face contorts with pleasure.

She's enjoying this, and it fills me with a sort of satisfaction I've never felt before. I've never felt this anxious about pleasuring a woman, never been this desperate to make any woman enjoy my touch before now.

But it's different with Vivienne. I'd be satisfied just watching the sheer pleasure tearing up her emerald eyes.

She jerks forward when I push up another finger inside her and curl it up to her G-spot. Her jaw falls open, and she gasps for air, for my name. "Antonio."

"Who does this pussy belong to?" I ask, peering into her eyes.

Those beautiful emerald-green globes bore into mine with the intensity of wildfire. "It's..." Her chest heaves, her nipples hardening even more. "It's yours."

"Good girl," I purr, drowning in the taste of her. I'm fucking high and thirsty to stretch her out with my cock. "Whose body is this?"

"Yours," she whispers under her breath.

"I want to hear you say my name, *gattina*. Who do you belong to?"

"You... Antonio." She lets out a cry of pleasure as I press my tongue firmly on her clitoris and start to pump her with my fingers. She's fucking wet. "I belong to Antonio Mancini."

I groan at the way she calls my name, like it's a blend of whiskey and sin. I want to hear her scream my name when I break into her and fuck her like the world is about to end. "Flaunt what belongs to me like that again, and I'll kill every man that looks your way, Vivienne."

Her moans grow more desperate. "I won't. I think I'm... I'm going to come."

"Come for me, baby." I pull out my fingers and thrust them inside her again while my tongue dances aggressively with her sensitive organ. "I want you to come in my mouth."

She cries out as her orgasm sears through her. Her grip on my hair tightens, and I throw my arms around her to keep her steady as she starts to jerk.

I lick off her orgasm before I raise myself to my feet and carry her to the bed. Pulling my pants down, I crawl on top of her and kiss her ravenously, feeding her the taste of her juices.

She snakes her arms around me and kisses me harder.

Her teeth gently nibble at my bottom lip, and I groan into the kiss. Her taste still lingers on my tongue, and I want more. I want to feel her under me, around me. I want to possess every inch of her body.

Lifting myself slightly, I position myself at the entrance of her wet, eager pussy.

She looks up at me with eyes burning with desire and a hint of fear, as if she's not entirely sure what's about to happen.

But I don't give her time to think too hard about it—with one swift motion, I thrust myself inside her, causing her to cry out in a mixture of pain and pleasure.

I stop moving to look at her. "Does it hurt too much?"

She opens her eyes. The tears in them make me want to freeze. The thought of causing her pain is somehow unbearable. It's something I've never felt before now. "It does, but don't stop. Please don't."

I lean in and start to kiss her again, and then I push inside her with another powerful thrust.

She screams, breaking our kiss as tears run down her cheeks. She looks so vulnerable and in pain, and it completely breaks a part of me. I would stop if she wanted me to, but she holds me tighter, urging me to go on.

"I'm sorry," I whisper as I pepper kisses down her neck and chest.

She shakes her head. "It hurts, but I'm enjoying it too. I want it. Don't slow down."

Her eyes lock with mine, her emerald gaze filled with a hunger that matches my own. I thrust deeper, matching the rhythm of our breaths and the sounds of our flesh slapping together.

After a moment, her moans are filled with nothing but pleasure.

"Fuck me, Antonio," she whispers, her voice hoarse with desire. "Don't go easy on me."

I oblige, slamming into her with all my strength, our bodies slick with sweat and passion. I'm lost in the sensation of being inside her, feeling her tremble beneath me.

Her nails dig into my back, leaving small red marks that I know will fade within a day or two. Her grip is strong and assertive, and I can feel her heart pounding against my chest as we kiss, the intensity of our passion seeming to grow with each passing moment.

As I continue to thrust into her, her moans grow louder and more desperate. Her emerald eyes are locked onto mine, filled with a raw, primal desire that only fuels my own hunger.

I can feel the tension building within me, the pleasure coursing through my veins like wildfire. The thought of climaxing inside her makes my cock twitch even more, and I know that this is what I've been waiting for all this time.

A fiery need takes over me. I want to possess her completely, to feel every part of her body shaking and moaning under my touch. The thought of her wanting it as much as I do sends a wave of exhilaration through me.

I pick up the pace, feeling myself nearing my release. She whimpers, her eyes wide and wild, as if she's not sure she can take anymore, but instead of slowing down, I intensify the rhythm.

"Antonio!" she cries out, "I'm going to come again."

Her words send a jolt of electricity through me, making me slam into her harder. My fingers are gripping her ass tight, but it's still not enough. I need more contact, more friction. More of her.

"Come for me," I whisper in her ear, my voice low and

filled with lust. "I want you to come with my cock inside you, baby."

Her walls clench around my dick, her legs curling tighter around me. She screams out my name as she comes once again, her muscles clamping down on me fiercely.

The sound of her moan, along with the way her body shudders beneath me, drives me over the edge.

I groan when my orgasm hits me like a tidal wave, and I thrust harder and deeper into her than ever before.

Her muscles contract around me, milking me of every drop of cum I have until I start to soften inside her.

As her orgasm subsides, she wraps her legs around me tighter, holding me close as our breaths slow down.

I kiss her forehead and then her lips. I can't get enough of this woman—my wife—and as much as I want to deny it, I know this is not just sex. I'm getting addicted to this woman; I feel possessive and protective over her as well, as if I could burn the world down just for her, which is strange because I've never felt anything like that before.

Not just because she is my prisoner, but because of a deeper emotion I don't understand.

She lets out a breath. "That was better than I expected."

"What did you expect?" I ask, curling her hair around my finger.

She shrugs and thinks for a moment. "I don't know. Maybe I just didn't think I would enjoy it as much as I did." Her cheeks turn red with embarrassment. "I need to wash up."

What a smart way to change the topic.

I pull out of her, and for the first time, I notice the trail of blood between her thighs and how my cock is covered in blood, her blood. I took her virginity tonight, and I've marked her as mine.

She can't escape from me now. But regardless of all I have taken from this woman, I know there's a part of her that will always hate me. There's a part of her that will never be mine.

I'll never have her heart.

An alarm goes off in my head, and memories of Dante's lifeless body flash before my eyes. I don't need her heart. All I need is to find Dante's killer.

Rising to my feet, I throw a blanket over her. "Don't move."

She sits up, clutching the blanket to her chest and looking confused. "What is wrong?"

I smirk. "You'll find out soon."

I take my phone out of my pants' pocket and take three pictures of her. She throws her hand over her face to block it out, but it's too late.

"What the hell do you think you're doing?" she barks.

"Proof of life for daddy dearest." I find Peter's number and forward the pictures to him. "I wonder what he'll think when he sees them."

She glares at me with so much spite that I feel my chest tighten. I hate it when she gives me that look. "Is that why you did what you did? Just say you can take pictures and torment my father with them?"

A pang of guilt makes my pulse race, but I don't let it deter me. I don't have to explain anything to her. "Will it make it better if I say no?"

Her eyes glisten with tears, and she shakes her head. "It won't. I blame myself. I must've forgotten how much of a bastard you are."

My phone buzzes with an incoming call. It's Peter.

"Go get cleaned up," I tell her. "Your daddy might need another picture before he agrees to my terms."

"Asshole," she spits at me. She wraps the duvet around herself and starts for the bathroom. Each step she takes is slow and calculated, as if she's in so much pain.

I can't take it anymore, so I stride over to her and lift her into my arms. Surprisingly, she doesn't fight me. She allows her to lower her into the bathtub and fill it up with water.

Minutes later, she's done bathing and falls asleep.

I take a shower and go to my study to tend to business.

The first thing I do is call Peter back. I can bet on my life that the old man is raging and thinking of all the ways he can kill me. Unfortunately for him, I am not that easy to get rid of.

It rings just once, and he answers immediately, as if he were waiting for me to call back. "What did you do to my daughter?"

"Do you want me to go into details?" I muse. "It'll take a while, and you might die of a heart attack before I get to the main part."

"Antonio—"

"What part do you want to hear first?" I ask, cutting him off. "The part where I slid my ring onto her finger... Or would you rather hear how it felt to be inside her?"

"I'll kill you," he growls with so much rage and threat in his voice. "I'll find you, and I will make you die miserably."

I huff out a mocking laugh. "Not if I kill your daughter first."

"I won't let you off if you harm her."

Another chuckle escapes my lips. "I don't think you understand me, Peter. Now, let's start over. You're not in the position to make threats or even be angry. If you want your daughter safe, all you have to do is tell me what I want to know."

There's a moment of silence as if he's considering and

weighing between his pride and his daughter's life. "What do you want to know?"

"Who killed Dante and why?"

He sighs heavily. "I can tell you anything but that. They'll come for my entire family if I tell you, I can't risk it."

There's a knock on the door. Lorenzo and Luca walk inside. Lorenzo sits on the mesh chair across my desk, and Luca rests his back against the wall, folding his arms and watching me.

"I see," I drawl. "You're afraid of whoever it is. But you see, I lost something, and I have nothing else to lose. You know the type of man you should fear? The one who has nothing to lose."

He remains tight-lipped, my clue that he's not going to give up the answer easily. It looks like I went through the stress of kidnapping Vivienne and forcing her into marrying me for nothing.

Either way, I intend to get my answer, and I don't give a flying fuck if I have to force it out of his fucking mouth.

"You have three days to give me the answer I need, or I'll torture your daughter each day. I'll tear her apart limb by limb until there's nothing left," I threaten, keeping my tone low and icy. "When I am done with her, and there's nothing left, I'll come for your other daughter and make you watch as I kill her."

"Antonio—"

I hang up before he can finish. I already know men like Peter enough to predict he's trying to negotiate, not give up whoever is behind Dante's death.

"That fucker won't talk, will he?" Luca says, his eyes burning with as much rage as the one I feel in my gut.

I rise to my feet and grab my car key from the table.

"Select two guards to watch Vivienne. She must not be left unsupervised."

I'm about to walk out the door when Lorenzo's voice brings me to a halt. "Are you really going to torture her?"

That question makes me feel like I've just been hit with a sledgehammer. Swallowing suddenly becomes too hard. "I'll do whatever I have to."

But deep down, a part of me knows I'll never be able to hurt her. And I'll kill anyone who dares to.

13

VIVIENNE

Rage. Betray. Confusion.

I'm feeling all of those emotions at once, and the problem is that I have no freaking idea why I feel that way.

I knew what Antonio was before I decided to seduce him. I know he hates me, and all of this is just his perfect plot for revenge, but I think a part of me died when he took those pictures of me last night.

Whatever hope I had that a part of him was human, at least, is long gone. I only have hatred left to offer him now.

Slipping out of bed and sliding my legs into the fluffy slippers next to the bed, I walk to the vanity mirror to tie my hair in a bun. Surprisingly, I no longer feel any pain or burn like I thought I would.

I'm not even bleeding or spotting. I read online that many girls do.

The red hickey around my neck catches my attention when I raise my hair.

It's so red, like an imprint. A mark to show that I was now fully his and there's no going back. I'd given him my virginity—it was the only thing I could give to earn his trust, but that wasn't even enough.

God, I want to hate him so badly. I want to curse him until my tongue dries out, but as I run my finger over the hickey, all I can think of is the way he kissed and fucked me last night. The way my body reacted to each thrust of his cock inside me and the flicker of his tongue on my clitoris.

My scalp prickles with need, the hair at the back of my neck rising on end as I imagine him standing behind me and doing all of those things to me again. My heart starts to race, and heat simmers in my stomach.

Good heavens, I don't think I'll be able to get over last night quickly. It's a memory engraved in the nastiest part of my mind.

But Papa... My God, Harper... I hope she doesn't see those pictures because she'll think the worst of it. She'll be in so much pain if she thinks I'm being tortured and raped here.

As for my father, I don't care what he thinks. It's not like he cares about me that much anyway. I'm probably nothing but tainted goods to him right now. If he does react to those pictures, it will be nothing but a matter of his reputation and ego, and not because he truly cares for me.

I'm so lost in thought that I flinch when someone knocks. I hold my chest and inhale deeply. "Who's there? Come in!"

The door creaks open, and Agatha's head pops into the room. With the way she's standing, someone could think she's a floating, bodiless head.

"Good morning, Mrs. Mancini," she says.

I roll my eyes. I'll never come to terms with that, too. "Just call me Vivienne," I correct her.

She nods. "Good morning, Vivienne. It's time for breakfast."

After last night, I would have to be a beast to have an appetite to sit at the same table with that Italian asshole. I don't care if I'm starving. I would rather that than share a meal with him. "I'm not hungry."

"Mr. Mancini—"

"I don't care what Mr. Mancini said or what he'll do. I'm not eating with him." I force a smile to hide the anger raging in my veins. Agatha did nothing wrong to me; it's not right for me to direct my anger at her. "Please, tell him I am not hungry."

She reluctantly nods and leaves the room.

Minutes later, the door swings open, and Antonio marches in. His face is stone cold, as blank as a white wall. "Come downstairs; you do not get to turn down breakfast," he says.

I pretend not to hear him and keep staring out the window. A bird perches on a tree miles away, and I watch in amusement as it starts to groom its wings.

"Vivienne!"

I flinch at the tone of Antonio's voice and turn around to face him. "Goodness, you almost gave me a heart attack." I push my hair behind my ear and act as if I didn't notice him walk inside minutes ago. "When did you come in?"

"Don't play games with me, Vivienne."

"Games?" I scoff at his audacity to get mad after what he did last night. "You took photos of me after we had sex and sent them to my father, and somehow, I'm the one who's playing games?"

"Watch it, *gattina*. You don't want me to cut off that sharp tongue of yours and ship it to your papa, do you?"

A shiver runs down my spine. How can such vile threats

slip out of his tongue so easily? I don't understand. My heart begins to pound faster with fear, but I don't back down.

I'm a Cole, and Coles don't tremble in front of their enemies. My papa used to tell me that all the time when I was a kid. "Do it."

His brows shoot up to his hairline.

"What's that look? Are you surprised I am not on my knees begging you?" I chuckle sardonically, holding his gaze. "But remember this: In the end, I plan to repay my debt. An eye for an eye, Antonio. I might even repay double, you fucking monster."

I don't know what part of what I said provokes him, because, in the blink of an eye, he's across the room with his fingers around my throat. He's pressing me to the ball, pressing his body against mine.

I inhale him like he's the most intoxicating thing to have ever existed. And I think he is because I can't get enough of that citrus scent or the heat rolling off him. My head instantly becomes mush, filled with filthy thoughts.

Behave, Vivienne. You're not supposed to find this hot.

"I think you've forgotten where you are and who your life depends on, *gattina*," he whispers harshly, his breath a hot tang along my neckline.

It feels like a lover's caress, and I wish he'd just kiss me instead of talking. "I know where I am and who I'm with," I tell him, straightening my spine and refusing to back down. "It's impossible for me to forget how you kidnapped me and forced me to marry you."

"We're not going through this again, *gattina*," he says calmly.

"We are," I shoot back sharply. "Insult me again like you did last night, and I'll kill myself before you have a chance to blackmail my father with my half-naked pictures, pig."

I expect him to go crazy with rage, but instead, his eyes crinkle with amusement. He's stunned by my guts, but not in a bad way. "We have to put that mouth of yours to some good use."

We both look at the bulge in his sweatpants at the same time, and he winks at me.

I gag, pretending I'm absolutely disgusted by the idea of it. But I'm not. My mouth waters at the thought of having him fill it up with the size and length of his dick. I wonder what he tastes like and how much it'll ache sucking him up.

"Now, what dirty thought is running through that perverted head of yours?" he drawls mischievously.

My stomach flutters, and my face heats up with a blush. "I'm not disgusting, asshole."

Too embarrassed to face him, knowing he can see right through me fully, I shuffle past him and head downstairs. I'm hungry anyway, and I might as well eat since he came to ask me himself.

I stiffen when I hear him walking behind me. I wonder what he's thinking or looking at. "Stop looking at my ass, Antonio."

He huffs out laughter and starts to walk down the stairs even more quickly. "For someone who was a virgin until last night, your mind is nasty." He doesn't give me a chance to muster a retort as he jogs down what is left of the stairs.

He's already sitting at the head of the table when I join him, and I take the chair furthest away from him.

Filling my plate with eggs, bacon, and fruit, I grab a fork and dig in. "I need new clothes."

He glances at me with his brows shot up, but he doesn't say a word.

"Unless you'd prefer taking me home so I can grab my

things and let my sister know I'm still alive," I say, straining the last word.

He drags his attention back to the food. "I'll take you after breakfast. You can buy whatever you need."

"Why do you need to take me?"

He sighs as if that's the dumbest question ever. It could be, and I asked just to piss him off. "Should I let you go on your own so you can run off?"

I scoff and roll my eyes. "For someone who dared to kidnap me from a restaurant both my father and Enzo were at, you're smart. I'll give you that."

"One more thing, you're going to have new bodyguards from now on. I'll introduce the two of them after breakfast. They can take you out when I'm unavailable, and you're not to move around the mansion without them."

Ice trickles through my veins. Having bodyguards watching me means it'll be close to impossible to escape this place. I mean, it's already that with all the bodyguards around and all.

But having personal ones... Oh God. I'll never be able to leave. I may never see Harper again or get my freedom, not unless Antonio dies.

My chest tightens, and I struggle to breathe as my panic surges through me like wildfire. I glare at Antonio, cursing him in the back of my mind and hoping he dies in an excruciating way. His death is the only way I can regain my freedom; it's the only way I'll truly be happy.

"Bodyguards?" I laugh manically. "More like prison guards. You're only giving them to me so they can watch me. You want to be sure I don't escape from here."

A smug smile creeps up his face, and his eyes darken. "You're right.

His phone beeps, and he shifts his attention to it,

ignoring me completely. He doesn't notice the way my chest heaves with each breath or the tears welling up in my eyes.

Fine, he can laugh now, because it won't be long before he'll be breathing his last. And I'll have a good last laugh while I kill him.

Heck, I might even fuck him before I send him straight to hell.

14

ANTONIO

Vivienne has been ignoring me since breakfast this morning. She doesn't like the idea of having bodyguards because she knows all too well that I'm trying to keep her from escaping.

I could see right through her last night, and I could tell she'd enraged me on purpose. She'd thought giving me her virginity would be enough to earn my trust, but that is one thing she'll never have, even if she gives up her life for me.

She is Peter Cole's daughter, my enemy by nature. I'll never trust her; it'll snow in hell before I let her come within an inch of my heart.

Sexual attraction and love are two different things. I've never felt the latter, and I'm more than certain I will never feel that way for her. No matter what she does or how crazy she drives me.

My heart will never beat faster or flutter for her, no matter how hard it is to keep my eyes off her or the thought of her legs crossed around my waist off my mind.

The driver pulls over at the parking lot of a three-story shopping mall, and we both climb out of the car.

Vivienne stares up at the tall, white building towering above us, and her lips curl with a wicked smile. "I've heard a lot about this place. Most of the designer companies have a store in this building, am I right?"

I nod.

The place is far away from Peter's and Salvatore's territory. No one will recognize her here.

She hisses. "I wonder how many women you've been with know this place. Man whore."

I narrow my eyes at her. "What did you just call me?"

She shrugs. "Nothing. Did you hear me say anything?"

I heard her, but I pretended I didn't. She's trying to get on my nerves—she's good at it. But I won't let her, not while we're in public.

"I'll warn you, though, I'm a big shopper, and I like expensive things," she says with a lopsided grin before walking away gingerly as if she owns the entire world.

My brow furrows, and a smile curls my lips before I can stop it. No woman has ever dared to warn me or act like this to me, but Vivienne is not just any woman, I suppose. She's a thorn in my flesh, one that infuriates me deeply yet somehow softens the part of my heart I didn't even know I possessed.

I should hate her, but I can't. There's just something about this woman I find intoxicating. Maybe it's her fierceness. I'm not too sure yet.

I follow her inside, walking closely beside her as one of the bodyguards leads the way. Vivienne is wrong. I only know this place because I'd done extensive research on the best shopping mall in the city, and this is the result I came up with.

My relationship with women has always been fairly the same. Meet at the club, suck my cock in my office, and be on your way. Vivienne is the only woman who's been successful at making me shop with her, even though I can sense she hates every bit of my presence around her.

It's fine, though. I love her presence, and that is all that matters.

I catch two men in a corner ogling her from where they're standing. One of them has his eyes on her ass as we walk by.

Rage filters through my system, and I'm suddenly possessed by jealousy and the need to protect what it is. I wrap my arm around Vivienne, marking my territory.

We're out in public, so that is all I can do. On a good day, those *bastardi* would have lost their fucking lives by now. She's my wife, and I would rather they keep their disgusting gazes to themselves.

Vivienne's gaze flits to my hand on her shoulder, then she glances up at me, her eyes filled with curiosity. "What the hell do you think you are doing?"

"Don't ask questions and keep moving, *gattina*. I don't have all day to hang around with you," I say, struggling to sound as if I'm not thinking of a million ways I could torture those bastards before I kill them.

Aiutami, Cristo! Help me, Christ.

We arrive at the store she'll be shopping from moments later, and Vivienne takes in the place in awe. She's Peter Cole's daughter, which means she usually shops in places like this, so I doubt her expression is shock at how expensive the place is.

"Why are we the only ones here?" she notices.

I spot the store manager and two other women as they approach us with wide smiles. "I reserved the entire store for you. I need you to be comfortable while you shop."

Her laughter hangs heavy in the air, as if she's calling my

bullshit. "Really? I think you reserved this entire place so people won't find out you're nothing but a criminal."

The store manager reaches us before I can think of a comeback for her.

"Good afternoon, Mr. Mancini," the manager, Grace, greets with a smile. She turns to Vivienne. "And..." she trails off as if she isn't sure whether to refer to Vivienne as my wife or not.

"My wife, Vivienne," I introduce.

"Ah." Grace's smile widens. "Welcome to our store, Mrs. Mancini. We have a lot of new arrivals. What would you like us to show you first?"

"I'm a sucker for red heels and black dresses," Vivienne answers, smiling back. "You can show me either of those first."

I don't realize I'm no longer breathing as I stare at Vivienne. I hate how I'm a total idiot around this woman.

Dante's rotting in his grave six feet under. Peter Cole is running around, hale and hearty. I should be torturing his daughter, breaking her until he has no other option than to tell me what I am, but here I am, losing myself every time she smiles.

It's hard to resist this feeling, not with the way her eyes crinkle and her cheeks double in size when she smiles. Not with the way her skin glows under the overhead light. No woman I've ever met holds a candle to her.

I sit in the waiting room while she selects several bags, shoes, and dresses to suit her taste. An hour passes, and then another thirty minutes before she finally steps into the waiting room wearing a long, black dress with a deep v-cut in front and a slit to the right that runs down the entire leg.

My mouth drops, and my eyes devour her ravenously. She looks ravishing in that dress, and the way it highlights her curves and everything... *Mio Dio,* I can't take my eyes off her.

She notices because scarlet red burns her cheeks, and she bites her bottom lip. "Why are you looking at me like that?" she asks in a voice that is barely above a whisper.

"You look breathtaking in that dress." The words slip from my mouth before I can stop them. Dammit, I don't even think I want to stop them.

"Thank you," she says, her voice shaky with nerves.

I wonder if she's feeling the same way I do. If her insides are burning with a ravenous need for me. If every hair on the back of her neck is rising and her core is throbbing, aching, and dying for a feel of me.

Because mine is.

Every cell in my body is on fire. My cock keeps twitching, and my pulse is beating at a rate that could send me straight to hell. My thoughts are unholy, and only she—Vivienne—can make me well again.

My gaze drops to the pair of red shoes she's holding.

She holds the shoes forward. "I want these."

I narrow my eyes at her, confused. "So? Get them."

"They cost three thousand dollars," she says, watching me for a reaction. "Are you sure you can afford to get them for me? I mean, I've wanted them for a while, but I can—"

"I said, get them," I repeat. "Get whatever you want."

"I'll max out your credit card."

A chuckle rips from my throat. She has no freaking idea how much I spend in bars some nights. Fifty of those shoes won't even come close to maxing out my card. "That's a challenge I welcome, *gattina*. I'll hold you to your words."

She squints and starts to feast on her lower lip. She looks even more confused than I was seconds ago. "You sure you're not gonna regret saying that?"

Striding over to her, I gently push her down on the sofa and take the shoes from her.

She tries to stand, but I don't allow her as I take one of her feet and slide off the slippers she's wearing. God, even her foot is pretty and soft. Is there a part of this woman that is not perfect?

I take out one of the shoes she brought in and help her put it on, and then I do the same with the second one.

She tenses at my touch, her eyes wide and searching mine.

When I'm done with the shoes, I stand up and extend a hand out to her.

A moment passes before she finally takes my hands and stands up. She's only tall enough to reach my shoulders, even in those heels.

"Those shoes were made for you, baby," I whisper as I wrap my arm around her waist and pull her closer. "And I never regret anything I say."

An hour later, we're done shopping and driving back home. Vivienne is ecstatic to show Agatha the dress she got for her. We also stopped by a jewelry store to get a bracelet for Ginny.

I appreciate how she cares for everyone—how she wants to share whatever she has with those around her.

We're driving on the highway when the driver suddenly starts speeding and glances at the rearview mirror.

"There's a problem, boss," he says calmly. It's a common rule in the Mafia. Panic is the enemy of logic. It does more harm than good when a person is in a dangerous situation. "I think we're being followed."

I whip my head around to stare at the cars behind us. They're all the same black Mercedes with tinted windows, and they're driving at a high speed.

He's right, we're being followed.

I take out a gun from a spot under the car seat where I store them for emergencies.

"What is happening?" Vivienne asks with a panicked voice.

I cock my gun. "We're being followed. Get down, and don't raise your head until it's over."

She nods and does as I say.

The bodyguard in the passenger seat calls the others to alert them to the situation, so they're on guard in case anything happens.

The tires screech as the impact from behind jolts us forward. I grit my teeth, keeping my grip on the gun firm. The car swerves slightly, but our driver maintains control, steering us back into the center of the lane.

"Hold on!" the driver barks, his voice steady despite the chaos.

Another crash. This time, they ram us from the side, trying to force us off the road. My jaw tightens, adrenaline spiking as I glance at Vivienne crouched low in the seat, clutching the dress bag like it's a lifeline. Her trust in me to protect her fuels the fire roaring in my chest.

"Step on it," I command, my tone sharp.

The driver nods and accelerates, weaving through the traffic on the highway. The engine roars, and the speedometer needle climbs. My men in the other cars will catch up soon, but we're on our own for now.

"Boss, they're trying to box us in!" the bodyguard in the passenger seat shouts, pointing to the black Mercedes closing in from either side.

I roll the window down and lean out slightly, taking aim. The wind howls in my ears, but my focus narrows to the target—the driver in one of the cars chasing us. I fire. The windshield of the Mercedes cracks, and the car veers off course, slamming into a barrier.

"Good shot!" the bodyguard yells. But there's no time to celebrate. Another car pulls up, and the muzzle of a gun glints through its open window. A barrage of bullets pelts our vehicle.

"Down!" I shout, ducking as the windows shatter. Shards of glass rain over us, but I don't care. My priority is to get Vivienne out of this safe.

The driver turns sharply onto an exit ramp, tires screeching as we narrowly avoid slamming into a truck. The maneuver throws off one of the enemy's cars, but two others stay on our tail.

My phone buzzes, and I glance at the screen. It's Lorenzo. "We're two minutes out," he says.

"We don't have two minutes!" I snap, ending the call.

The second Mercedes comes alongside us. Its passenger leans out, gun in hand. I don't give him a chance. I fire three quick shots, and he slumps forward. Their car swerves and collides with the one behind it, taking both out of the chase.

Only one left.

The driver floors it, and we speed onto a narrow stretch of road. The final car closes in, its front bumper nearly kissing ours. My bodyguard fires at their tires but misses. They ram us again, and we spin briefly before the driver regains control.

Enough of this.

"Slow down," I order. The driver hesitates but complies, letting the enemy's car pull alongside us. I aim carefully, waiting until their window aligns with mine. The moment it does, I shoot. The bullet finds its mark—their driver. The Mercedes swerves violently before crashing into a guardrail.

Silence.

Our car slows to a stop on the side of the road. I glance back at Vivienne, who's still crouched low. "It's over," I say, my voice softer now. She looks up, her emerald eyes wide with fear and something else—relief, maybe?

The convoy of our cars pulls up moments later. Lorenzo jumps out, scanning the scene. "You good, boss?"

I nod, handing him my gun. "Clean this up. I'm taking her home."

Vivienne looks at me as I settle back into my seat. Her hands tremble, but she says nothing. She doesn't have to.

The horror in her eyes is enough for me to decipher what she wants to say. The half-dead guy in the smoking Mercedes works for her father. He somehow figured out we'd be here and sent them to retrieve his daughter.

If he thought getting her back would be that simple, then he underestimates me. I need to get a message across to him in a language he'll understand.

I slide out of my seat and round the car to drag Vivienne out of hers. "Do you recognize any of these Italian bastards?"

She shakes her head. She has the guts to lie despite the obvious fear in her eyes and the way her body is trembling. "No... I... I don't recognize any of them."

I smirk. My little wife is not a good liar. "That will make my job easier then." I fill my gun with more bullets and point it at one of the men, but she grabs my hand just as I'm about to pull the trigger.

"What are you doing?" she yells.

"Getting rid of them." I scrutinize her expression. "They

tried to kill us. I should make sure that never happens again, shouldn't I?"

She huffs out a shaky breath. "You can't do that."

I cock my brow. "Why?"

"Because..." She pauses, and her throat bobs as she swallows. "They're... my father's men."

"So, you lied to me?"

"I couldn't just let you kill them," she shoots back, her eyes wild with rage. "I thought you'd hurt them if you knew."

I chuckle at her naivety this time around. "Their fates were decided the moment they decided to chase my car, *gattina*. Only one of them will be leaving here alive."

A shot rings in the air as I pull the trigger on the first guy.

Vivienne screams, but Luca holds her back before she can lunge at me. "No! Antonio, don't!"

It's a little too late for that, as I pull the trigger three more times, until only one of the men is left.

Prowling toward him, I drop to a squat in front of him and press the gun to his temple. "Tell Peter I'll be sending his daughter's head to him if he pulls a shit stunt like this again."

15

VIVIENNE

Sigh.

Groaning, I roll over on the bed, lying on my back as I stare at the ceiling. It is another day to start again. Well, it's more like *try* again in my case. How does the saying go? *If the going gets tough, rather die trying?*

That can't be it. I'm not going to die trying. I'm going to fucking succeed in getting out of this place, by any means necessary.

I sit up, lean against the soft headboard. The covers slip below my breasts, and I don't even pull them back up. What's the point anyway? I went to sleep naked and frustrated, and woke up even more so. I might as well act like the captive that I truly am.

Each time I remember the icy look in Antonio's eyes when he unashamedly admitted to kidnapping me from the restaurant, I want to put a dent in that perfectly handsome face of his. Heartless bastard!

Folding my arms, I brainstorm alternative options I might need to use to find a way to escape from Antonio

Mancini's fortress, but the only solution that presents itself is sex.

Mind-blowing continuous sex with the cold-hearted monster.

In a normal world, where ordinary, innocent people carry on their day-to-day lives, it is understandable to advise a girl my age not to consider such a hopelessly degrading option—*sex*. I should maintain my dignity, prioritize my self-respect, rather than sacrifice myself, than willingly present my body to the Italian devil.

But there are two major problems.

The first one is that this world of guns, violence, and rivers of red is anything but normal. And here, a girl has to compromise to save herself.

The second one is, in this complicated case of mine, even compromising is not enough. *Having sex* with Antonio will not be enough to earn his trust and finally be rid of him. He is a man of means, a man with the looks. A man with *everything*. And every single fucking thing—power, charm, charisma, intelligence, and all of those potentials—works to my disadvantage. Sex with me can be sex with any other woman. One snap of his slender fingers or a commanding bat of his short eyelashes, and a hundred of them would gladly fall at his feet.

Sunken by the weight of burdens, I slip back into the covers, finding no strength to continue the rest of the day. The air is warm, the sheets are comfortable, but my life is officially a mess, and I miss my sister so much. My chest aches like a sledgehammer slammed right through, leaving a big, fat hole behind. My father always said I was the stubborn one, the one who preferred things to go her way, the one who pretended to listen but hated to do what anyone else demanded of me.

I used to think he was right, until now.

Now, all I desire is to go back to sleep and pretend that I can dream the rest of my life away till it's all over. With the rest of my future looking bleak, sex can be put on hold, but sleep can't. I am sure as hell not going to cry.

A soft knock on the door startles me. My heart lurches into my throat at the idea that I might have accidentally conjured the man himself from my thought, but soon enough, the hammering stops.

Antonio Mancini waiting by the door for my permission to come in? Ha! Laughable, indeed. If it was him, he wouldn't bother to knock. Only normal people with respect for others do that.

I don't get up, but my ears strain to pick out the smallest sound that can help me identify the stranger at the door. "Who is it?"

"Agatha."

Oh.

Dragging the covers to my chin, I sink my head deeper into the pillow. The thought of how I threatened this woman with a knife to her throat lingers. *A fucking knife,* for Christ's sake. Maybe I'm burying my head in subtle shame, or maybe I'm just pretending to be sick. She can interpret it either way when she comes in.

"The door's unlocked." Because the man himself would stir up a disastrous storm if he finds out I keep the door locked.

Again, Vivienne, you are not the owner of yourself.

Like hell, I'm not.

The door clicks shut behind the old woman as she shuffles into the room, bearing gifts: toiletries and something that looks like a pink maternity gown. Sitting up, I clutch the covers to my chest. Her brows dip, and a pout takes shape on her lips. She places the gown and tubes of toothpaste, cream, and other items at the foot of the bed, then walks over to the side to gently rest the back of her hand on my head.

"Are you well, child?"

I'm looking into her eyes, melting under her motherly touch, wondering—*Am I?*

Are you well, Vivienne?

The answer is, of course, a very solid N-O.

"Yes, sure." Being more self-conscious, I stretch the covers higher up and shift my gaze away from hers.

Her kindness surprises and overwhelms me. Perhaps, she doesn't remember, but the memory is as vivid as the day I was kidnapped—glinting steel held to her throat. *God,* how pathetic could I be? I wanted to run away from a killer, and I harassed an old woman.

Calming down, I encourage myself. It is not my fault that I am here. Again, compromise.

"Then why are you naked? Did you have a fever?"

"I might as well have. It's hot in here."

The air-conditioners are working just fine. I didn't turn them on. Maybe I low-key just wanted to wallow in frustration. Who knows? The point is, I feel suffocated and need a way out. But my conscience pricks like a freaking needle, and I know I cannot continue a conversation with Agatha until I—

"I'm sorry."

Wide-eyed and startled, she takes a step back. "Whatever for?"

What does she mean by "whatever for?"

I could have hurt you, woman!

"For the other day. The knife episode."

A hearty chuckle leaves her lips, and she goes around

the bed again, picks up the items she dropped there, and starts moving about the room to fix them where they belong. When she is done, she ambles toward me and hands me the dress. When I take a closer look, I am relieved to notice the laces dangling at what I suppose is the back of the flowing dress.

Taking it from her, I keep it beside me on the bed.

"We all have our crazy days. That was your day, and I perfectly understood your need for fight or flight. I was available and vulnerable. If I were in your shoes, I might have done the same thing, child. I hold nothing against you. I couldn't even if I wanted to. You are Nio's own. No good can come out of holding a grudge."

I almost bite down on my tongue when she indirectly points out Antonio's ownership over me and focus instead on her ability to forgive. How is it possible that a woman with such a golden heart and an invisible halo hovering over her head works for a man like Antonio?

It's almost enviable. If I had a shred of her piousness, I might have settled in twenty-four hours after my abduction.

Thinking about it stirs a flame in my chest that I thought I could sleep away.

Settling in? Bullshit.

My father *was* right. I am resilient *and* stubborn. And I pretended to listen and subdue, but hated it when anyone else demanded something from me.

Antonio didn't play fair with me, so I wasn't going to either with him, and as long as I am concerned, he dragged in the wrong fucking cat.

I am Vivienne Cole, and I am prepared to rain shit on Antonio Mancini's parade. If he thinks he'll easily break me, he has another thing coming.

"Thank you, sincerely. You will make my stay here a little

less awkward." I hold my head up high and stare out the window. "Say, Agatha, I've been wondering, what can a girl like me do for fun around here?"

I don't look at her, but catch a glimpse of shoulders moving from the periphery. "Fun? I'm not sure, child. This fortress wasn't designed to be a kid's playground. But I guess... It is a sunny day. You can lounge by the pool. I can ask someone to buy and bring up a selection of the finest bikinis for you to choose from. Nio wouldn't mind, as long as you behave."

Kicking the covers off with a wide, lopsided grin, I strut to the bathroom.

Of course, he wouldn't.

Before I shut the bathroom door behind me, I don't fail to appreciate the old maid for her kind-heartedness and naivety.

"Thank you, Agatha. Really, *thank you*."

ONE HOUR LATER, and I'm emerging from the cool, crystal-blue waters of the swimming pool like a water goddess on a mission to teach the mortal men on the island a lesson they will never forget.

The scorching sun beats down on my skin, making the water droplets sparkle like tiny diamonds. I feel the warmth seep into my pores, and I don't bother reaching for a towel to dry off. Instead, I let the sun do its work, evaporating the water from my skin as I bask in its radiant heat on the pool chair.

The warmth is exhilarating, and I feel alive, refreshed, and rejuvenated after my swim.

But something else prickles at the side of my face and

makes my body tingle in an anxious awareness. I don't need to crack my skull to know what it is. He's watching me.

From the moment I stepped out into the sun, wearing the sleaziest one-piece swimsuit from Agatha's selection, Antonio had his eyes on me. From the window in his room, he has the perfect view of everything, from the beautiful sight of nature to the glinting diamond reflection of the pool, and the crisscross ropes on my lemon bikini that barely shield my assets.

A huge shadow falls over my poolside chair, and when I open my eyes to the sight of hard eyes and long hair, the curve on my lips tilts higher.

What *Nio* doesn't know is that I wasn't built to behave. I'm only prepared to give him an even more perfect view.

I brush my hair behind my ears and smile up at Lorenzo. His gaze brushes over my body and lingers for a second, until he seems to remember that action, as brisk as it was, can get him killed.

"What are you doing here?"

"It's obvious, isn't it? Like you, I thought the pool would be a great way to clear my head."

I nod, pretending to understand. "Busy day?"

He shrugs, and there's a look in his eyes, like he's trying not to see me. "Something like that."

I hadn't noticed it before, probably because I got off on the wrong foot with almost everyone in this house, but Lorenzo is... kind of cute. *If cute was any way to describe a hot man with a hard exterior.*

He starts to move away, and I jump to my feet to follow him. "Hey, Lorenzo, can we be friends?"

That makes him pause and turn to stare at me, first with wide eyes, and then they grow a fraction wider. I think it was my question that put that look of concern there, but I should have been a bit more observant.

If I were, I'd have noticed that Antonio's window was now empty, and the man who should have been standing there now lurked behind me like a second shadow.

I don't make it through a protest. Lorenzo spins upside down when Antonio throws me over his shoulder, and marches off wordlessly with his strong hands clamped down on my ankle.

In a matter of seconds, I'm in my bedroom, the door bangs shut behind us, and I'm flung on the bed like a rag doll.

"Turn the fuck around, *gattina*. Right now."

"What are you going to do?" I glare at him. "Spank me?"

The growl that rips through his throat is beastly when he lurches forward and, with unearthly strength, flips me around so that I'm lying on my stomach.

Blunt fingernails dig into my thighs, strong hands go around my waist and grip my hips, and—

A loud smack echoes in the room when he spanks me across the butt cheeks. He smacks me again, hard palms connecting with my soft flesh, and I gasp.

My fingers curl into the sheets, grasping as I struggle to suppress a moan. And I may or may not have arched my ass higher against his crotch. I don't think I've ever seen Antonio as livid as he is now, and it excites me because the source of his anger is, in fact, *me*. His obsessive possession of me.

I shouldn't like it. I shouldn't want him to keep spanking me, but I do anyway.

I feel him move away before I hear the thunder in his voice.

"The next time I see you flirt with another man, he's going to lose his fucking head, I swear to God."

Nostrils flaring, fingers clenched, and jaw set like a man on a mission to obliterate his adversities, and yet, I still *unashamedly* find him hot.

Rolling off the bed, I pretend to be upset and narrow my eyes at him. My ass stings, but pleasure zaps through my body rather than pain.

"Have I ever told you how much of an asshole you are, Antonio Mancini? If yes, then I don't think I have told you enough."

I stomp toward the bathroom, intentionally brushing past him as I move. "You are an asshole, and, it doesn't matter how many times you act like it, *I* don't fucking belong to you or anyone else."

I slam the door shut.

16

ANTONIO

When I arrive at the club, Luca and Lorenzo are already seated, waiting for me.

I collapse on the velvet sofa beside theirs and swing an arm above the rim. Luca lifts a tumbler to his lips with his brow raised, and when the light flashes in his direction, I see the question in his eyes directed at me. I ignore him.

Lorenzo pulls his gun from the holster at his belt, drops it on the center table, and runs a hand through his hair as he leans back.

"Judging by that look on Nio's face, I doubt that whatever's going on is anything good. Another round, on me."

The corner of Luca's lips tilts upwards, and he stares into his tumbler. "It's literally on the house, Lorenzo."

"Well, I'm the one placing the fucking order, so at least my name's going on the book."

Stupefied, Luca shakes his head and gulps down the entire drink. He brings his head back up and reaches for the bottle of Kauffman on the table. "The clock's ticking, Nio. I thought we came here to cool off."

I rub the crease between my brows. "We are cooling off."

They are. *I'm not.*

I'm teetering on the edge, boiling and brewing at the same time. It's fucking uncomfortable, and there's a constant ticking somewhere at the back of my head, like a bomb that might go off at any minute.

"Then why do you look like you want to shoot somebody?"

I see Lorenzo's smug smirk and immediately want to wipe it off with the back of my hand. The bastard knows exactly why I'm all riled up. If it wasn't for his years of devotion and loyalty to Dante and me, I might have put a fucking bullet in his head this afternoon. He'd seen my anger, smirked at my jealousy, and shook his head before strutting off.

"I don't think I want to talk about it."

They share a look, and Luca shrugs. Like Lorenzo, he stretches backward on the sofa and doesn't take his eyes off me. "It's that serious, huh? You hear about Joey's trouble with his wife?"

Lorenzo chuckles, but Luca's poker face stays intact. I'm not sure I get it at first instance, but if I do, it means I have to also deal with the men sticking their nose in my fucking business.

Glaring at him, I reach for a tumbler on the table and fill the glass. "Who the fuck is Joey?"

"Some guy."

"Then how the fuck am I supposed to care about some random guy and his fucking wife, huh? Please, enlighten me, Luca." That bomb is close to fucking detonating.

Realizing that I'm better off hearing what he has to say without beating around the bush, his shoulders sag, and a small smile tugs at the corner of his mouth. "Joey's you, Nio.

Respectfully, you look like shit. Like a tornado blew through. Everything good with your new wife?"

"My best guess is no."

I neither have the strength to deal with Lorenzo nor to answer Luca's question. I shake my head and take the glass to my lips.

It wasn't any of their fault that Vivienne intentionally wanted to drive me nuts. She is so fucking stubborn, I find it hot, and infuriating at the same time.

"I guess that's a good thing then."

I raise my eyes to Luca, and when he sees that I'm not catching on, he clarifies. "We've never thought you could put up with a submissive woman anyway, the giggling idiots —that kind."

Lorenzo barks a short laugh, collecting his hair in a tight bun atop his head. "You fucking like them feisty, and Vivienne matches that description."

"Why the fuck do you enjoy your blood pressure going up and down like that?"

"He likes the rush, keeps his energy going."

The conversation practically twists into a back-and-forth tease between my two men. My head falls back as I watch them laugh their fucking heads off, while they throw subtle jabs, and take hits at me, one after the other.

Colorful flashing lights rhythmically resonate with thrumming music, and at the center stage, neon hoops glow on the strippers twirling on poles. Three of those girls walk over to our section, prancing seductively with their boobs and asses barely covered.

My teeth clench when an image of Vivienne coming out of that fucking pool crosses my mind. The ray of sunlight shimmering on her golden skin like tiny crystals, the tempting dip and curve of her fucking body, and the fiery blaze in her green eyes told me she knew exactly what she was doing.

"Hello, ladies."

When I look up, Luca and Lorenzo have welcomed their pick from the whores, and the last one standing comes up to me. The blonde one. I recognize her from a few nights ago.

Lowering herself, she straddles my lap, smiles at me, and brushes her finger under my jaw. "Hi, *Daddy.*"

Luca picks it up from where he's seated and laughs. "You should let her check your blood pressure, *Daddy.* Who knows, she might be your remedy?"

I glare at him and turn to the beaming girl. I brush her hand away from my face. "I'm not your daddy, and I'm not in the mood." Even to me, I sound unnaturally calm, and I believe that the girl has gotten the message.

She hasn't.

Her hand floats back to my face, and her thumb strokes my jaw. "I can get you in the mood, if you let me."

There's only one woman on my mind, and it's not her. Not her, not anyone else. Coming to that conclusion, that ticking time bomb finally detonates.

"Get the fuck off."

"But—"

Before she finishes, I'm on my feet, and she falls to the floor, staring up at me with a look of horror and disgust. I don't owe her an explanation, and I don't acknowledge Luca or Lorenzo before marching off.

As it turns out, the one place I thought I could cool off is the very reason I wanted to cool off in the first place. Even from a distance, she still manages to rile me up and infiltrate my thoughts.

If anyone's the remedy, it might just be my fucking wife.

When I get home and into the bedroom, Vivienne is nowhere to be seen. I'm already bulldozing my way toward the door to cause hell if my men let her escape, when soft sounds from the bathroom make my feet stop.

Dropping my keys and phone on the nightstand, I kick off my shoes and slip into the bathroom.

The shower is on, so she doesn't hear me come in, and unintentionally offers me the full view of her back.

Leaning against the wall, I take off my belt, let my pants drop to the floor, and stroke my cock at the sight of her perfectly shaped ass and sexy legs.

The water runs in a rivulet down her back, and she tilts her face up toward the water to rinse off the soap on her face. I catch sight of her pink tits, and a haze fills my vision. All I think about at this moment is filling her up with my dick and feeling her walls squeeze hard around me.

I don't wait for her to turn off the shower before taking the initiative.

Stepping into the shower, the water seeps into my shirt as I mold her back against my front and bury my face in the crook of her neck. She freezes and then relaxes in my touch. I expect her to protest, push me away, and yell about how much of an asshole I am, but she doesn't do any of those things, and I take it as a cue to believe she craves this moment as much as I do.

She smells clean and exotic, like soap and coconut shampoo. I suck the water off her nape, biting down lightly on the golden skin under her ear, and she sighs.

Wrapping an arm around her waist, I bring her even closer and close a hand around her breast. I test the weight of each and pinch her perky tits. Desire blinds me, my body quakes, and my cock strains painfully between my legs. How is it possible for one woman to command my entire attention this way? She doesn't even know, but she's somehow gotten me wrapped around her tiny fingers.

She shudders against me, and I slip a hand between her legs, lifting my finger to her core.

I clench my teeth, feeling the blood thrum in my ears when I stroke her clit.

Vivienne arches into me, pressing her ass hard into my hand. Her knees buckle, and her hands fly to the wall to grasp for support.

I add another finger and squeeze into her tight pussy.

"*Antonio...*" Her eyelids flutter shut. Hearing my name pour from her lips ignites a fire in my groin, burning, consuming, until I'm not thinking straight.

"That's it, call my name, *gattina*."

My nails dig into her hips, and I move my fingers in and out of her. I am almost fucking shaking when her moans grow louder, echoing off the bathroom walls, hitting my ears like they're begging for more.

Her walls clamp down on my fingers, squeezing tighter, and I know she's close, but I take my fingers out, and she whines in protest.

Vivienne flips around, green eyes clouded with desire, and before I mumble a word, she drags my lips to hers and rips my shirt open. I lift her legs off the wet tiles, and she fists my hair with her fingers.

When I thrust into her, she cries into my mouth, writhing in pain. I'd gone in too hard, too quick. But she doesn't tell me to stop. So, I kiss her gently, pull out of her, and slide back in, slow enough to soothe the sting.

I shouldn't care that I physically hurt her, but I do.

And I fuck her slowly, peppering her neck with tender

kisses I didn't know I was capable of giving. She shuts her eyes, parts her lips, and squeezes me hard when her orgasm hits like a storm.

I don't remember what I mumble in Italian, or what she whispers into my ear, but her beautiful face is all I see when I explode and come inside her.

17

VIVIENNE

"Twelve bloody... *argh!*"

I'm almost pulling my hair out as I reach the thirteenth CCTV camera mounted on the side of the house, partially hidden by a bunch of overgrown leaves from a nearby tree.

This wasn't the initial plan—spying, moving around the large estate, counting the security cameras. No, as hard as it might seem to convince anyone who accidentally catches me in the act, this wasn't the plan.

It's a warm afternoon, one I initially planned to enjoy with an aimless stroll around the vast estate, and surprisingly, it was going well. I mean, after spending one week indoors, reliving the heated shower sex moment, I needed a break and a change of scenery.

The sun shone on the big house, and other dwellings littered around. The grounds looked amazing, and the structures blended seamlessly with the surrounding trees and grass.

The lawn was perfectly cut, the flowers blooming beautifully, the air smelling sweet and fresh. I heard the birds chirping and leaves rustling in the breeze. Hidden behind the house were some orchards. Rows of fruit trees stretched toward the sky. I wandered in and out of the orchard and stood on my toes to gaze into the distance. It looked like rolling hills, green pastures, and I longed to watch the sunset over that scene.

Life, in that small nick of time, seemed good and normal. As normal as it was when I played with Harper in our make-believe garden back at home. As normal as it was when I moved about with my head held high, breezing in and out of any club I saw fit.

That was until I was reminded about how I got here in the first place. Absolutely nothing about that was normal. Yes, I was kidnapped by my husband, and with that came the responsibility to recall my plans to escape from all of this.

The memory burns in my mind, a vivid and unrelenting image that refuses to fade, no matter how hard I try to suppress it. I can still see Antonio standing amidst the terror, his dark eyes cold as ice, as he moves like a predator through the bloodied remains of my father's men.

It isn't just the violence that haunts me—it's the reason why he did it. Taking men's lives to pass a message of just how cruel he really was. Men who had served my father for years reduced to a pile of lifeless bodies.

I could still feel my heart pounding in my ears, the fear seizing me as I realized that day was probably just another day for him, nothing special.

Every time I remember, Antonio doesn't look like a monster, and that is the most unsettling part. He was always controlled, almost regal in how he carries himself, as if what he'd done was beneath him, but necessary—it was terrifyingly composed.

That is what led me to start this devious act of mine, and my mind was almost blown at the number of security cameras in the house. How many did someone really need?

It doesn't matter.

I can't stay here, anyway. Not in this life, not under Antonio's shadow. Whatever my father had done to bring this upon us doesn't matter either.

Antonio might think he owns me, that I'll cower like some obedient pawn in his games. But he's wrong.

I would find a way out. Out of his reach, out of this nightmare. No matter how long it took, no matter what I had to do, I would escape Antonio and this fucking world he thinks he's trapped me in.

I start making a turn around the house, back to the front, when movement at the entrance makes me pause.

"Agatha said I'll find you roaming around the house, and she was right."

At least she didn't say you'd find me counting the CCTV cameras, I think, as I turn to the source of the voice.

It's Ginny, and she looks just as beautiful as the first time I saw her. She is dressed simply but elegantly, wearing a tailored black dress that hugs her curves just enough to highlight her figure without being overly ostentatious. Around her neck is a single gold chain, delicate and understated, but on her, it seems to gleam with purpose.

And she's wearing that pleasant, friendly smile on her face, one that has me smiling back at her.

"Liked what you saw?"

I blink when I realize what she's speaking of. "What?"

She joins me on the lower step and gestures to the surrounding environment. "I asked if you liked it—the estate. I know you do. I've been here a couple of times and enjoyed taking strolls around. You might not believe me because, well... living with these men is anything but peaceful. But the surroundings here are incredibly serene. Have you seen the orchard?"

"Yes, I have. It's beautiful and abandoned." Strangely, I feel relaxed around her. "And I believe you. I experienced it myself. Walking around this place, you'd never believe that the men here sleep with knives under their pillows."

Ginny snorts. "Just knives? Sometimes, my husband keeps the gun on the vanity when he's in the shower."

I roll my eyes but can't suppress a chuckle. It's amusing that she finds her husband's habit absurd, but the subtle crinkle at the corner of her eyes and the lingering smile on her lips tells more than she does: The thought of her husband is like having a breath of fresh air.

She loves him.

Despite the uncanny bond and connection forming between us, that is one thing we'll probably never have in common: love for our husbands.

I'm pretty sure I'm on the verge of detesting mine and everything about him. Except for sex with him.

That's *tolerable*, at least.

We slowly go around the house again, but I no longer bother noting the security installations. This moment, chatting with Ginny, is liberating, as if I am finally getting something I've lacked for a long time.

We talk about everything and anything we think of; what my life was like before Antonio, my sister, my father, friends, if I ever had any, and her life with Dario.

She's happy. I'm not.

But we both like salted caramel popcorn and ice cream and Netflix, and a bunch of other things that are truly silly.

I like Ginny. I like that we share interests. But she

reminds me of my sister, and how much I miss chatting like this with her.

"And Agatha? How's your relationship with her?"

I kick a stray pebble and knot my fingers behind my back. Ginny doesn't see the red stain on my cheeks, but I feel the heat creep up my neck when I remember nearly slicing off Agatha's neck.

"Cordial? I guess we're cool," I say instead. There's no need to go down that memory lane with Ginny, although I am surprised that she isn't aware.

"She is generous, isn't she? After you tried to use her as an escape route."

Of course, she'd heard. The whole house must have heard, too.

We're by the orchard when we stop walking. Ginny turns to me, and the smile that once was on her face is no longer there. She brushes loose strands of her hair behind her ear and nibbles on her lower lip.

"Look," she sighs. "I know this isn't the best life you're living, and I'm sorry you are stuck in this situation. I know what it feels like first-hand to feel trapped."

Does she?

She seems to read the question in my eyes and further clarifies. "Dario and I weren't always in love. We were enemies at first, even though I always found him really hot," she says with glee. "But now we mean the world to each other. I'd give my life for him, and I know he'll do the same for me. I believe there's a chance you and Nio will fall in love with each other."

Before I can stop myself, my protest flies out of my mouth. "I doubt it. Nothing will change."

"Vivienne..."

Maybe I should stop now, before I say anything more, before I incriminate myself.

"No. A girl doesn't see the carcass of her father's loyal men and happily marries the man who killed them."

"That's your father's business."

Her bluntness stirs tears in my eyes for one reason: She's right. Those men's deaths were my father's business. Not mine. "He had a gun to my father's head."

"Vivienne, that's still your father's business."

A teardrop spills on my cheek, and I angrily wipe it away. "But he kidnapped me anyway. And you can't say that's my father's business because *I'm* here. It's *my* business. And I will get out of here before I join the list of victims hung on Antonio Mancini's wall."

In the midst of this emotional turmoil that wracks through me, I can't help but feel thankful that I didn't have to marry the old bastard my father initially planned for me, but it doesn't make being married to Antonio any less scathing.

Ginny is quiet for a while before she shakes her head with a conviction that I don't share. "Antonio won't hurt you, Vivienne. I'm sure of it."

Well, I'm not.

And before we find out which one of us is right, it'll be too late. I'll be long gone by then.

GINNY LEAVES EARLIER than I want her to, before dinner, leaving me to wallow in the lingering effects of our conversation. It feels like there's a hole in my chest, an ache I need to feel, and maybe that's why I miss Ginny's company more than I should.

I'm seated in the dining room with an array of delicious food spread out before me when one of Antonio's men steps inside with an unmistakable aura of intimidation, dressed in black. I recognize his fresh buzz cut and unsmiling face from the night when Antonio was a pretend gentleman. He drove us home.

"Luca, is it?"

His brows dip, and the frown on his face deepens, like he doesn't expect me to be talking to him. "It is. I am."

Strange response, but I can't exactly peg him to be the talkative type. He wasn't chatty that night, either.

I should focus on ripping my chicken and broccoli to shreds and eating in silence, but I blink, and this man before me doesn't look so made of stone anymore.

If anything, I dare myself to think I can hold a five-minute conversation with him.

"Nice to be in the same space with you. I'm Vivienne."

Luca's brows rise in greater surprise. "I know who you are."

He didn't expect me to introduce myself. Did everyone else really think I'd go around parading as the popular Antonio's wife?

"Oh, okay. That's good, then." I take a bite of the tasty broccoli. "Care to join me? I'm afraid they made too much of all this goodness, and there's no way I'm eating all of it."

"I'm good."

"If you say so. Prepare to have the waste of the good stuff on your conscience."

I see a ghostly smile tug on his lips.

"I'm sure I can handle more than that on my conscience. If I have one."

Did he make a joke?

I doubt it. He was under the category of men who slept

with knives under their pillows and dropped their guns on bathroom vanities while they had their showers. It's possible that Luca lacks a conscience.

"What brings you to these parts of the house then, if you weren't reeled in by the aroma?"

He looks around, then back at me. "I'm on duty."

"Watching the mansion tonight?"

"Exactly that."

I nod and nibble a juicy chicken part.

The conversation between Luca and me goes back and forth in a friendly tone. He turns out to be more engaging than I thought he would be.

We beat five minutes and end up laughing like old buddies. The summary? He likes his job, and is thorough with even the most minute responsibility Antonio gives him. I don't ask any further questions to know he's one of the loyal ones. One who would possibly kill or die for my *husband,* if the situation were life and death.

I know all these things, and yet I ask anyway, because I feel warm enough toward him, and I think it will kill *me* if I don't.

"Luca, this is abrupt, but can I make a request?"

Luca tilts his head, watching me warily. "Will Antonio approve of this request?"

Fuck Antonio.

"I don't know, but if it's not important, I won't risk my neck by asking. Can I please use your phone to call my sister?"

The warmth that flowed easily between us changes so fast, I think I imagined it. An icy cold replaces it when he pushes himself off the chair and starts for the door.

"Luca…" I'm grasping at straws to bring him back. "Luca, please."

His broad shoulders are almost past the door when he turns back with a frown that is deep enough to put a dent in his features.

"I asked if Antonio was going to approve, but you already knew the answer, didn't you?"

Heavy boots thud on the polished floor when he marches out of the dining room, and that marks the end of our conversation.

18

ANTONIO

"How many dead?"

"Ten."

"How many injured?"

"Twenty-five."

My fingers curl around the edge of the desk, the sharp edges of anger slicing through me, and my teeth clench hard enough to start a fucking headache. "Damn it! And are they being tended to? At the hospital? *Fuck!*"

Giovanni barks off in Italian at the other end of the line to someone, and I hear him walk away from the background noise. "Twelve now confirmed, Nio. Twelve dead. And yes, those injured have been rushed to the hospital. Nio, we can't fold our arms and do nothing about this. This was a direct target. Whoever the fucker is knew we were offloading shipments today. They fucking knew we'd have more people inside that warehouse."

There is no doubt about that. The warehouse by the docks was one of our biggest. Built and structured to be untouchable. My mind is already running through possibilities, calculating the losses, and, most importantly, who had the balls to pull this off.

It is bad enough that we have twenty-five men injured, but twelve men dead is a punch to the gut.

I'm losing control, trying not to lose the last shred holding me together. "How?"

"I don't know." I feel the frustration and anger radiating off him and know that the rest of the men would be out for blood. "One of the workers here said everything happened so fast. People in masks came in fast, armed to the teeth. Looked professional. We're still piecing it together. But someone has to pay, Nio. They have to fucking pay."

I stand, and the chair scrapes against the floor. My blood burns under my skin, but I subdue the urge to crash something against the wall. Allowing anger to rule my thoughts is a weakness, one I can't afford right now.

"Call everyone back to the house," I say. "I want eyes on every detail—surveillance, witnesses, anything. If someone so much as sneezed near that warehouse, I want to know. Tell Lorenzo to meet me here in ten minutes."

"Yes, boss," Giovanni says, and the line goes dead.

My best guess on who's responsible is the Camorra. Salvatore fucking Russo. But I can't act on an assumption even if everything inside screams that I am right.

I toss the phone onto the desk, pacing the length of the room. This wasn't just an attack—it was a message. And whoever sent it will regret making me their target.

THE MEETING with the men is long and strategic. Every one of my men is affected, and, though they don't try to show their distress, their anger is palpable.

Luca says it will take more than a few days to trace the culprit. Lorenzo's already sharpening blades, ready to go on a foot hunt, no matter how long it'll take. I give him permission, appoint more men to accompany him, and dismiss the meeting.

Tomorrow's going to be a long day, and the day after that. They are going to need a lot of rest tonight to face what's ahead of us.

By the time I get to my bedroom, I'm already crumbling under the weight of fury and exhaustion. I don't bother with asking Agatha to send up my dinner, or going to check on Vivienne in her room. Without a doubt, one look at the hands of the clock striking midnight on my phone screen, I know she'll be asleep.

I toss my phone on the nightstand, drop my gun beside it, and take a quick shower. Fifteen minutes later, my head hits the pillow, I drag up the covers, and it's night out.

At least, I think it is.

I'm not sure how long I'm out, but there's a movement that groggily pulls me out of a dark dream. My gun lies on the nightstand, but I don't reach for it. I don't move. Hell, if I'm even breathing.

Keeping my eyes closed, I listen intently, taking note of every movement. The door creaks gently, then there's a shuffle of feet. It's soft, so soft, I might still be dreaming. Only, I'm not.

I'm more certain of this idiot's presence when the bed dips beside me, and one of the pillows brushes my arm.

There's a sudden stillness, a familiar one.

The first time I ever shot someone, I placed my finger on the trigger, looked him in the eyes, and... hesitated. I fucking paused, because I knew, if I took the shot, there was no coming back from it, ever. The reason I can recall it now is because I took the shot.

My eyes open, and, with precision and mastered skill, I twist to my side, snatch the pillow, and flip the culprit on his back.

I frown.

Correction: *her* back.

Wide-eyed and stricken with fear, Vivienne's chest heaves, and she tries to push me off her. I don't budge.

"So, you're the idiot."

Unlike her usual spitfire self, she looks frozen, and I can't tell if it's because I interrupted her plan to suffocate me to death or because I'm hovering over her like a predator. On any other day, I'd let her off easy with a slap on the wrist. But today was far from regular. I lost twelve men, and twenty-five were fighting for their lives. I wasn't in the mood to entertain the idea of my wife sending me off to an early grave.

"You tried to fucking kill me?"

"Antonio..." Her voice is barely a whisper. "You... you're naked."

I glance down the length of my body. As a matter of fact, I am stark naked, and somewhat displeased to see that my dick isn't matching my fury. Instead of shrinking, it stands erect, *hard*, poking her thigh like it seeks permission to go inside.

I'm furious, but even in the heat of the moment, I cannot deny that I want her. That her body calls to mine like a fucking siren and, instantly stands at attention.

So, my anger takes a different turn.

Without her permission, desperately, I crash my lips against hers and kiss her as fiercely as the turbulent storms brewing inside me permit. She gasps and moans into my mouth, eyelashes fluttering as I devour more of her.

This is one of those moments when I expect her to punch my chest or bite my lips until I hiss in pain and throw her out of my bed.

She wants to kill me, and I am torn between a decision to physically cause her pain or pleasure. But we're both insane, because neither of us let go.

Vivienne drives her tongue into my mouth. It's warm and wet, evoking a growl from the depths of my soul, and I nip on upper lip, sucking deeply while she angles her head to give me deeper access.

She wriggles so much, her nightdress rises higher above her thigh, and when she sighs, I pull away from her mouth, latching instead on one of her breasts through the silk fabric. She arches into me, filling my mouth and nose with the scent of flowery perfume.

Tugging the fabric lower, her pink tits peek above the white lace above the loose neckline, and I graze one with my teeth.

"Oh, my God."

Lust clouds my vision, and I leave a hot, messy trail of kisses from her breasts to her collarbone. I get to the spot on her nape that leaves her as weak and jiggly as jelly, and I make sure to mark her with teeth. The spot glows a faint red, and I slip my hands between her legs.

She's already wet for me. I expected nothing less.

My finger finds her clitoris, and I press my thumb against her, rubbing intentionally to see her lips part and legs stretch wider in pleasure. There's something about watching her revel in such intimate vulnerability that stirs a heavy possessiveness inside me.

I want it to stay like this, longer than I should. Just me and her, and moments like this that I could call mine—*ours.*

Any more observations at this moment, and my chest would explode from foreign emotion.

With one last flick, I eject my fingers and grab her hips closer.

"I want you inside me, Antonio," she whines.

I clench my jaw, positioning my throbbing head at her entrance. One moan is all it takes to melt my resolve, and I slide inside her.

We curse at the same time. Her eyes roll backward, and my eyes slam shut briefly.

She's so fucking warm, all I think of is staying buried inside her.

Her legs go around my waist, and her hips move, demanding.

I thrust, slamming deep enough to hit her G-spot. Her toes curl behind me, and her fingers fist into the sheets beneath us. She mumbles something incoherently, but my name is a repetitive mess on her lips.

It fuels me, knowing how desperately she wants me. Knowing how desperately *I* want *her.*

I drive into her again, hitting her just where she needs me.

And when I feel her slipping, letting go, ready to release...

I pull out of her and don't go back in.

Her questioning eyes fly open, and her mouth hangs agape.

"Anto—"

"You can't always get what you want now, can you?

The smile on my lips is dry and wicked, and very much intended to be so.

Deep down, I'm restless and aching to slide back in and come inside her, but my intention from the start was to punish her, and the forlorn look on her face is sufficient proof that I've succeeded.

"Antonio, please, don't—"

"The next time you try that stupid shit, I'm going to fucking punish you more than this, *gattina*. You keep proving that I've given you much more freedom than you deserve."

I don't even think she realizes it, but her eyes are pleading, asking me to reconsider, and I know it has much more to do with me finishing what I started than my annoyance at her action.

Knowing she gives no shit about me and rather prefers having sex, it leaves an uncomfortable squeeze in my chest that coerces me to climb off her.

She tries to speak again, but I beat her to it.

"Get out."

19

VIVIENNE

I stab my fork into the scrambled eggs on my plate, glaring at the yellow mound as if it personally offended me. The clink of metal reminds me of the handcuff keeping my wrist tethered to the chair, and my blood boils anew.

I take another stab at the egg, remembering the anger in his eyes...

Asshole!

The taste of his lips when he kisses me, the feel of him over and inside me, the sound of his growls and grunts in my ears, letting me know I made him feel good, too.

Bastard!

And, finally, to crown it all, the disappointment in his voice when he ordered me to get out of his fucking room.

Arrgh!

"Is this really necessary?" I snap, my voice echoing off the kitchen tiles.

Did it really bother him that I tried to kill him? I mean, weren't men like him supposed to expect things like that—

death lurking around every corner? Didn't they sleep with guns under their pillows?

But, to be fair, his gun lay on the nightstand by the bed. Still...

He. Kidnapped. Me.

And constantly keeps me from communicating with my sister.

I get that acts of violence aren't exactly news to anyone's ears anymore, but doesn't it at least mean something?

Agatha sits across from me, calm as ever, buttering her toast with the precision of a surgeon. She doesn't even glance up.

"You keep trying to run, I guess," she says, her tone infuriatingly matter-of-fact. "The boss has to take precautionary measures."

"I wasn't running," I huff, jabbing at my eggs again. "I was walking—briskly—toward the door. There's a difference."

Okay, I didn't exactly tell her the *true* story. But when Antonio's men marched into the kitchen this morning to interrupt breakfast by handcuffing me to a chair, I had no choice but to think up something slightly convincing in seconds.

Agatha finally looks at me, one perfectly arched brow lifting. "With a suitcase, Vivienne? And shouting, 'You'll never catch me alive'? Sounds an awful lot like running to me."

My cheeks flush, but I refuse to back down. "It was a figure of speech."

Imagine the look of horror on her face if she knew I tiptoed into her boss's room to suffocate him with a pillow. *His* pillow.

Pathetic.

I took a knife to her neck and, last night, a pillow to her employer's head.

Behind me, one of the bodyguards coughs, clearly trying to stifle a laugh. I whip my head around, glaring at him. "Something funny, Andre?"

His name isn't Andre, but that's the point.

No one else knows what happened. Not the stupid attempted murder, the brief intense sex I couldn't get out of my mind, his punishment, or rejection. Absolutely nothing.

And I intend for it to stay that way.

Andre straightens immediately, his face going blank.

"That's what I thought," I mutter, turning back to my eggs and stabbing them again for good measure.

Agatha sighs, setting her toast down and fixing me with her exasperated motherly *you're being ridiculous* look. "Vivienne, this is for your protection. You know that."

"My protection?" I scoff, rattling the chain of the handcuff for emphasis. "I'm in my kitchen, eating breakfast. Who's going to attack me here? The toast?"

Agatha's lips twitch like she's trying not to smile, but she schools her expression quickly. "No one wants to keep underestimating how far you'll go to escape."

I roll my eyes so hard, and it's a miracle they don't get stuck. "Well, maybe if he voluntarily offers me freedom, I wouldn't feel the need to 'escape.'" I make air quotes with my free hand, the one not shackled to the chair.

Agatha doesn't reply immediately. Instead, she takes a slow sip of her tea, her calm demeanor only fueling my frustration.

"And we're back to the pointless argument. It's not happening, child. Take your mind off it."

"Fine," I say, slumping back in my chair. The handcuff

pulls tight, and I wince, yanking my arm back. "But I'm not saying I won't try again."

Agatha smirks. "Oh, I'm counting on it."

The audacity.

Before I slam back a quick-witted retort of mine, there's a quiet entrance made into the kitchen, and I never thought I'd be happier to see her face again.

"Ginny!"

Finally, a more friendly face, and someone who will actually understand. Agatha swiftly whips up another plate of scrambled eggs and a steaming cup of tea for my guest, and, regardless of her protest, she shoves it in front of her anyway.

Ginny grabs a high stool, settling beside me, as her eyes journey from the steel shackles on my wrist to the silver fork hanging over the scrambled eggs on the plate.

"Elated to see you too, Vi, but what's going on here?"

I thought I wanted the truth to stay between Antonio and me, but seeing Ginny, I'm not sure I want to keep anything bottled inside. The chaos is already too much, I feel I can't handle it, and I might explode.

Except maybe the sex part. It feels too private to share.

My eyes dart around the room, glaring at the guard who laughed, and to Agatha, who gives an understanding nod before she excuses us.

"About the guards, it's no use asking them to leave. They won't. Antonio's orders."

Ginny chuckles. "You mean your *husband's* orders."

I shove a chunk of egg into my mouth and wave the fork dismissively. "He's the same person." I sigh. "I'll have to whisper."

She leans in, encouraging the secret conversation, and I

end up spilling everything about my secret mission last night, and how it ended. *Including* the sex part.

Amazing.

By the time I'm done, Ginny is laughing her head off, her silky hair swish-swaying over her shoulders as she wipes off tears from her eyes.

Disbelieving, she shakes her head. "No way any of that happened. I mean, I believe the *other* part, but the pillow? Come on, Vivienne. Just... No."

I raise my hand, gesturing toward the handcuffs to prove it *did* happen, and she bursts out laughing again.

"You know what this is, don't you?"

Stabbing another huge chunk of eggs, I shovel it into my mouth. "If it isn't punishment for my evil deeds, then I'm sorry, but I don't know what this is."

"Don't be naïve, Vi. You guys are having a lovers' spat."

It's a miracle I don't choke on the eggs going down my throat. I feel my eyes widen in their sockets, and I glance around to make sure no one else heard that.

"What? Lover's... *what*?"

Chuckling, she leans in and repeats. "Lover's spat. You know, the phase where two lovers have intense arguments or fights, just like you two are. Antonio's probably just upset that you tried to kill him and still wanted him to satisfy you. Now *that's* pure evil, girl."

Swallowing the eggs, I try to swallow the information she tosses at me. It doesn't digest.

"No," I shake my head, disagreeing. "He's just pissed that I tried to bruise his ego. You know, a pillow? Of all the things I could have used? Imagine the headlines: *NOTORIOUS AND RUTHLESS ANTONIO MANCINI DIES A SAD, PAINFUL DEATH AFTER WIFE SUFFOCATES HIM WITH PILLOW.*"

Ginny literally guffaws, and her happiness forces a genuine smile to my lips for the first time this morning. If it wasn't for the guards around, there is a high chance she'd be rolling on the floor in joyful tears.

Collecting herself, she flicks a teardrop from underneath her eyelids and surprises me with a warm hug.

"Soon, Vivienne. Very soon, your eyes will be opened. You will see and understand."

I doubt it, but I don't bother saying anything because, in my heart, I know I hate Antonio Mancini.

But I enjoy every moment spent with him more than I should.

AT SOME POINT between lunch and immediately after dinner, the handcuffs come off. I don't even give *Andre* the common courtesy of a thank you before stomping off to the living room to watch the sunset through the tall glass windows.

Drawing the curtains apart, I fold my legs on the couch and nuzzle my head on the soft arm. Antonio is away on business, Agatha is busy as always, the guards leave me to wallow in loneliness, and Ginny is gone, too.

It's just me, alone, left to ponder Ginny's words from breakfast.

Soon, Vivienne. Very soon, your eyes will be opened. You will see and understand.

It doesn't make sense to me, and I doubt that it ever will.

I'm watching the beautiful canvas of red and orange as the sun kisses the sky, when a haze of sleep clings to me like a heavy fog.

I know I fall asleep, but I don't know for how long.

When I stir, my body sinks into something firm yet warm, a soft sway rocking me.

My eyelids flutter open, and I realize I'm moving—not by my own will, but because I'm cradled in Antonio's arms.

His face is shadowed in the dim light of the hallway, but his jaw is set, his expression hard. I glance at his chest, where my hands are now resting, fingers curling instinctively into the soft fabric of his shirt.

My heart skips a beat.

I'm possibly dreaming. This *has* to be a dream.

"Antonio?"

He doesn't look at me, but he answers my unspoken question. "You looked uncomfortable on the couch."

My cheeks flush, warmth spreading through me that has nothing to do with sleep.

He was mad at me, livid even. He shouldn't care, but he does because I doubt there's any other explanation for why he bothered to lift me out of that uncomfortable couch.

The steady beat of his heart vibrates against my palm, and for a moment, I just let myself feel it—the strength of him, the way he carries me without hesitation, as if it's the most natural thing in the world.

It's in me to argue, and, though halfhearted, I try to play cool. "I could've walked."

He glances down at me, and I think I see a small, amused smirk tugging at his lips. Although with this lighting, I can't be sure.

"You could barely open your eyes. Until I lifted you."

I don't argue.

Instead, I nestle closer, my cheek pressing against his chest, letting myself enjoy the rare moment of vulnerability. His scent surrounds me—musk, man, and entirely him.

We reach the bedroom, and he nudges the door open with his foot.

The room is dark, but Antonio lowers me gently onto the mattress, his hands lingering at my back before he lets go.

The cool sheets contrast with the warmth of his touch, and I shiver slightly.

He notices, of course. Antonio notices everything.

"Don't move."

Because maybe, just maybe, we'll finish what he started last night.

I fall silent, watching him as he adjusts the blanket over me, his fingers brushing against my arm briefly. The warmth of his touch lingers long after he pulls back, and I realize I'm holding my breath.

He straightens, his expression shifting back to calm, but there's tension in his shoulders and hesitance as he lingers by the bed.

Then, as if reconsidering something, he turns his back to me, pulling his shirt over his head in one smooth motion. The fabric falls to the floor, but my eyes are locked on him.

I've lost count of the number of times I've seen him like this before—shirtless, perfectly sculpted—but this time, something catches my attention, something I've never noticed before.

It stretches diagonally across his back, faint but unmistakable, like a faded line marring smooth skin. The edges are slightly jagged, but healed long ago, and look deep enough that I know it must have been brutal when it was fresh.

A scar.

"Where did you get that?" I ask before I can stop myself.

He pauses, his shoulders tensing ever so slightly. For a

moment, I think he's going to ignore me, to brush it off like he does with everything he doesn't want to discuss.

Instead, he turns his head slightly, just enough to glance at me over his shoulder. His eyes are unreadable, dark, and distant. "It's nothing."

Standing, the covers fall to the rug behind me, and I step closer to him. "Antonio, it doesn't look like nothing." My fingers itch to reach out, to trace the scar, but I hold back. "How did it happen?"

His eyes narrow like the question annoys him. "A long time ago. When I was seventeen. I handled it."

"Handled it? That's not an answer, and you know it."

"Vivienne, drop it."

It's the first time Antonio has called me by my name in... *Ever*. Not *gattina*, or anything else, just Vivienne.

And that means whatever happened was gruesome enough to be kept locked in his big box of secrets.

I search his face, trying to piece together the fragments of his story he refuses to share. As if challenging himself, he stares at me, his jaw tight, his eyes locked on mine. Then, as if deciding against whatever words he might have said, he shakes his head.

He says nothing, picks up his shirt, and slips it back on.

Knowing Antonio, the conversation is over, but I'm sure I'll never forget the image of that scar.

Why, Vi?

This shouldn't concern me. *I* shouldn't care.

And yet...

I do.

I want to know all the secrets that lurk behind those guarded eyes of his, but most importantly, I'm suffocated by an indescribable need to crush whoever hurt him that way.

20

ANTONIO

"Peter's a stubborn son of a bitch."

Dario's the first person to break the silence.

Since his arrival in my office, we'd done nothing but stare wordlessly at each other; now his expression is carved from stone, and his eyes burn with restrained fury, matching my own.

My fingers drum rhythmically against the edge of the table, and I lean back. The buzz of the club rattles in a silent hum against the walls of the office, but it barely distracts us.

More serious issues are at hand, like figuring out who launched the attack on the warehouse by the dock.

"Stubborn doesn't even begin to cover it." My jaw tightens. "His daughter's life is hanging by a thread, and he still won't talk."

"You'd think with family on the line, he'd fold. But no. He might be protecting someone—whoever's behind this," Dario says.

I nod, running a hand down my face as I try to push down the anger threatening to consume me. "And that someone sent a message with that attack. Peter's either scared," I meet Dario's gaze, "totally clueless, or he's in deeper than we realize."

"Peter Cole can't be innocent."

"Doesn't matter what he can or can't be. Whoever did it is trying to cripple us."

"You know who it is."

"I have my best guess."

Dario sits up, folding his arms across his chest. Curious eyes meet mine. "Who?"

My chair scrapes against the floor as I stand, unable to sit any longer. The weight of this shit presses down on me, suffocating. Every second we waste leaves us more susceptible.

"Salvatore Russo."

Dario shakes his head. "No."

"No?"

Dario rises to his feet as well, sticking his hands into his pockets. "That surprise attack was a sneaky one. We've been against Russo for years, Nio. Salvatore's style is bold. He'd walk in dressed in a fucking suit, burn the place down, and leave his fucking signature on the cameras. I highly doubt that he did this."

"Don't put it above anyone; a man can change."

"A man?" His eyes narrow, and his frown deepens. "Salvatore's not just *anyone*, Nio. You know this. He's a fucking beast. He's been that way for years. Why send masked men now? Or launch a surprise attack when he can just do it anyway? Doesn't make sense, does it?"

No, it doesn't.

The whole thing is frustrating, and I quell the urge to smash into something. But Dario has more than just a fucking point.

We've never known Salvatore Russo to be a coward. It's

one of the reasons we take his threats seriously.

"Talk to Peter again. Push harder. Remind him of what's at stake."

"You think he'll crack?"

I stop, turning to face him. "He has to. If not for himself, then for his daughter. No man alive can watch his child suffer and stay silent forever."

Dario exhales sharply, shaking his head. "We don't have forever, Antonio. We need answers now. If he doesn't give us what we need…"

He doesn't finish the sentence, but he doesn't have to. We both know what comes next.

"Handle it. One way or another, Peter's going to talk. And when he does, or if he doesn't, we'll find whoever's behind this and make them regret the fucking day they decided to cross us."

Dario leans forward, his elbows resting on the table, his eyes locking onto mine. "That's the only option. If we don't, they'll come for more than just the warehouses next time."

When Dario leaves, I pick a random tumbler from the mini bar at the corner and throw it against the wall.

ANOTHER DAY WASTED. Peter refuses to break, and neither Dario nor Lorenzo has good news for me.

The faint aroma of something cooking greets me when I step through the door—spice, chili, something warm.

It's comforting, but it doesn't settle me. Nothing does. My chest feels too tight for that.

I follow the sound of clattering dishes to the kitchen, and I find Vivienne there, moving between the stove and the counter with a strange efficiency.

She's wearing an apron that's slightly too big for her, tied tightly around her waist, and her hair is pinned back, a few loose strands framing her face. She doesn't look up when I enter, but I know she's aware of me.

"Dinner will be ready soon," she says while shuffling a pot and waving a spatula in the air.

Dinner?

I must've entered the wrong house, because Vivienne *doesn't* cook.

Agatha's leaning against the counter, arms crossed. She meets my gaze briefly, and I raise a brow. She looks away with a shrug, silently advising me not to bother asking her anything.

Vivienne turns to me. "Take a seat." She gestures to a high stool drawn out from the kitchen island.

I hesitate, but there's something in her demeanor that disarms me. It's calm and new. Reluctantly, I pull out a chair and sit.

Vivienne continues working, and I lean back in the chair, my eyes darting between her and Agatha.

"What's going on?"

The question is directed at Agatha, but she just shrugs again and nods toward Vivienne.

"You'll have to ask her."

And with that, the old maid leaves the kitchen.

The silence is immediately disturbed by the occasional clanging of pots and ceramic.

I turn to my wife's back. "Over to you. What the hell is going on?"

Vivienne doesn't respond immediately. She stirs the pot on the stove, and I can see her shoulders rise and fall with a deep breath.

I grip the edge of the table. "Vivienne."

She turns then, holding a wooden spoon in her hand like it's the only thing keeping her steady. Her eyes meet mine, and I see something she never gives me access to—her anxiety.

She gestures to the food in the pot. "You had a long day. I thought... I thought this might help."

Her answer is not what I was expecting, and her genuineness throws me off guard.

"I always have a long day."

She rolls her eyes, a small smile playing on her lips. "I've not always known how to cook. Just... I don't know, Antonio. Today's a special day. Take it that way, okay? I thought I'd do something nice."

"Or maybe the pillow didn't work, and now you're trying actual poison with a mix of niceness to deceive me."

The smile melts off her lips, and quietly, she turns back to serve the meal into the arranged plates. "I deserved that."

She does.

But I feel like an asshole for bluntly pointing it out.

Exhaustion rolls off my shoulders, and I rub between my eyes. "Vivienne—"

"You've stopped calling me *gattina*." She places a steaming plate of pasta before me with a brow raised and goes back to grab her plate from the counter.

Dragging her stool, she lifts a wine bottle from the island and fills each glass, half full.

I'm too stunned to speak. Everything is happening so fast, it feels surreal. The last time I had a conversation with her, she poked at my past, and I shut her off. The Vivienne I knew should have done anything else but cook me dinner.

I exhale. "You know what? I'll taste it. If it kills me, I have men that will willingly shoot you in the head, execution style."

Vivienne doesn't flinch under my threat; she just raises her glass in an air-toast and takes a sip while watching me through unguarded eyes.

I twirl a forkful of pasta and lift it to my mouth, expecting something disastrous at best, but the flavors surprise me.

The sauce is rich, perfectly balanced between the tang of tomatoes and the warmth of garlic.

The pasta itself is cooked just right, not too firm, not too soft. The traditional way.

I set the fork down, taking a moment to process.

There's no point hiding my opinion from her. By the time I'm done with the plate, she'll figure it out.

"This is good. Really good, *gattina*."

Across the island, she lets out a soft laugh, almost nervous, like she wasn't sure how I'd react.

"I'm so glad you like it. For a moment, you had me there. But I had help." She brushes her hair behind her ear. "I practically begged Agatha to show me how to cook something decent. She gave me a crash course today."

"Looks like it paid off."

I take another bite. The warmth of the meal spreads through me. It's rare for anyone to go out of their way for me like this.

She shrugs, but Vivienne's not one to hide the pride in her expression. "I didn't want to embarrass myself. I figured... it's about time I learn something useful."

Her words make me pause, the fork resting halfway to my mouth. "My honest opinion? You don't give yourself enough credit."

Fidgeting with the edge of her napkin, she murmurs. "Maybe."

I decide to change the subject, shifting the focus away from her self-doubt.

"I'm going to tell you something. Promise not to judge."

She raises her hand. "I swear, I won't."

"I'm not much in the kitchen myself." I lean back slightly. "But I can manage a few things. Omelets, mostly. Pasta, if I'm in the mood."

Vivienne bursts out in a shocking laugh that shoots a tingle down my spine. Her green eyes light, and the strands framing her face brush her cheeks.

"Antonio Mancini making omelets? You, in the kitchen? How does that even work?"

A small smile tugs at my lips. "You swore."

"I didn't think a man like you would have time for cooking. I expected something else, maybe a hobby of carving out people's eyeballs. Not *cooking*."

"No," I admit. It's been years since I did. "But sometimes it helps to keep my hands busy. Keeps my mind quiet."

Her gaze softens at that, like she understands more than she lets on.

The more we talk, the more I take note of the tiny details that might have passed off as insignificant if I didn't look closely. She's laughing, not the polite, measured kind, but the kind that bursts out loose and genuine.

It's fucking infectious. Before I realize it, the corner of my mouth lifts more.

This woman is not just beautiful. She's... *alive*.

Every word she says, every gesture, fills the space around her like she's somehow stolen all the light in the room and made it hers.

Many times during the conversation, I catch myself leaning forward, drawn in without knowing it. Her smile carries warmth, the kind that seeps into places I thought I'd closed off long ago, and I realize I want to see more and more of her smiles than scowls.

Whatever's going on inside me can't just be attraction.

Lust is fleeting, simple.

But what I'm feeling now? It's something heavier, something that settles in my chest and refuses to let go.

I shake the thought, but it clings stubbornly, and the realization hits me quietly, like something I don't want to admit out loud.

It's not just her beauty, though that's undeniable.

It's all of her.

"Thank you for this," I say, breaking the quiet. "You didn't have to, but I'm glad you did."

Her cheeks flush, but she doesn't look away this time. "I'm glad I did, too."

And as I take another bite, I realize it's not just the food that's warming me—it's my *gattina*.

21

VIVIENNE

The ceiling above me blurs into shadowed shapes as I stare at it, and my voice grows louder in my head. Technically, it's Ginny's voice— the prophecy thing that haunts me.

My eyes open—seeing, understanding.

Could this be it?

It might as well have been because I can barely get a wink of sleep after having dinner with Antonio. No matter how hard I try, I can't stop thinking about him.

I toss and turn, tangling the sheets between my legs even more as sweet memories resurface. His voice lingers in my head, from when he boasted about his kitchen skills—and despite his efforts to hide it, I saw the vulnerability he kept so carefully locked away.

His humanity. I felt it in the weight of his words during our last conversation.

I turn onto my side, clutching the pillow like it might somehow ground me. It doesn't. If anything, it makes the ache in my chest worse. Maybe this side of him had always been there, but I never wanted to see him as anything more than what I believed.

But now...

Now I'm not so sure.

The way he spoke, the way he looked at me, there was something raw, something real that chipped away at the walls I'd built.

I try to convince myself that I hate it. I hate how I'm starting to question everything I thought I knew about him. How I can't shake the image of his eyes, dark but not cruel.

I close my eyes, willing the memories away, but they only grow stronger. Flashes of his voice and the beautiful curve of a smile on his lips, like it belonged there. The faintest trace of amusement when I surprised him with my special pasta.

I caused this turmoil in the first place, and now I have to suffer the consequences.

My heart twists.

This isn't who I am.

Before Mancini, I was Cole. Somewhere, despite the nagging voices in my head saying otherwise, I still believe I am more Cole than Mancini.

I've always known where my loyalty lies, with my family, my blood. But Antonio is like a storm, tearing through everything I thought was solid.

How did it come to this?

I take a deep breath, forcing myself to sit up in the dark room. My fingers tremble as I run them through my hair, frustration rising under the surface.

I know I can't let this continue. Antonio is the enemy. He has to be.

But then why does the thought of him feel like anything but fury?

I desperately have to talk to someone.

Flinging the covers off, I practically hop off the bed and tiptoe toward the door. I press down on the handle and hold my breath when the door eerily creaks open.

Antonio and I went up to our rooms at the same time, so without a doubt, I believe that he's already out cold.

Shutting the door behind me, I step into the hallway and push my anxiety aside.

They'd already turned off the lights.

The house is cloaked in darkness, the kind that stretches long shadows across the walls and muffles every sound. My heart thuds in my chest as I tiptoe down the staircase, and it sounds like everything is creaking under my weight despite my best efforts.

But I am not deterred. I know my mission—to retrieve Agatha's phone.

I know exactly where she keeps it—on the small table by the kitchen, tucked neatly under a pile of papers.

She never explains why she hides it there, and I never ask because she doesn't know I've caught her stashing the small device there. Whatever her reasons are, I could fall on the ground and worship her for making this task too easy.

I hold my breath, pausing at the bottom of the stairs, ears straining for any sign of movement. The air feels heavier, like the walls themselves are watching me.

But there's no sound, no hint of anyone stirring.

I dart toward the kitchen, my steps quick and silent.

Just a few hours ago, the place was lit up with genuine laughter, sweet wine, the delicious aroma of pasta, and conversation between the lord and the lady of the house. Now, all that was, but another priceless memory, and the faint glow of the moon filters through the curtains, just enough to guide me.

My fingers skim the edge of the table, and there it is—the phone.

Grabbing it, I duck into the pantry, closing the door behind me. The small space smells of spices and bread, but I am in a hurry to reconnect with home.

I press the home button, and the screen lights up, nearly blinding me in the dark.

My fingers shake as I dial my father's number, memorized from years of repetition.

It rings once. Twice. My breath catches, but then the voicemail clicks on.

"Damn it." I bite down on my lip.

Hanging up, I immediately type in my sister's number. The phone rings, and this time, relief floods through me when she answers.

Her voice comes through, sleepy and confused. "Hello?"

"Harper!" I lower my head, almost blinded now by a rush of tears in my eyes. I press the phone closer to my ear. "It's me. Vivienne. I'm so sorry it's late, but I just had to talk to you. I had to hear your voice."

"Oh, my God. Vi!" If I know my sister as well as I do, I know she's already drenched in tears. "Vi! Oh, you don't know how much I've missed you. Are you okay? What happened? Where are you?"

My heart aches at the sound of her voice. It's been too long. "I can't tell you all the details right now, but I'm fine. I just... I needed to hear from you, to know you're okay."

"Vi..." The worry in her tone almost breaks me. "If you're so fine, why aren't you calling with your number? You're hiding to call me, aren't you?"

I blink back tears. "Yes, but you have to trust me. I'm okay where I am. I'm being well taken care of." *With handcuffs, pasta, and conversations that leave me more confused by the second.* "I can't explain everything, but I need you to know that I'm safe. You don't need to worry about me. I'm the older one, let me do the worrying."

"I miss you," she sniffles.

"I miss you more." The words catch in my throat, threatening to bring tears with them. "I'll come back when I can. I promise. But for now, I just need you to hang on tight, okay? Don't do stupid things."

She manages a small laugh. "That's all you, Vi. You're the one who does stupid things."

I want to laugh, but fear that something might hear me. Or worse, I might burst out in tears instead. "Harper, I'm serious."

There's a long pause on the other end, the kind that makes my chest tighten. Finally, she whispers, "Okay."

I smile, though she can't see it. "Thank you. I love you."

"I love you, too," she says softly before the line goes dead.

I stare at the screen for a moment, my heart heavy. I slip out of the pantry, returning the phone to its exact spot on the table.

As I creep back up the stairs, I move slowly, cautiously, every step calculated to avoid the creaking beneath my bare feet, and pray no one heard me.

But the joke's on me because prayers aren't being answered tonight.

When I reach the top of the stairs, I freeze.

Antonio stands there, cloaked in shadow, his dark eyes lock onto mine, sharp and more furious than the night I tried to suffocate him.

I feel my stomach drop, and the first thing that comes out of my mouth is the cliché, "Antonio, I can explain. It's not what you think."

"Sure, you can explain falling for it, can't you? She just randomly leaves her phone lying around, and you don't think it's a test?"

Shit.

I blame desperation. I blame a million and one related and unrelated reasons right now. But I don't want Antonio stomping off with the wrong impression.

"I promise, it wasn't like that. I—"

"Proved yet again that I've given you much more freedom than you deserve." He eliminates the distance between us, and I see the other thing burning in his eyes—disappointment. My chest squeezes. "Your promises don't mean shit to me, Vivienne. You saw an opportunity, and you took it."

"No!" I try again, stepping forward, my hands clasped together in a desperate plea. "I wasn't betraying you, Antonio. You have to believe me. I just had to—"

A strong pull on my wrist kills the rest of the words on my tongue.

"Antonio..."

But he doesn't stop.

Yanking me harder, he drags me toward my bedroom, and my vision is excessively blurred with tears to notice when we reach the door.

He opens it and throws me inside like a weightless doll. I land on my knees, falling flat on the rug, and scraping my palms as I try to protect my head from the force of impact.

I'm crying now. I'm a total mess, but knowing that he feels stabbed in the back by me, surprisingly, makes me feel like a truckload of shit.

I glance back at him, hoping for some sign of leniency, some crack in the armor, but all I see is stone-cold determination.

"You're not fucking leaving this room until I say so."

"Please, Anto—"

His back disappears into the darkness, and the door slams shut with a heavy finality.

The locks click into place, and I hear the jangle of keys, the sound of him pocketing them before his footsteps fade down the hall.

The silence in the room is deafening, and I crawl back to the bed to bawl my eyes out.

22

ANTONIO

"I know the difference."

Startled, I raise my head to find Dario smiling. Across the table, he's seated cross-legged, flipping through a magazine like a gentleman.

"What?"

Keeping his eyes on whatever it is he's looking at, the pages of the papers rustle when he flips again. "I said I know the difference. You know, when we meet to discuss business, and when the problem is your woman, there's a difference. And I know it."

Clenching my jaw, I grab a pen and start clicking it. "Good for you."

"Interesting." He turns the pages again. "I also know that, if you keep it all bottled up inside, it's going to distract you. Best you let it out now."

I'm not the sharing type, but I'm also not the type to condone distractions when we have more important things to attend to. So, if sharing was going to help offload the shit, then I'll share.

I'd never done it before. I'd never had to do that to her,

regardless of her excesses. But last night, she crossed the line, and I got upset more at myself than her for feeling betrayed.

I reach for the magazine in Dario's grasp and snatch it away. When his eyes meet mine, I tilt backward. "I locked her up."

Dario's brows twitch disapprovingly. "You locked her up. You do realize she's your wife now, not your fucking whore or prisoner."

"I know what I did," I snap, more harshly than I mean to, and rake a hand through my hair, exhaling slowly to rein myself in. "It's not something I wanted to do."

"Then why did you?"

"I made Agatha randomly leave her phone in a place where anyone could easily find it."

He shakes his head, understanding. "You set her up. Wanted to see if she'll fall for it and betray you."

"Great minds think alike. Only, she wasn't thinking. She didn't know I had that planned out."

"And she fell for it."

I nod, incessantly clicking on the pen to distract myself from remembering the fear and horror in her eyes when she saw me on the stairs, knowing I'd caught her.

"If that's the case, what are we going to do?"

Dario loses me, and I'm back to asking, "What?"

"If I'm following, you just said you set up your wife. She fell for it and betrayed you. In this context, I'm assuming a betrayal means calling reinforcements to spill her location and take her out of your custody, right? In summary, you're probably someone's moving target. Either that, or your wife is planning to silently leave you without killing you."

I don't answer. Maybe I can't.

"I didn't..." I trail off, and slam the fucking pen on the desk. Whoever said being honest with oneself is easy?

Dario's interest piques, and he leans forward.

"You didn't what?"

"I didn't hear the conversation."

Momentarily, he's stunned. Silence hangs between us, stretching for seconds more until a deep laughter I'm not sure I've ever heard pours from his lips.

"You didn't... Are you fucking kidding me, Nio? You locked up your wife because of your shitty insecurities."

The fuck?

"Insecurities? Dario, she took the fucking phone."

"Doesn't mean she called an airstrike on your mansion. Damn. You didn't even hear her out or bother to get proof. Since when did you start acting on emotions? And don't bother denying it. What you did is a clear sign that you acted on your feelings. You thought she intentionally wanted to hurt you, and you fought back the best you know how—by equally hurting her."

"Dario—"

"You can't keep running from this. From her. You're not going to figure it out by locking her away or burying yourself in this work." He gestures to the stacks of documents on my desk.

Running?

"Running from what exactly?"

"Okay," he scratches his head. "Let's take it from this angle. I'm going to ask you a question, ready?"

"No."

"I'm asking anyway. Why the fuck do you care so much if she betrays you? Wouldn't be the first time someone's sticking a knife to your back, would it?"

It wouldn't, but I don't answer aloud because I know

where Dario's heading, and I'm not sure I'm ready to face it just yet.

"No answer?" he smiles. "I'll help you, and I'll be blunt: Don't hold back, Nio. Give yourself a fucking chance—for once in your damn life. You've spent years building walls, shutting people out. Maybe it's time to let someone in. Go against your strict rules, and just fall in love."

Fall. In. Love.

It's the strangest thing anyone has ever told me, ever advised me to do. I don't even know how to fucking react to it, and, when I try to press on with more questions, Dario changes the subject like he didn't just drop a fucking bomb.

"Russo's hosting a party. Big one. The kind where people talk too much after too much wine."

"We were just talking about—"

"How you should bring your wife out of captivity? I thought we were done with that?"

The sly curve on his lips tells me the bastard knows exactly what he's doing, playing a fast one when the seed has already been sown.

"And what about the party?"

I'm grateful for the distraction.

"We need to be there. He's been cozying up to some new faces lately. Potential links we can't afford to miss. And maybe we'd finally get to uncover something helpful."

I nod. "Fine. We'll go. Keep your ears open."

Dario stands, his usual smirk returning. "Always do."

As he heads for the door, he stops and glances back at me. "Think about what I said, Antonio. You can't protect her and keep her at arm's length. One of those is going to give."

When the door closes behind him, his words linger, pressing against the guilt I already feel, and I'm forced to confront what I've been avoiding.

Maybe he's right.

Maybe it's time to let someone in.

LUCA IS DRIVING when I meet his gaze through the rearview mirror to tell him about my meeting with Dario, and the man's advice.

I expect Luca to be the most concerned one, more serious. I expect him to offer other advice, one that would feed my counter-thoughts to convince me that Dario didn't know shit about what he was talking about.

But Luca literally swerves the car to the corner of the road and steps on the brakes to laugh his heart out.

I sit awkwardly at the back, wondering whether or not to whack the back of his head with a bunch of folders I grabbed from the office.

When he raises his forehead from the wheel, I glare at him through the rearview. "Done?"

He leans back in the passenger seat, arms crossed, his smirk annoying as hell. "Done? No. I'm just getting started. This is my session now, and I say you should do something sweet for her."

I keep my eyes on the road, because I might blow someone's brains out, and it won't be mine.

"Sweet?" I narrow my eyes at him. "Like what?"

He waves a hand like he's reciting from a checklist. "Flowers. Chocolate. Something fucking romantic, I don't know."

I grunt.

Romance has never been my strong suit. If I wanted to impress someone, I'd handle it the way I handle everything else—directly, efficiently. But with Vivienne, nothing feels straightforward.

"Try again. I'm not the hearts and flowers type."

"You're telling me?"

"What the fuck does that mean?"

He laughs, loud and obnoxious, again. "It means women like that stuff, Antonio. You might not be the type, but you have to go out of your way to do it. That's what makes it special, the effort."

I stare at him like he's grown two heads overnight. When did Luca become the love master?

I don't say anything, but with a roll of my eyes, I give him the go-ahead, and together, we *go out of our way.*

The car slows as we pass a flower shop, the kind with buckets of blooms spilling onto the sidewalk. My eyes land on a bouquet of red roses, their petals so vivid they almost glow under the streetlights.

I point at it. "The roses. What do you think?"

Luca grins. "Classic."

He pulls over, and my gaze lands on something even more ridiculous as we step out.

A massive teddy bear sits in the shop's window. It's at least four feet tall, fluffy, and wearing a red bow around its neck.

"Luca," I call his attention to the bear. "That's good, right?"

Luca leans out the window, takes one look, and bursts out laughing. He laughs loud enough to draw stares in our direction.

"You're kidding, right?"

"Why not? Women like stuffed animals."

"Yeah, but that thing is bigger than her!"

I ignore him and head into the shop, grabbing the roses

and pointing to the bear. The cashier looks at me like I've lost my mind, but rings it up without comment. By the time we get back to the car, Luca is doubled over, still laughing.

"You're serious about this?" He shoots a glance at the bear, wiping at his eyes as I shove the bear into the backseat. Its head lolls forward, almost brushing the dashboard.

With a growl, I toss the roses on the passenger seat. "Shut the fuck up and drive."

He snickers the whole ride back, but I block it out, focusing instead on how Vivienne might react. Romantic gestures might not be my thing, but if this stupid bear and a bunch of flowers make her smile, it'll be worth it.

We get to the house, and I brush past Luca, grabbing the huge bear and flowers up to her room.

I unlock the door. Pushing it open, I step inside. She's sitting on the edge of the bed, her arms wrapped around her knees. Red hair falls forward, framing her face, but her head snaps up when she sees me.

For a moment, neither of us speaks.

My conversation with Dario plays like a broken record in my mind—*Maybe it's time to let someone in*—and I hold up my gifts like sacrifices that can fix everything.

"I brought these."

A softness fleets through her gaze as they land on them, but she doesn't reach for them right away.

I set them on the nightstand and stand there, awkward, feeling out of place in my own space.

"I was wrong." I slide my hands into my pockets to stop them from fidgeting. "About how I handled it."

She doesn't respond, just watches me with those eyes of hers.

"I'm sorry."

Vivienne's lips press together, and for a second, I think

she's going to turn me away. But then she nods, slow, almost hesitant, and something in my chest loosens.

"I don't blame you. I just wish you'd heard me out first."

"You wanted me to apologize before you were going to say anything, weren't you?"

That familiar mischievous twinkle appears in her eyes for a brief second before it fades off.

Cautiously, I take a step closer. "We're okay?"

Slowly, she nods. "I called my sister."

I sit on the edge of the bed, close enough to feel her warmth but not close enough to touch.

I want to trust her.

God, I want to believe every word that comes out of her mouth, but my world doesn't work that way.

Still, as I look at her now, I feel an ache I can't ignore, and I know that it's not just guilt or the need to make things right.

It's her.

I'm falling for her, and I don't know if that's a good thing.

If it isn't, then she will definitely be the beginning of my undoing.

23

VIVIENNE

A throng of people, specifically the male folk, gyrate on the floor, spreading green mint bills on the pole dancers. The music is loud, throbbing hard enough to pound on the walls of my chest, and the moving stage lights are brighter and almost more blinding than usual.

Someone shouts, more like cheers loudly, and there are concurring whoops and shrieks. Champagne bottles are popped, a group of girls laugh, and a bunch of young-looking crazy men join the strippers on the lit rotating stage. Is this even allowed?

The juveniles get even crazier, forming a PG-13 orgy, groping, kissing, making a mess. The scene is slightly nauseating, far from fun.

Looking away from their lustful eyes, cheeky grins, and the semi-nude strippers who appear to be enjoying themselves, I turn around, facing the broad back of my husband.

For a fleeting moment, I'm stunned by his biceps flexing underneath the burgundy T-shirt that clings to his body like a second skin. The expanse of his shoulders calls to my fingers, tempting them to touch him, *to hold him.*

When I stood in front of my mirror earlier this evening, after rummaging through my closet for the perfect outfit for tonight, I promised myself that I would relax and enjoy the night, *without* thinking of pouncing on him every minute.

I seriously have to work on getting my head out of the gutter. It's the first time he's willingly requested my company to his club, and it might not be a big deal, but to me, it is.

After the surprise bouquet of roses and a giant human-sized teddy bear a few days ago, I'm not sure what to think of Antonio Mancini anymore.

It was all very confusing; first, he locked me in, then ambushed me with the most unexpected gifts.

What was I supposed to do?

I froze on that bed, sensing a wave of shock ripple through my entire body. I had tried to process it, imagined what he'd looked like, searching through the aisles, picking the gallant bouquet, and dragging the items through the doors.

My heart melted that afternoon and turned to mush when he crowned his efforts with an actual, purposefully articulated apology.

There was nothing else to do but forgive him and leave the whole thing behind as swiftly as he wanted to, because whatever unexplainable insanity was going on between us was affecting him, too.

Shaking my head, I'm back to the present, where my hand is tightly linked with Antonio's as he leads me away from the noise and sweaty bodies.

His little finger locks with mine, and the thrill is like electricity, traveling straight to my toes.

Biting down on my lip, I disperse the image of dragging him to a corner to put that naughty finger of his between my legs. Not tonight.

"This is unusual."

I practically have to shout over the noise to get Antonio's attention. He glances over his shoulder at me.

"What?"

Green light pours on his face, flashing against his schooled features before swirling into a fade. My heart skips a beat at his heightened level of attractiveness, and I clear my throat before asking again.

"I was saying, tonight feels a bit unusual. It's a bit louder, somehow. Or maybe it's just me. But why's everyone jumping around?"

"Unusual?"

He'd only heard that part. The rest got lost in juvenile shrieks. Chuckling, I don't bother repeating.

"Yeah!"

We're both shouting above the noise and smiling at how ridiculous it sounds. Finally, we get to a private VIP section. Security guards stand on either side—more like secret bodybuilder soldiers— and nod in acknowledgment when we pass the lush red ropes.

Antonio guides me forward to a velvet sofa, placing his large hand on the small of my back. I'm wearing a red halter dress that stops mid-thigh, and the back is cut low. The warmth radiating off his palm scorches my skin, and I am hyperaware of how close we are sitting together.

"Some kid's twentieth birthday," he says after we settle comfortably beside each other. "Father's a politician. He rented out the club for tonight."

That explains it.

A dark brow raises on his face. "Does it bother you? If it

does, we can go elsewhere. I have a couple more places you haven't seen yet."

I smile at him, shifting closer to bask in his scent. It makes me heady and weakens my knees, leaving me wanting to bury my face in the crook of his neck.

Instead, I focus. "It doesn't. But is that why you brought me here? To eat some cake?"

"You know that's not why. I thought you should come out of the house, see a bit more than the four walls of the bedroom."

"How thoughtful."

He leans forward and kisses my nose, and by the time he pulls away, I know I'm blushing red like a tomato. My heart is hammering so loudly that I forget to breathe.

What's wrong with you, Vi?

He starts talking about trying different ways of living with me, twirling a strand of hair around his finger, but I get distracted by a movement near the security guard.

It's a woman. She's blonde, with shiny straight hair, skinny with long legs, and smoky eyes. There are barely any clothes on her body, except for the gothic lingerie-like contraption that narrowly covers her breasts and glides down to the valley between her thighs.

She's looking—no, *glaring* at me. As quick as a flash, she walks past some guy and disappears.

Antonio's voice reels me back. "Are you listening to me?"

"I'm sorry, you lost me for a minute there. What was that?"

"Is there a problem?" He tries to look over his shoulder, tracing my line of sight with narrowed eyes. "Someone irritating you?"

"No, no, everything's good. I'm fine. Just those crazy youths doing more weird stuff there."

That's what comes out of my mouth, but my pulse is racing with uncertainty for a different reason. The mysterious woman managed to leave an impression that had nothing to do with the effects of a strip tease.

"Sure?"

I manage a smile at Antonio. The concern in his eyes is a big distraction, and soon enough, I forget the stripper with the killer eyes.

"Yeah, I'm sure."

Something about sharing this moment with him reminds me of the first time we met, at the club, when he was the pretend gentleman.

Only now, it feels better, more real, and intimate. Like a promise of something that might just stand the test of time.

Antonio kisses me on the cheeks, standing up to leave after he receives a phone call. There's a grave expression on his face after the call ends. For a week now, I've had the feeling that something else is going on. Something serious enough to rattle Antonio. But he doesn't tell me, and I don't ask because it's clear he doesn't want me involved.

He has a meeting to attend and will have to leave me shortly.

Shortly, he says. Yet, it sounds like I'll have to wait for an eternity until he returns. When he pulls away, like a force of magnets, I rise on my feet, too. When did I become this clingy?

"Promise you won't stay too long."

Antonio's gaze softens, and he wraps me in his arms, dragging me close enough to suffocate me with all that manly cologne. "*Gattina,*" he murmurs under his breath and utters a string of Italian. "If I could take you with me, I would."

I breathe him in before pulling back. "You haven't promised."

A sigh leaves him before his lips come crashing down on mine. Automatically, my eyes flutter shut, and I allow myself to fall deep into the maddening desire that overshadows reasoning.

When my fingers curl into his shirt, he has to let go.

"I promise." He sticks his hand in his pocket and pulls out a phone. "I thought you should have this."

My jaw falls open as I take the phone from him. "Wait, is this my phone? You're trusting me with this?"

His lips curl with a smile. "Yes. Don't get any ideas, though. I won't let you off if you do. Here..." He takes the phone from me and types in his number. "Call me if you're bored or need anything."

My attempt to fight back my smile is useless. It just breaks through me effortlessly. I can't believe he's starting to trust me. "Thank you."

He presses a kiss to my forehead. "I'll be back in a moment."

Watching his back as he retreats, there's a painful tug on my chest, and I collapse on the sofa with an annoyed huff. This man had officially turned my brain cells to scrambled eggs, because how is it possible that, one minute, I hate him, and the next second, there's a possibility that I may or may not be able to live without him?

The hands on the clock are ticking, I'm sinking deeper into the arms of boredom, and there are no signs of him. Even the juvenile party appears to have dulled considerably. Most of them are worn out, while a few others, hurdle at a corner, grunting and cackling as they engage in—*I'd honestly rather not say.*

"Ma'am."

My eyes snap away from the wasted youths and turn toward the intruder. It's one of the security guards, and I glance at what he's holding. A tall glass full of what appears to be wine.

"The boss asked us to give you this—a little entertainment to keep you busy until he returns."

How thoughtful.

I smile at the man and politely dismiss him after I grab the drink from the tray.

I take a swig and then another, stopping only when the entire contents are almost gone. It's nice, sweet and fruity. It fizzles in my mouth, and a certain pressure in my bladder alerts me that I need to use the bathroom. Even before I entered the club with Antonio, the pressure had been there for a while, but I ignored it.

Can't evade nature's call for too long, can I?

Grabbing my phone, I ask for directions to the ladies' room and make my way there. It's bright and quiet when I go in. The place is clean, too. After knocking on the doors, I go into one of the empty stalls to handle my business, and that's when the eerie, calculated clicking of shoes on the marble tiles echoes around the bathroom walls.

My heart catches in my throat, and I'm not sure why I hold my breath, but I do. Crouching low enough to peek through the gap underneath the door, I spot a pair of glossy leather boots.

I arrange myself, stand to my feet, and take a few seconds after flushing down before I leave the stall.

When I see the owner of the glossy leather boots, the blood in my veins turns to ice.

It's her.

The stripper with the killer eyes.

She stares at me through the mirror, patting down her blonde hair after washing her hands. Glaring, I fold my arms across my chest and step away from the bathroom door. "I'm starting to believe this meeting is more than just a coincidence."

"Oh, it's not." She laughs, baring pearly teeth. "It's perfectly planned, Vivienne."

So this one knows my name and thinks she's smart and intimidating. I smirk. "The last time I checked, I didn't have a stripper on my contact list. Who the fuck are you?"

The blonde shrugs, turns off the faucet, and spins around on the heels of her boots. She crosses one leg over the other and leans back against the porcelain sink. "No one of importance. Or maybe I am just a girl who's trying to get back what rightfully belongs to her."

That stuns me for a moment, and I try to think of all the possible ways I could have established any link to this psychopath. It isn't through my father, not Harper either, and nothing else I can think—

When it clicks, I almost can't wrap my head around it.

I take another good look at her. Her eyes glower with undiluted hate, and there's a small crack in her false smile that makes me see right through her innocent sexy girl bullshit.

No way.

No fucking way this childish ambush is about Antonio.

I burst out laughing, and her smile wobbles. Of course, it is. She'd passed by us only a few hours ago, looking like she wanted my head for dinner.

"You think this is funny, don't you?"

"I don't think it is, sweetheart. It is not only funny, but

also fucking crazy that you stand there and lay a claim to someone who doesn't give even half a fuck about you. You, my dear, are sick in the head if you think you can intimidate me with your Hades Halloween outfit and vampire eyes. My advice, even though you're not worth it, is to go back out there and shake your booty. I'm sure there are more than a few teenagers who would gladly make you theirs."

Anger flashes through her eyes, and the crack in her calm composure stretches. "Such a pity that you're a foul-mouthed bitch. My poor Antonio married a piece of trash."

Playtime is officially over. In seconds, I'm ready to show this crazy slut who the piece of trash really is, after I put my foot in her mouth.

"What did you just say to me?"

"You think I'm scared of you?"

"If you're not, you should be. Get out of here and leave me the hell alone. It's not a plea, but a fucking warning. I'm willing to put this stupid conversation behind me and move forward like I never encountered someone so desperate and insignificant."

She's quiet for a moment, considering whether or not to match my words with hers. Just when I think I've finally baited her into a fight I know she'll lose, she flashes an overly confident smile and flicks her hair behind her shoulder.

"Who gets scared of a dead bitch anyway?"

Now, I'm more certain that I'm going to kill this stupid, motherfucking— "Is that a threat?"

"A threat? I see you haven't heard." She cackles like a fucking witch, eyes glinting wickedly under the lights. "Dear Vivienne, I'll be attending your funeral."

I lurch forward, willing every fiber of my being to grab

her stupid hair and drag her down to her knees until she begs for mercy. However, my body fails.

Sudden weakness cripples my knees, and the world sways around me.

What the hell is happening?

The ground feels like it's giving way under my feet, and I flail my arms for the nearest support.

The stripper's laughter rings in echoes, amplifying as it fades into the distance, like a sound from a million miles away.

"I hope you enjoyed your drink, because it's the last one you'll ever have." She sneers, rolling her eyes contemptuously before she turns around and starts to leave.

A gasp chokes in my throat. *The boss asked us to give you this. A small entertainment to keep yourself busy before he returns.*

A growing fog takes over, weighing heavily on my mind. I grip the vanity, and tears well up in my eyes when I hear the harsh pounding of my heart beating like drums in my ears. I struggle to breathe, gasping for air.

Warm tears spill on my cheeks.

Antonio.

My phone. I remember my phone.

It's in my grasp, but my sight blurs, so I barely see the contact that pops up on my screen when I hit the message box.

But I type anyway, even as the black stars dot my vision.

Before my strength fails, and the bright world I once saw turns to an empty black hole, I hit send.

24

ANTONIO

I stare at her body, curled up in my arms.

The moonlight bathes her in a soft glow as we walk past the shadows on the pavement. Her skin is pale, her body light and almost weightless. Her pulse is weak, and she is barely breathing, but shallow rises of her chest give me hope.

Regardless, I can't help but blame myself for not being there, for not protecting her the way I should have.

[10:26PM] Gattina: *Antonio... I'm dying.*

For fifteen years of my life, I thought I knew what anger was.

That is, until now.

Now, it's a wildfire, consuming every corner of my mind. There's a tightness in my chest, the pulse pounding in my temple, the way my fist clenches so hard my nails bite into my palms even as I hold her. I'm shaking; my hands vibrate from the force of my futile attempts, but miserably failing to hold back.

"Antonio."

Luca's already standing by the car by the time I get there.

His eyes hold both a message of understanding and rage, and he stretches out his arms to carry her. My eyes stay on her the entire time while he carefully places her in the back seat of the car.

I kiss her forehead, allowing my lips to linger before I shut the door.

My hand goes to the holster at my belt, and Luca slides into the driver's seat. I barely look at him. "She's weak but alive. Get her home safe and get the doctor to check on her."

He nods and steers the car down the road.

I turn back to the club, gripping the gun like an extension of my hand.

I'm going to kill them. I'm going to fucking kill them all.

When I march back inside, I head to the center of the stage and raise my arm in the air. I hold the gun steady, my chest rising and falling with fire coursing through my veins. And I pull the trigger. Four shots fired in quick succession.

Glass shatters, loud, terrified screams rip through the air, and some lights go off.

The music stops, and I know I have everyone's attention.

Wide, frightened eyes lock onto me. A couple of them tremble, but none dare move. A cluster of young people huddle in the corner, some crouched beneath tables as though cheap wood could shield them from me. They think it can, but it won't. Nothing fucking will.

My gaze sweeps across the room. "Someone here spiked my wife's drink. Some fucking idiot here believed that they could somehow do that and walk away unscathed. Now, here's the thing: If you had a hand in this, I assure you that you won't be leaving here alive."

Someone lets out a muffled whimper, and my eyes snap to them. It's a girl, one of the juveniles. She shrinks back into a corner with tears streaming down her face, and I narrow my eyes at her.

Silently, I dare any one of them in the room to speak, to *breathe* wrong.

"Whoever you are, you have sixty seconds."

No one steps forward.

"Forty fucking seconds now. You all have a chance to tell me who it was, or I'll start deciding myself. Don't make me ask again."

Still, no one.

"Thirty... Twenty..."

My mercy—what little I had—is buried beneath a sea of boiling anger. I don't care who's afraid. I don't care who's innocent. My eyes find one of the security guards near the stage. He was one of them stationed by the VIP section.

His eyes meet mine, and he starts to tremble. Guilt gleams in his eyes, and sweat beads on his forehead as I step closer and press the gun to his head. "Weren't you supposed to keep fucking watch?"

Dropping to his knees, he clutches his arm, drawing ragged breaths like a wounded animal, and his voice cracks when he speaks. "I'm sorry, boss. She asked me to give Vivienne the drink, but she said it was from you. I didn't know."

Anger claws its way up my throat like acid as I look in the direction he's pointing.

The light shines on a blonde woman, her teary eyes pinned on me as if she's just seen a beast. Her fingers are ash, and she looks like she's barely breathing.

It's her—the stripper I rejected.

I laugh mirthlessly as I shift my attention back to the security guard. "You were supposed to protect her. How could this stripper have tricked you? You're a worthless piece of shit!"

Before he can say a word, I pounce on him, landing a punch that makes his jaw crack and leaves a trickle of blood on my hand.

More rage flares in my chest as I prowl over to the stripper and fist her ponytail. She whimpers at my grip but doesn't try to fight back. I guess one stupid action is enough for one night. "Do you know she's barely breathing? If she dies, I'll make your entire family suffer!"

Her voice breaks as she speaks. "I'm sorry... I—I was..."

"I don't want to hear any excuses from you," I growl at her. Through the corner of my eye, I see the security guard stagger back to his feet. Trembling with rage, I pull out my gun and point it at him. "I could put a bullet in your fucking head if I wanted to."

But I can't.

I can't kill a woman, not when she looks so terrified of me. I can't kill the security guard over a mistake, even if I wanted to—though the thought of Vivienne being hurt is driving me insane. Vivienne wouldn't like it. She already sees me as a monster. She'll hate me if she finds out what happened.

It's a struggle as I lower my gun and yell, "Get out! Both of you, get out before I change my mind! And pray she's still alive—because if she isn't, I won't stop until I find you, and you pay for her death. If I ever see your faces again—or even hear of you being near my wife—you'll regret being born. I'll fucking kill you!"

∽

WHEN I GET BACK to the house, I don't make any stops until I'm in the bedroom.

She's already awake.

I can see the soft rise and fall of her shoulders as she stands by the window, her back to me, her silhouette framed in the soft light spilling through the glass. Her head turns slightly, just enough to let me know she knows I'm here. Her eyes meet mine over her shoulder, but they're unreadable.

"You shouldn't be here, *gattina*. You should be resting."

Vivienne faces me fully, tugging on the loose shirt that hangs above her thighs. "I tried to sleep but couldn't. I was waiting for you to come back."

I cross the room, closing the distance, keeping us apart. There's something eerily calm about her that unsettles me. Brushing my hand against her cheek, I tilt her chin up. "How are you? Are you feeling dizzy? Does your head hurt?"

She shakes her head. "Luca had a doctor come over. I'm better now."

Her eyes widen as her gaze shifts to my shirt, stained with blood.

"There's..."

"I handled it."

"You handled..."

"I didn't kill them. I just gave them a good lesson. They'll never come near you again."

The relief on her face makes me glad I didn't kill those idiots.

Her eyes meet mine, and understanding fills them. I don't expect her to burst out in tears, and I stiffen when her head collapses against my chest.

"Antonio, I thought I was going to die."

"Shh." I rub her back, soothing her the best way I know how. My heart clenches at the tears shimmering in her eyes. "You're not going anywhere. I'm not going to let that happen ever again, you hear me? I'll be by your side to protect you, I swear it, Vivienne."

She's still shaking with sobs, fisting my shirt tightly like she's scared to let go.

I place my hand over hers and, slowly, peel her fingers away to get her attention, and when she looks up, I do what I should have done the second I walked through that door.

I kiss her.

With slight hiccups, she sighs, closes her eyes, and wraps her arms around my neck. Gripping her hips effortlessly, I lift her from the ground, and she locks me in with her legs around my waist. Cupping her bare ass underneath her clothes, I squeeze, and I break our lips apart briefly to kiss the tears from her eyes.

"Nio..."

My lips find hers again, and I'm gentle, sucking on each of her lips with a tenderness I have known myself to be capable of. I feel the strength in her grip, the vulnerability in her embrace, and the possession oozing all over her from the way she holds me close.

She breathes against my lips, runs her fingers into my hair, and when her palm connects with my scalp, I groan against her mouth.

My cock pulses in my pants, a rush of ice and warmth enveloping me at the same time. My skin rises in gooseflesh, and my heart thumps against my chest walls, echoing her name over and over again.

I can't count the number of times Vivienne and I have had sex, and there have been variations: rough, wild, angry, passionate. But never... this.

Now, she kisses me like she can't get enough, holds me like the most precious diamond she has, and I take her like we have all the time in the world.

Lying her on the bed, she reaches for my shirt and rips it

open. A few buttons pop out, and when I look at her, she shrugs. "I can't... It's just... the blood."

And I understand.

No more words need to be said, and we don't bother taking off the rest of our clothes tonight. The burning need to connect is more overwhelming than foreplay.

Nudging her shin with my knee, her legs spread wider, and my breathing escalates at the wet sight of glistening pink between her thighs.

I take my erection out, holding her close to me as I slide inside her. Pressing my mouth over hers, I swallow her gasp before it escapes.

Her nails dig into my bare shoulders, her soft cries sounding like a melody to my ears. Slowly, she whines her hips, taking me in, and I jerk forward, filling her up. I press closer, feeling her every breath, every pulse beneath me as we move together.

She shudders beneath me.

Her hands grip my hips, her nails digging into my skin, pulling me deeper and harder, as if she's afraid that if she lets go, this moment will slip through her fingers.

I feel the slick heat between us, the tightness of her body, her tight walls squeezing me in, the way she arches into me. I groan into her neck, thrusting deeper, *harder*.

Her eyes are half-closed, lashes wet from her tears, and when they open, I catch a glimpse of that unspoken affirmation in the way she watches me.

She's holding nothing back.

And I don't either.

Her lips part, her toes curl behind me, and she convulses beneath me when her orgasm wracks through her, leaving her spent before I'm done.

I ride her through it, through the rising swell of ecstasy, through the spiral of pleasure that pulls us both under.

I don't want to stop. I want to hold onto this longer, maybe forev—

The coil bursts from within me like a snapped string, and I surrender myself into that wild, desperate release that leaves me breathless, trembling, and truly vulnerable for the first time in a long while.

I collapse on her, and she hugs me close; our breathing is ragged, and we stay like that. Again, we don't say anything. But I know we don't have to.

In the heat of passion, we'd said it already.

Neither one of us was sure we were ready to let go.

25

VIVIENNE

"Nope."

Lifting a bowl of raisins and oats to my nose, my stomach churns in response, and I nearly gag. I shake my head and push it away. "Nope."

The young maid, with short dark hair, blue eyes, and an oversized gray shirt, sighs, and her eyes bulge when she realizes it is loud enough for the entire room to hear. Offering her an apologetic smile, I shift the large tray with six different meals toward her.

"I'm sorry, I don't know what's wrong with me, but everything is making me nauseous. Could it be something I ate, maybe?"

Varya's cheeks glow a bright shade of red, and she ducks her head while retrieving the platters. "Oh, ma'am, please don't apologize. You have every right to select your preferred choice of breakfast. It's just..."

She trails off, chewing the insides of her cheeks while staring regrettably at the apple pie I persuaded her to bake. Varya doesn't have to say more; I know the exact thought that crosses her mind, because it crosses mine too.

I cross my legs on the high stool, leaning forward on the kitchen island with one elbow propped up and one hand under my chin.

Varya and I had gone through a long list of things I could have for breakfast, and still, I'd chosen nothing. The pancakes, waffles, fruit bowl, apple pie—they looked delicious, but made me feel queasy.

Varya doesn't have a clue what could be wrong; I don't, either. In addition to this mystery, my body temperature rises and falls at will. It fluctuates between hot and cold, then reverts.

I rub the crease between my brows. This phenomenon had been an occurrence for a couple of weeks, and I initially let it slip by, not giving much thought to the nagging exhaustion or the twists in my stomach. I always chalked it up to stress, maybe something I ate; the unease lingered.

"Ma'am, it can't be something you ate, because you haven't exactly eaten properly these past few days. The only reason I haven't informed Agatha, who would inform the master, is because you've asked me not to."

The only reason I made that request was to purposefully keep Antonio from finding out and having to worry. He is away on business, and I don't intend to cause any more distractions with unimportant domestic issues than he already has to handle.

I know Antonio; he definitely would go apeshit on somebody.

No. I don't want any innocent person's blood on my conscience.

"It might be a stomach bug," I say to the retreating back of Varya, who starts to put all the untouched food in plastic containers.

Her chuckle is very light and girly. "I am not a nurse, ma'am. Honestly, I wouldn't know." Her hands hover above the apple pie, hesitating to pick it up and store it somewhere else.

"Take it."

Surprised blue eyes snap to mine. Her jaw drops. "What?"

"The apple pie? You can take it. I wouldn't eat it anyway, and Antonio's not a big apple pie fan."

"Wow! Thank you, ma'am. You're so... you're so kind." I think I see tears well up in her eyes, and her cheeks are an even brighter shade of red now, tilting more to the shade of pink. "You'll surely be a great mother."

Her sincere joy and childlike happiness force a smile on my face.

And after a fleeting second...

After her voice echoes somewhere at the back of my head, the smile falls, and I jump off the stool.

Shit!

My heart starts racing, and Varya calls out after me as I make a beeline out of the kitchen, heading to the room. Slamming the door shut, I grab my phone and scroll straight to the calendar.

Diligently, I'd been tracking it, until I lost track of the goddamn thing.

The reality lands like a stone in the pit of my stomach, heavy and undeniable. My heart skips a beat, then races, my pulse thrumming in my ears as I replay the days in my mind, counting backward, trying to pinpoint when last I bled, and if somehow, perhaps, my calendar was wrong.

Shit!
Shit!
Double shit!

The numbers don't add up in my favor. My period is officially late.

Panic swerves around the corner like a fucking crook, launching a surprise attack on me. I sit on the edge of the bed, and my hands tremble slightly as they press against my thighs. The world around me is suddenly too quiet, and the voices in my head only grow louder.

My stomach twists into knots so tight I can barely breathe. My mind races, each thought more chaotic than the last when it replays the signs I've been ignoring—the fatigue, the nausea...

Oh, my God!

My chest tightens even more, and I dig my nails into my thighs, trying to ground myself, but it doesn't work. This is real. This is happening!

And then, like a freight train, the next thought crashes into me.

Antonio.

Everything slows down rather dangerously, and I feel myself teetering on the edge of uncertainty. In the end, it's not only me in this, is it? He's as much a part of this situation as I am. But I don't know if he'll receive this news with joy. Joy as sincere as the one on Varya's face earlier.

I'm not sure if my husband is ready to become a father. The topic has never been one for discussion before, and now, it is hard to tell Antonio's stance toward fatherhood and children.

Prickly tears sting the back of my eyes, but I catch myself before I cry.

Is Antonio ever going to be ready for this?

Am I?

I can picture his face now, but in my mind, his expression falters and cracks. What if he doesn't want this? What if the weight pushes him away?

My breath comes out in shallow gasps, and I grip the sheets for support.

There's a soft knock at the door before the handle rattles, and Varya pokes her head through. "Ma'am?" She's worried. "Is everything okay? You sort of left—"

"Varya?"

I'm seeing her, watching her brows crinkle with greater anxiety, but my mind is still fixed on running through the possibilities of uncertainty. I close my eyes, but that only makes it worse.

"Varya, I'm..." I lick my lips, trying to gather strength. "I'm fine. It's nothing too serious. Which one of Antonio's men is on watch today?"

Slipping in through the door, she edges closer into the room. "Luca. Lorenzo's away with the boss. Himself, Giovanni, and Dario."

Mild relief settles in my chest, and I ask again to make sure. "Luca's here?"

"Yes, ma'am."

"Great." I summon strength and push myself to my feet and pad over to the closet. "I need to change first. Send a message across and tell him to wait for me downstairs."

"Your fingernails might disappear before we get there."

Turning to the side, I look over my shoulder at Luca, who'd been strangely quiet throughout the ride to the hospital. He has his eyes pinned on the road and his jaw set in a stubborn clamp. I can feel the tension radiating off him in waves.

Convincing him to take me without Antonio's knowledge and permission had been a tedious drag. The man was as stubborn as a mule. Thank God, I managed to succeed after several attempts at emotionally blackmailing him. I deserve an award for my efforts.

Sighing, I drop my fingers from my mouth and sink deeper into the car seat. The nerves wracking in my stomach and chest are threatening to kill me before I have the opportunity to carry out the test.

"You don't understand."

Luca gives me an unreadable side-eye before his jaw flexes, and he looks back at the road. "Maybe you should take a look in the mirror. You look like a ghost, Vivienne. I don't need to understand; what I see is enough. That's the reason I'm doing this."

Antonio and his men are not exactly vocal about their emotions, but I can identify care and concern when I see one.

Before I can respond, the hospital comes into view.

Luca presses down on the gas, and my heart lurches as he swerves sharply into the lot, tires screeching louder on the pavement than they should in the quiet midday sun. When he cuts the engine, there's an abrupt silence that follows. It's deafening, and, at the same time, it makes everything louder—my heartbeat, my ragged breathing.

"You don't..." I take a deep breath. "You don't have to come in with me. I can do this on my own."

"Sure, and have Nio slice my dick off when he hears I left his pretty wife without protection," he says dryly.

His seatbelt whirs when he unbuckles it, and the car seat dips under his weight when he turns to me, his face hard and unsmiling. "Look, I'm going to tell you a short story. You can't tell anyone I told you."

"Um, okay."

Luca telling me a *story* now is the last thing I expect, but I welcome a diversion from the current situation glaring at me in the face.

"When I was a kid, maybe nine or ten, my father took my brothers and me on this family hike—said it'd be a bonding experience. It was supposed to be a simple trail, you know, easy enough for a kid like me. So we get about halfway up this trail, and it's fine at first—trees everywhere, birds fucking singing, or whatever. But then we hit this ridge, and out of nowhere, the path just... disappears. Erosion or something. There's this steep drop on one side and nothing but loose rocks on the other. My father urges me to move forward, but I'm fucking terrified, convinced that if I move an inch, I'm going to fall."

Luca's jaw moves a muscle, and he runs a hand over his hair.

"My father is like, 'Luca, don't look at the whole thing. Just look at your next step. That's all you have to do.'"

I hold my breath; his father's talking to me.

"So I did. I focused on the one rock, then the next. One step, then another. Before I knew it, I was past the ridge, standing on solid ground. And when I turned back to look, it wasn't as scary as I thought. I realized the hardest part wasn't the trail—it was getting out of my own head."

His eyes search mine before he opens his door. "You don't have to figure it out all at once. Just take the next step. That's all you need to do."

The door closes behind him, and the knot loosens in my chest, just a little. Though strange and completely out of the blue, I appreciate Luca for sharing a bit of his past to encourage me.

I stare up through the windshield at the towering hospital. Its glass panels harshly glint under the sun, and my throat feels dry, my palms damp.

Swallowing, I whisper, "Next step," and step out of the car and into the blinding afternoon.

Inside the hospital, the entire process goes by in a blur. Luca is at my side before I can even steady myself, taking charge. I force my legs to move as we follow the nurse, one shaky step at a time, to the room she leads us to.

The seconds drag, feeling more and more like a stretch of eternity, and when the doctor finally exposes his white teeth in a smile, my throat tightens.

Positive.

The office is no less claustrophobic. Shock grips me, and it's sharp and cold. I guess I'd known from the moment Varya made the comment about children, but hearing now is… surreal.

The shock gives way to something else, and I feel it rise to the brim.

It's that stubbornness I'd never managed to get rid of. The same one Papa identified one time too many.

Fuck anxiety.

I'm not breaking or running.

I'm pregnant. *Pregnant!* There is a real seed, a real baby forming inside me, and it doesn't matter what comes next; I'm going to fight for us if I have to.

Once we leave the doctor's office and head straight to the car, under the burning rays of sunlight, Luca steps in front of me and blocks my path. His tall shadow looms over me, his dark eyes brimming with more fierceness than when I'd first ambushed and coaxed him to bring me to the hospital.

"Remember the ridge and the rocks? Well, Vivienne, now's the time to take that step. You're telling Antonio. End of story."

26

ANTONIO

From the moment we stepped through that door, the eyes hadn't stopped following us. I blame Vivienne for being so irresistibly tempting tonight. As far as I am concerned, she's the only jewel in the room.

Her red dress clings to her every curve. It's silk—or something that looks like silk—that ripples with every step she takes. The plunging neckline is just a shy of scandalous, and the slit along her thigh seems designed to test every man's self-control.

My hand rests possessively on the small of her back as we take our seats, but it feels like a futile gesture. I take a chair out for her, watching as she gracefully sits, before I occupy the space beside hers.

She's radiant. Her red hair cascades in loose waves over one shoulder, her lips painted a deep, intoxicating crimson to match her dress. I spot a man, standing not far away in the midst of company. His drink is halfway to his lips as he gawks at her. The fucker doesn't even bother to hide it as he drags his gaze over her like he's entitled to it.

My jaw tightens, and I hook my fingers under her chair, pulling her closer.

It's that she doesn't notice, or she doesn't care.

She doesn't turn toward my direction, which unsettles me, and, when I think about it, I realize she hasn't looked at me once since tonight, not at home or on our way here.

I slip an arm around her waist, leaning closer to whisper against her neck. The whole room is watching; I can feel it, but I don't pay them any heed.

"*Gattina*." I feel her melt against my arm, but she catches her lower lip between her teeth. "Are you hungry? Do you want to eat something?"

She shakes her head.

"How about a drink? Thirsty?"

She shakes her head again, and I grow concerned.

A quiet Vivienne is not a good sign, and I'm unsure how to handle the situation, but I know there's something wrong. I feel it in my core.

The music swells around us, and, feeling utterly helpless and annoyed with myself for not being able to do something, I try to focus on the conversation around the table. I have never been a big fan of these types of gatherings. Phony faces with practiced smiles, feigning delight to see you, all the while hiding the secret wish for your downfall. All the same, it is necessary to attend, socialize, and establish potential connections. And maybe uncover those secrets while at it.

I reach for the Kauffman bottle on the table to fill my glass when someone in a blue suit approaches our table with a line of bodyguards behind him. He fucking occupies the empty seat beside my wife like he owns it.

The conversations around us subside to a quiet hush,

and the side of my face sizzles with an awareness that this unprecedented collision has taken center stage in the hall.

Tilting his head to the side, he raises the cigar between his fingers, and the corner of his eyes crinkles when he smiles.

"Antonio Mancini," he drawls dryly, but the wide smile on his face doesn't give away anything else. "Pleasure meeting you here."

I take my glass to my lips, glaring at him over the rim. It's been a while since he made an appearance in this type of public gathering. I don't trust this man, and having him near me, close to Vivienne, sets me on edge and boils my blood. But the people are watching, waiting to point fingers at the one who makes the first move.

"Salvatore." I tilt the glass toward him. "Can't say the same."

Grinning, he looks away from me, and the blood in my body boils hotter when he releases a crude and unrefined whistle, gazing desirously at Vivienne. She stiffens when he curls a finger underneath her chin and crooks her head to face him.

"And who's this vixen? My, my, my... Can I have you as my plus-one for tonight, pretty one?"

I grit my teeth with anger swelling in my gut. "The only thing you'll have tonight is a bullet in your brain if you don't take your hands off my wife."

One of his bodyguards reaches to grab his gun, but I'm faster. I pull my gun from my holster and aim it at him.

The loud crack of a bullet splitting through the air makes someone scream. Murmurs and hushed whispers spread like wildfire across the room.

"Next time, I won't miss."

I drop my gun on the table, aiming the barrel at Salvatore's chest with my finger still on the trigger. He has a brow raised and a smug smile plastered on his face when he drags his gaze from his bodyguard back to me.

"Interesting."

"Let's see how interesting you'll find it when my heels are buried deep in your balls," Vivienne hisses, her emerald eyes filled with more disgust and rage than I've ever seen them. "Get your dirty hands off me," she grits out.

A burst of pride ripples through my chest. That's my wife.

Like an arrogant son of a bitch he is, he raises his hand in mock surrender, and another crack splits through the air.

The music stops completely. The hall falls into pin-drop silence.

Vivienne gasps when I pull the trigger, and the brown cigar falls to the table.

"*Fucking—son of bitch!*" Growling, he rises to his feet.

Satisfied, I release my finger from the trigger. "*That w*as to ensure you *never* touch her again."

He points at me with his middle finger. "You're going to regret this, I swear to you, Mancini. No one, absolutely no fucking one, dares to disrespect me and goes scot-free."

"Get the fuck out of my face, Russo, before I change my mind about letting you leave here with a hand."

Seething, and probably regretting his choice of sharing a table with me, he stomps off, his back and bodyguards disappearing between the crowd.

The people are still staring, but softly, the music rises, and soon enough, the party resumes as if nothing had just happened.

I cup Vivienne's chin, lifting it.

The shock is still visible in her eyes when she searches my face and licks her lips. "Antonio?"

I raise a brow to let her know I'm listening.

"Did you really have to do that?"

I lean back on my chair and closely watch the phonies in the room. If Salvatore wasn't out for me before, he certainly is now.

"Except you enjoyed it, yes, and even if you didn't enjoy it, yes, I really had to do that. And if I have to do it again, I'll do it a hundred more fucking times, *gattina*. No one gets to fucking touch you like that except me."

I don't look at her because I'm still fuming and don't want her to feel like I'm redirecting the heat. After a brief moment of quiet, she mumbles a quiet, "thank you," leans forward to press a kiss against my cheek, and withdraws into the shell the drama brought her out from.

Before I can interrogate her, Lorenzo appears from out of nowhere, shoving his face between hers and mine.

Expression taut, and eyes hard, he lowers his voice. His hair falls forward, and he brushes the loose strands behind his ear. "Nio, there's an update."

I narrow my eyes, giving the crowd a quick once-over before I tell him, "Go on."

"We found something. An encrypted phone recording of someone discussing the warehouse on the dock, and there are more recordings with Dante's name mentioned. We haven't yet been able to trace the person on the end of the line, but you can guess whose voice we recognized."

We share a look, and his eyes dart to the man in the blue suit glaring at me from across the room while he talks to his men.

Lorenzo grits his teeth and tucks his hand into his jacket. "He knows more than we thought about the attack on the warehouse. About Dante."

This information hits me like a punch to the gut, and I'm pulling out my gun again.

"Are you sure?" Because if he is, I'm raining hell on that pompous piece of shit, here and now.

He nods once, his jaw set. "You can ask Luca. I know you think my methods are rash or not as organized sometimes, but this time, I swear, Nio, we've done the necessary checks."

I glance across the room, my eyes zeroing in on Salvatore. He's laughing now, with a woman, his head tipped back as if he doesn't have a single worry in the world. What he doesn't know is that he has me to worry about now.

My blood boils, the heat of anger rising to the surface, threatening to spill over.

He's always been good at playing these fucking games, but never like this, like a sneaky crook who's scared to show his face and get the job done himself.

In the end, I am right, and Dario is wrong.

Salvatore is involved somehow, and that's all I need to know.

I drain the rest of my drink, the burn of vodka igniting my fury. "Tell one of the men stationed outside to get the car ready," I say, checking the magazine in my gun. "Vivienne and I will be out in five minutes."

There's a familiar psychotic glint in Lorenzo's eyes when he smiles. "We're doing it here, aren't we?"

Standing to my feet, I smile at my wife. "Whatever you do, put your head down, and don't get up until you hear the sound of my voice. Are we clear?"

"Antonio, what are you—"

"Down, Vivienne." Aiming my gun, I signal Lorenzo. "Now."

Tapping the earpiece in his ear, he barks off in a hot rush of Italian orders and takes his gun out of his pocket. While he's talking, I notice Salvatore no longer stands where he should. Not a good sign.

I scan the room, and his men are nowhere to be—

The air explodes with multiple gunshots, and we can't see him, but I hear his voice boom in a thunderous echo. "Take them down!"

A woman screams—high-pitched, strangled—as she drops to the floor, hands flying to her face in a desperate, frantic attempt to shield herself from the madness. Another shriek follows, and voices rise in frantic, disjointed screams.

Salvatore's men surge forward like unleashed hounds, their guns raised high, the metallic glint catching the reflection of lights from the chandeliers.

Lorenzo and I retaliate, but barely have time to duck. Instantly, a dozen of my men flood the hall, and Lorenzo ducks behind a concrete pillar, returning fire with a craziness in his eyes.

I know how this is going to end eventually. More men will end up in a crumpled heap, and people will be caught in the crossfire.

I want to stay, to finish off Salvatore Russo once and for all after getting his confession firsthand, but one glance at the woman in the red dress crouched by the table makes all thoughts of vengeance fly out the window. The primal need to protect her overrides all other desires and takes precedence.

"Vivienne!"

She's frozen for a heartbeat, her eyes wide with terror, as she wraps her arms around her stomach, shielding herself.

Another bullet ricochets off the pillars in the hall near us, and something inside me snaps.

I reach for her, grabbing her arm and pulling her toward me.

I don't wait for her to catch up. My grip is tight, almost bruising, as I force her to move, weaving through the chaotic web of people running for their lives.

Shots ring out around us, and I throw a glance at Lorenzo. "*Ritirasi!*" Fall back.

He gives a curt nod, and I focus on Vivienne. "Keep your head down!" I shield her with my body as we dart between panicking guests.

Her breath is ragged, panicked, and we're almost to the car, where one of my men stands with his gun firing, when another shot cracks too close.

I shove Vivienne to the side, catching her before she stumbles, dragging her upright again. When my man sees us, he fires a shot above our head before fumbling with the doors.

When he wrenches the door open, we get in, and immediately, Vivienne wraps her trembling arms around me as the engines roar to life. Burying her face in my shirt, her rough sniffles disturb the silence as she cries her heart out, and I don't try to stop her.

Pulling her close, I kiss her hair.

I don't say anything. My pulse still pounds in my ears.

But the thought won't leave my head.

I'm going to fucking kill Salvatore.

27

VIVIENNE

The first rays of sunlight warm my face, and the gentle sound of waves lapping against the shore stirs me awake. My eyes flutter open, and I'm met with a breathtaking view through the glass walls of the room.

The endless expanse of the ocean stretches before me, its surface glistening like scattered diamonds under the early morning sun.

I sit up slowly, the soft linen sheets pooling around my waist. The air smells of salt and something fresh, like jasmine.

My gaze sweeps across the room—minimalist yet luxurious, with whitewashed walls and rustic wooden furniture. My bed is massive, draped with gauzy white curtains that billow slightly in the sea breeze coming through the open sliding doors.

Curiosity gets the better of me, and I swing my legs over the edge of the bed, my bare feet meeting the cool hardwood floor.

Nothing here looks or smells familiar.

The soft rustling sound reminds me that I'm wearing one of Antonio's oversized shirts, the fabric brushing my thighs as I move. I vaguely recall him draping it over me last night after insisting I rest.

The scent of freshly brewed coffee wafts in, drawing me toward the open-concept kitchen and living space. But it's the view that captures my breath. Just beyond the living room is a sprawling deck, complete with a small infinity pool that seems to spill directly into the ocean.

I step out onto the deck, the wood warm beneath my feet. The sand is just a few steps away, golden and untouched, as if this little stretch of paradise belongs only to us.

"Good morning, *gattina*," Antonio's voice cuts through the serenity, deep and rich like the coffee I smell.

I turn to find him leaning against the doorframe, a steaming cup in one hand and that ever-present intensity in his eyes.

He's dressed casually, barefoot like me, with the top buttons of his linen shirt undone. The sight of him here, so relaxed, feels almost surreal.

"Where are we?" I ask, my voice still rough with sleep. I can't remember much from last night. I remember chaos erupting at the party and Antonio whisking me away from it, but the last memory I have is falling asleep in the car.

He takes a step toward me, his expression softening. "Somewhere safe," he says simply, handing me the cup of coffee. His fingers brush mine, lingering for a moment longer than necessary. "I bought this place for when I need to get away from the chaos in our world."

I take a sip, the warmth spreading through me. Surprisingly, the smell doesn't make me nauseous. "It's beautiful," I whisper, looking back at the horizon.

"So are you," he replies, his voice low. And when I glance up at him, there's something in his eyes that makes me believe he means what he's just said.

Butterflies flutter in my stomach, and if I weren't early into my pregnancy, I would have sworn it's the baby dancing happily to the sound of its father's voice.

My chest tightens, a mix of guilt and fear swirling inside me—guilt for hiding the truth from him and fear that he may not accept our baby. What if he wants me to abort it?

"Are you okay?" he asks, his gentle voice dragging me back to the present.

I nod more than necessary. "I'm fine. I was just thinking about something."

"Do you care to share?"

I shake my head. "It's not something important." It's something beyond important.

"Do you want me to show you around the place?"

"Yes, I would like that."

He smiles. It's so warm and his eyes are so sparkly that I almost catch myself smiling back, save for the constant churning in my chest, reminding me of the secret I am keeping. I wonder if it'll ruin everything if I tell him today.

He nods at my cup. "Finish your coffee, and I'll show you around."

I hurriedly finish my coffee and follow him outside the building. The entire place is so serene and beautiful that I wouldn't mind living out the rest of my life here.

A smile plays on my lips as a mental image of raising our kids here and watching them run around forms in my head. I imagine Antonio running after them. He's not the grumpy mafia boss who eats the heart of his enemies for breakfast. He's just my husband—our children's father.

God, why do I keep dreaming of something I'll never

have? When did I go from looking for a way out of here to dreaming of a future with him?

My papa will be furious when he finds out. He'll hate me, and I wonder how Harper will react to it. Will she detest the idea of being an aunt to Antonio's daughter? To her, he's nothing more than a villain who kidnapped her sister after all.

I don't notice the tears sliding down my cheeks until Antonio reaches out to wipe them off. "Do you like this place so much that you're crying?"

I stop right in front of the water and narrow my eyes as the morning sun scorches me with its rays. It's hot, but not hot enough to leave a sunburn. "Yes, I do like this place. It's just... I've missed my sister so much."

There's a flicker of sadness in his eyes, but it lasts only a moment before his expression goes cold.

"I need to see my sister," I say, pushing my luck. This could go awry, but I don't care. I need Harper. Having her around me is the only way I won't lose my mind. "I want to meet her just once. I need to talk to her."

His eyes bore into mine. "And if I refuse?"

"You can't." The back of my throat starts to burn, and I sniffle to keep the tears welling in my eyes away. "You don't understand me because you've never had—"

He raises his hand to stop me. "Don't say it."

"You don't have a family or someone you love more than yourself. You can't understand how I feel."

His eyes suddenly grow so cloudy that I take a step back.

I've crossed the line. I shouldn't have said that. "I'm sorry."

He ignores my apology and remains silent for an uncomfortable amount of time. The tension between us thickens, the breeze suddenly cold enough to make my jaw quiver.

And finally, after what seems like an eternity, he clears his throat. "I, too, had a younger brother. I had parents, and I loved them very much. We were happy." He pauses. "Until that night when they were murdered. Everything changed."

It's the first time I've heard Antonio sound like he's in so much pain, and it breaks my heart to hear him sound this way.

"I'm so sorry about that. I mean, how did you survive all on your own?"

"I didn't," he answers. "I lived on the street for weeks until Dante found me and took me home. Mariana loved me at first sight, and they both raised me as if I was their son."

That is why he's so obsessed with getting justice for Dante. He wasn't just his mentor; he was his father, too. I wonder what my papa is doing. Can't he just give Antonio all the details he needs so all of this will come to an end?

"I'm sorry," I repeat, not knowing what else to say. Nothing I say can make him feel better.

He nods. "So you see, I know the feeling of loving someone. I've loved someone dearly, and I do love someone even now."

My chest constricts. By love, does he mean Mariana, or is there a woman out there with whom he's in love? I shrug the thought off before it can bloom further. I shouldn't be thinking about stuff like that.

When I glance at Antonio again, he is paying full attention to the sea. He's watching the water clap against the shore absentmindedly, lost in whatever thought that has clouded his mind.

I want to make him feel better. I want him to know he

could have a family of his own if he chooses, and that I will always be here for him.

So, despite my fear that he may not be ready to be a father, I decide to share what's supposed to be happy news with him. He deserves to know.

Reaching for his hand, I place it on my belly and wait for his reaction.

He lifts a brow. "Are you—"

I nod. "I'm pregnant," I say. "I found out not long ago, but I wasn't sure how to tell you. I wasn't sure you'd want the baby."

Some of the ice in his eyes melts away. "Are you saying I'm going to be a father soon?"

My eyes prickle with tears. These damn pregnancy hormones. "Yes, you're going to be a father, Antonio. We're going to be parents."

The world stops spinning for a moment. The sea stops crashing against the shore, and the wind stops whispering. Not even the bird dares to chirp.

For a moment, all that exists is me and Antonio. And all I can hear is the beating of our hearts in perfect sync.

And then Antonio yells out with excitement, picking me up and spinning me around gently. "I'm going to be a father!"

I laugh because his joy is contagious right now. I didn't expect him to be this happy about it. "Yes, you're going to be a father, Antonio."

"Oh, my God." He puts me down and touches my belly. "There is a little human inside your stomach who'll call me Papa?"

I smile and nod.

"Fuck! Yes!" He cups my face, and his eyes glisten with unshed tears. "Do you think it will be a boy or a girl?"

My cheeks heat with a blush. I'd been so busy worrying about his reaction that I hadn't even thought of whether our baby would be a girl or a boy. "I'm not sure, but I'll be more than glad if it's a boy."

He laughs heartily. "I want a little girl, one who looks just as beautiful as you. We'll give her everything she wants and spoil her rotten."

"A little girl or a little boy. Either one is fine by me."

"What are we going to name her if she's a girl?"

I think for a moment, but nothing comes up. "Don't be in such a rush. I'm only seven weeks in. We have more than enough time to think of baby names after we find out the gender."

"Right, we do." He takes my hand in his. "Thank you, Vivienne. Thank you so much for this gift. Thank you for everything."

I hold his hand. "Thank you, too, Antonio. A lot has happened, and I didn't plan to be here, but I somehow am, thanks to you. Regardless of all that, I am beyond happy for our baby, and I hope we get to raise it together."

He's breathing raggedly from all the excitement earlier. "We *will* raise our child together, Vivienne. It's a promise."

His thumb brushes my cheeks lightly. Heat from his thumb seeps into my skin and works its way all the way to my core.

My heart is beating faster, and my brain is fogged with images of him pinning me somewhere around here and fucking me until I cannot walk.

As if listening to my thoughts, Antonio leans in and kisses me passionately. I kiss him back, tipping myself on my toes and kissing him back.

His hands slide down to my waist, pulling me closer as our lips move in perfect harmony.

The world around us fades away once more, leaving only the heat between our bodies pressing against each other.

Antonio breaks the kiss, his forehead resting against mine as we catch our breath. His eyes, dark with desire, search mine. "Can we do this? With the baby, I mean?"

I nod, my fingers tangling in his hair. "It's fine. More than fine. I want you, Antonio. Now."

A low growl escapes his throat as he lifts me, my legs wrapping around his waist. He carries me to a nearby tree, pressing my back against its rough bark.

The contrast of textures—Antonio's smooth skin and the tree's coarse surface—sends shivers down my spine.

His lips find my neck, trailing kisses along my collarbone.

I tilt my head back, giving him better access as I moan softly.

His hands roam my body, caressing every curve in a way that makes my heart swell, and a pool of wetness forms between my legs.

"You're so beautiful," he whispers against my skin. "So perfect. So mine."

I pull his face back to mine, capturing his lips in a searing kiss. My fingers fumble with the buttons of his shirt, desperate to feel his skin against mine. Antonio helps, shrugging off the garment and tossing it aside.

The cool air hits my skin as he lifts my shirt over my head. His eyes darken further as he takes in the sight of me, half-naked, save for the lacy red thong I am wearing.

"Antonio," I breathe, pulling him closer. "Take me, please. I want you inside me right away."

He smirks. "You're the only one who can order me around like that."

He doesn't need any more encouragement. He slides down my panties, pressing a finger between my folds and gliding it back and forth repeatedly. "You're wet," he says in a deep, husky voice.

I gasp at his touch, my hips bucking against his hand. "Only for you," I moan against his lips.

Antonio's fingers work magic, circling my clit before dipping inside me. I moan loudly, not caring if anyone might hear us in this secluded spot.

"That's it, *mi amor*," he whispers, his breath hot against my ear. "Let me hear how much you want me."

I'm practically trembling with need as he continues to tease me. "Antonio, please," I beg, my nails digging into his shoulders.

He chuckles, a low, sexy sound that sends shivers down my spine. "Good girl. I like it when you beg me to take you just like that."

In one swift motion, he unzips his pants and frees himself. I feel the tip of his hardness pressing against my entrance, and I whimper with anticipation.

Antonio enters me slowly, filling me inch by inch until he's fully sheathed inside. We both groan at the sensation, our bodies perfectly joined.

"God, Vivienne," he breathes, his forehead resting against mine. "You feel sweet and tight. I love the way your pussy clenches around my cock."

I wrap my legs tighter around his waist, urging him deeper. "Fuck me," I plead. "Fuck me hard, Antonio."

Antonio begins to thrust, setting a steady rhythm that has me gasping with each movement. The tree's rough bark scrapes against my back, but I barely notice, lost in the pleasure Antonio is giving me.

His lips find mine again, swallowing my moans as he

picks up the pace. One of his hands snakes between us, his thumb finding my clit and circling it in time with his thrusts.

I cry out from the pleasure that cocoons me. I feel his touch everywhere as he explores my body.

The intensity builds between us, our bodies moving in perfect synchronization.

Antonio's thrusts become more forceful, driving deeper with each movement. I cling to him, my nails raking down his back as waves of pleasure crash over me.

"That's it, *gattina*," Antonio growls, his voice thick with desire. "Come for me. Let me feel you."

His words push me over the edge. I cry out his name as my orgasm hits, my body shuddering against him.

Antonio groans, burying his face in my neck as he follows me over the precipice, his hips jerking erratically as he spills inside me.

We stay like that for a moment, panting and holding each other close.

Antonio peppers soft kisses along my jawline, his hands gently caressing my sides.

"I love you," he murmurs against my skin, the words catching me by so much surprise that air stalls in my lungs. "I'm in love with you, Vivienne."

28

ANTONIO

Vivienne jumps up from the dining table when she sees me walk in. She's beaming with a smile that is so full of love and warmth, everything I need after all the bloodshed of the last couple of days.

It's been three days since the party, and I had the beach house guarded while I went out to hunt for Salvatore two nights ago. The old fucker did a good job hiding from me; I give him that. But he'll be crawling out of whatever hole he's hiding in soon enough, and I swear I'll get him then.

Vivienne runs up to me and wraps herself around me. I hug her back, lifting her and peppering her with kisses. I've missed her so much these last two days.

"How are you, *gattina*?" I ask, still holding her firmly against me.

She looks up at me and giggles. "Aside from my morning sickness, I think I'm fine. I was worried about you."

I pull back and drop down on one knee to touch her belly. I still can't believe I am going to be a father soon. I haven't had much time to process this, but the thought fills me with more happiness than I can put into words.

"How are you, little one?" I ask, rubbing her stomach softly. "You've been giving your mama trouble, haven't you?"

Vivienne's laughter rings in the air, so hearty and bubbly that it is contagious. I should laugh, too, but all I feel is my heart rate quicken and tears well in my eyes—tears of happiness.

So this is what being alive feels like. I've been dead for so long... but now, because of Vivienne, I feel alive.

"He's troublesome," Vivienne says. "I wonder who he gets it from?"

I glance up at her—my wife, the woman who somehow pulled me out from the darkest pit of hell and made me feel alive again. I still can't believe she's mine. I still can't believe that any of this is happening.

"He?"

"I'm just using that since we don't know if it's a boy or a girl yet," she says, her tone high with excitement. "I think he gets it from you."

I try to stifle my laughter, but it just erupts through me. "We're done for if he or she comes out with your smart mouth. Anyway..." I stand to my feet and snake my arms around her waist. "We're going home today. Ginny and Agatha are waiting."

She narrows her eyes. "Home? And Salvatore?"

"I've invaded his territory and taken down most of his men. He's gone into hiding," I explain. "He won't make any stupid moves for the time being."

She nods and cups her belly.

My chest tightens at that. She's already so protective over our child, and I feel so protective over both of them. I'll do anything to keep them safe, including following Salvatore into the depths of hell until he's no longer a threat to her and our baby.

I'd give my life to protect them.

"I'll get my things ready then." She turns around to leave but pauses and scrutinizes me. "You're not hurt anywhere, are you?"

I shake my head, despite the painful throbbing in my right shoulder. One of Salvatore's men managed to land two blows on me with his gun.

She smiles. "Thank goodness. I'll grab my things."

It's evening by the time we get to the mansion. I can hear Ginny's voice from the foyer as she orders Agatha around on what she thinks Vivienne will like to eat.

Vivienne's eyes light up at the sound of her voice. "Looks like someone really did miss me."

"Aye, someone did," a deep voice says.

We turn around to find Dario descending the stairs.

"She threatened to chop my dick off if I didn't bring her here and convince Antonio to bring you home," Dario continues with a shake of his head as he approaches us. "I heard from Antonio that you're going to be parents. Congratulations."

Vivienne glances at me, then flashes a wide smile at Dario. "Thank you, Dario."

Ginny raises her voice to get a maid's attention in the kitchen. "All right, I have to join them now," Vivienne says with a playful grin. "See you boys at dinner."

I nod in response, and she saunters off to the kitchen.

Turning to Dario, Lorenzo, and Luca behind me, I say, "We need to talk."

They follow me to my study upstairs and wait for me to

settle down. Dario sits on the chair across from mine, watching me as if he's trying to see through my thoughts.

"You're worried about her, aren't you?" he asks.

"Shit! Is it that obvious?" I ask, leaning back in my seat and steepling my fingers in front of me.

"As obvious as the color of the sky," he replies. "With Salvatore still in hiding, we don't know what the bastard will come up with. We need to find him before he allies himself with one of our enemies."

"How do we find him?" Lorenzo asks from where he's standing by the door.

"We scout the city," I suggest. "If he's gone into hiding, then I presume someone is helping him. We need to keep an eye on his allies. It has to be one of them."

Luca sighs. "Do you think there's a chance Peter Cole is helping him?"

I rub my jaw as I think. Peter is a tricky character in the midst of all this chaos. He definitely knows more than he lets on or shares. But there's one thing I'm certain of: He would never ally himself with someone who tried to kill his daughter. "It's impossible, but no—I don't think he's involved."

Dario and Lorenzo nod in agreement.

"I'll meet with Peter, see if we can get him on our side." Vivienne is carrying his grandchild; I hope we can use that to our advantage.

"And if he still refuses?" Dario asks. "Will we kill him? I bet Vivienne wouldn't want us hurting her father."

"I'll do whatever it takes to keep my family safe." I crack my knuckles. It's stiff from holding my gun for hours yesterday. "If that includes killing Peter, then so be it."

Vivienne will be upset, but I would rather she be angry at me than dead.

"I'll do my best to find Salvatore's hiding place," Lorenzo says. "I'll scout the city until we find whatever hole the mole is hiding in."

"Thank you." I flit my gaze to Luca. "Tighten the security around the house and make sure my wife doesn't go anywhere unprotected."

"Yes, boss," he responds.

"One more thing," I say just as he's about to leave. "Make sure Mariana's house is well-guarded, too. She won't be the top of their priority list, but they know she's a weakness."

He nods, and I dismiss them with a wave of my hand.

When they leave, my shoulders slouch, and I let out a frustrated groan.

Dario peers at me intently. "You're disturbed about something, aren't you? What is it?"

"It's Vivienne." My stomach churns as the image of her begging me to allow her to see her sister with tears in her eyes flashes in my mind. "I have to let her go when all of this is over."

"Why?" he tilts his head. "You're in love with her."

"I am." Fuck, I can't believe how easily I am admitting this. How easily I said it to her the other day. "That's exactly why I need to let her go. I can't keep her a prisoner forever. If she stays, then it should be because she wants to."

And God, I want her to stay. I know I'm a Grade-A asshole, but I want her here with me.

Dario smiles. It's the first time he's smiling at me in a while. "That's the right thing to do."

I imagine Dante saying the same words to me. He used to say things like that a lot—used to tell me how proud he was of me and the decisions I made.

I should feel anger, the urge for vengeance. But all I feel now is the need to protect, to not lose any of the people I care about again. To keep Vivienne and our unborn child safe.

"Do you think Mariana will like this decision?" I ask. As much as I am affected by Dante's death, I know Mariana is even more.

They'd known each other since they were kids; he was her soulmate. I imagine this will be harder on her than it will be on anyone else, knowing a boy she raised is in love with the daughter of her enemy.

"Mariana is like a mother to you, Antonio. She may not have given birth to you, but she and Dante loved you as if you were their own. Talk to her, make her see reason with you two, and it will not be a problem." Dario pauses and clears his throat. "She'll understand you better than anyone else."

Dario is right. Mariana won't hold it against me if she knows I am in love with Vivienne, but Mariana is the least of my problems. No one can stop me from loving Vivienne, not even the devil himself.

Vivienne's feelings for me are all I am concerned about. She's the only one who can break us, and even then, I won't stop until I get her back.

"I know" is all I can bring myself to reply.

His phone buzzes, and taking it out of his pocket, he sighs. "I gotta run, man. Talk later."

"Are you taking Ginny?" I ask.

Vivienne's happy to have Ginny around. She'd be disappointed if Ginny leaves now.

"No, I'll pick her up later." He pushes up from his seat and smooths his suit jacket. "Give it some more thought, and let me know when you decide."

"Thanks, man."

"Anytime." He leaves, and I drift back to my thoughts.

There's only one thing left to do now: Negotiate with Peter. I don't negotiate with anyone, but I have to for Vivienne's sake.

Pulling my phone out from my pocket, I dial Peter's number. Fortunately for both of us, he answers on the first ring.

"If it isn't the devil himself," Peter drawls in a gravelly voice. "To what do I owe this unexpected call?"

My nostrils flare, but I remind myself to remain calm. "I'll get right to the point, Cole. I'm inviting you for dinner at my house on Sunday night. You're to bring Harper with you."

He lets out a harsh laugh, his voice ringing in my ear like a funeral bell. "Dinner at your house? After you kidnapped my daughter. Do you really think I am stupid enough to dine with my enemy?"

I do think he is stupid; he wouldn't gamble his daughter's life away to protect a secret if he wasn't. But I don't tell him that. Instead, I say, "Trust me when I say sitting at the same table with you is the last thing I want. Vivienne misses her sister; we need to come to a compromise for her sake."

"And if I refuse?" Peter asks.

"Then you'll leave me no choice but to take your daughter."

"Are you threatening me?"

"I am. My wife needs to see her sister, and I'll make that happen in any way possible. I'll tear your entire mansion down if I have to," I state sternly, and I mean every word I say. "Friday night at seven. Oh, and we have one more matter to discuss when you come."

I hang up before he has a chance to argue.

Friday night will either end with us being allies... or with one of us dead.

29

VIVIENNE

Warmth rushes through me as Harper's voice washes over me. Hearing her voice is like sunshine breaking through a cloudy sky, filling my chest with so much love.

I jump to my feet and run down the stairs in excitement. I don't even watch where I'm going, and I can't stop smiling.

I suppose Harper is in the foyer, looking around for me.

The moment our eyes meet, her face lights up with a smile. She rushes toward me, and we both collide into each other's arms.

God, this must be what heaven feels like—my sister's jasmine-lavender perfume, warm embrace, and soft voice. I've missed her so much.

She pulls back but holds my hands as she scrutinizes me from head to toe. "Are you okay? They're not hurting you, are they?"

I shake my head. "I'm fine. Like really fine. I just missed you."

Tears well in her eyes, and she pulls me back in for another hug. "I missed you more. I was so worried about you. I was so excited when Papa told me we were meeting tonight."

Papa.

My papa is here.

Shit. I'd almost forgotten he exists. I wonder what he thinks of all of this. What he'll think when I tell him I'm pregnant.

My pulse quickens as I spare him a glance from over Harper's shoulder.

He's cold as usual, giving me that icy glare that is hard to read. I can't tell whether he is angry at me, the situation, or even angry at all. I wonder how Antonio managed to convince him to agree to this dinner.

I pull away from Harper and walk over to him. "Hi, Father."

He takes his time scrutinizing me before answering. "Hi, Vivienne. You look… well."

Maybe it's just my imagination, but it doesn't sound like he's pleased about the fact that I am… well.

"So do you." Which is a relief because I was scared he would have gone bald with worry for me by now.

"You made it in time." Antonio's deep, baritone voice comes from behind me.

I turn around, shaking my head to signal him not to cause trouble. It must've been hard for my papa to accept his invitation to dinner; infuriating him now will not yield any benefits for anyone.

Still, I am grateful to Antonio for this surprise. I steal a surprise smile at him, and he winks back at me.

"Why wouldn't I?" my father shoots back at him. "It's not every day a kidnapper invites the father of his prisoner to his home, is it?"

Tension fills the room, seeping into my veins and

making me tremble. My stomach churns, but I am unsure if it's the pregnancy hormones raging or my pulse racing. Whichever one it is, I hate the feeling of it.

I let out a nervous laugh. "Knock it off, you two." I turn to Harper, who nods at me, and then to my father. "Dinner's ready. Let's go to the table."

My husband and father exchange glares as if promising each other to continue their cold war later.

I sigh. Fine, they can kill each other if they want to. I won't be here to witness it, though. Grabbing Harper's hand, I lead her to the dining room and pull out a chair for her, not caring if Antonio or Papa are following behind us.

I round the table to the chair across from Harper and sit.

She narrows her eyes at me and stares at me intently.

I shift in my seat. "What is it?"

"You're glowing, Vivi." She leans over the table, grinning mischievously. "You're not just a prisoner here, are you?"

I press my lips together to suppress a smile.

"Ah," she drawls with glee. "You don't have to answer. Your face says it all."

Scarlet heat burns my cheeks. "Says what?"

"That you're in love with him. It's written all over your face." She pauses and exhales deeply. "Vivi, I want you to be completely honest with me right now. Are you truly happy here?"

I peer into my sister's eyes, fully willing to bare my soul to her. If there's only one person in this world I can be candid with, it's her.

"I am in love with Antonio, Harp," I say, the words coming out with a struggle. "That is not all." I cup my stomach.

Her eyes widen as her gaze shoots to my stomach, and then back up to my face. "Are you pregnant?"

The shock in her voice makes me shiver a bit. For a moment, I consider leaving this detail out of the equation for a while, but I don't. I'm not ashamed of the child growing in my belly, and I don't care about anyone's opinion on it apart from Antonio's.

I nod. "I am."

"How far along are you?" she asks in a barely audible voice this time.

"A few weeks." I suck in a deep breath, and in my gentlest voice, I say, "Look, Harp, I know this situation is not ideal to you. I mean, Antonio kidnapped me and forced me into marrying him, but this child—he didn't force this child on me, and I decided I wanted the baby. I'm having this baby because I love him… or her. I love Antonio, too."

She reaches for my hand across the table. "I'm okay with whatever as long as you are happy. I have your back, Vivi. Always."

A tear falls before I even realize I'm crying. "Thank you," I whisper.

She squeezes my hand gently. "Will you tell Papa about the baby?"

I shrug. "I have to. It's not like I can hide it from him forever."

"He won't be happy," Harper says. "You know this. He'll be repulsed."

I know it. I thought of it all night. I thought of ways to handle my papa with this news. "Do me a favor, Harp. Don't tell him about the baby yet. I'll tell him myself."

She raises her brow. "Tonight?"

Shaking my head, I think for a moment. "Not tonight. I'll pay him a visit later. I need to talk to him and make him understand my reasons—and Antonio's. The tension is too high for all of that tonight."

"I doubt he'll want to hear it, Vivi. But you can try."

The men enter the dining room, Antonio first, followed by Papa. Despite the blank masks they're wearing, I can tell they'd been discussing something outside, but it doesn't seem like the conversation or argument went pleasantly.

Surprisingly, dinner is peaceful. I almost choke on my food a few times from the palpable tension; still, it isn't all that bad.

Neither Antonio nor my father says a word throughout dinner. Harper and I share glances and a few stifled laughs a couple of times.

After dinner, my father hurriedly leaves while I hug Harper, and she rubs my belly. She whispers, "I'll get something for my niece next time" before she leaves.

As they drive away, I feel like a piece of my heart goes with them. I've missed Harper so much these last few months, and a few hours together doesn't make up for it.

Antonio takes my hand in his. He's standing so close that the warmth rolling off him heats me up instantly. "I'm sorry I couldn't make her stay longer."

I whip my head around to look at him, shocked he's apologizing. He's the only reason I got to see my sister after so long. "No, Antonio, thank you for letting me see her."

He shakes his head. "You don't understand, *gattina*. You shouldn't be thanking me for anything. You wouldn't have to stay away from her if I didn't kidnap you in the first place. It's all my fault."

"Hey." I reach for his face and cup it. "You're right. All of this is your fault, but we wouldn't have found the love we did if you hadn't taken me. We wouldn't have our baby. I would be married to that old bastard and have my life stolen from me."

His eyes soften in a way I've never seen them as he places his hand on mine. "Vivienne—"

I hold up a hand. "No, let me finish. None of this is ideal. Some might say I have Stockholm syndrome, but the truth is that you saved me from a fate I so badly wanted to be saved from, and there's nowhere else I would rather be than here with you."

"Vivienne." He wraps his arms around my waist and pulls me closer. "Did you just say love?"

My heart pounds in my chest as I peer up at him.

"Do you love me, baby?" he asks softly.

I swallow so hard that my throat burns. "Yes, I love you. I love you, Antonio. So much that it hurts."

"God, Vivienne," he whispers. "Tonight, I wanted to tell you it was okay to leave. I wanted to let you go, but a selfish part of me still wanted you to stay."

"Don't ever think of letting me go, Antonio. I'm never leaving you. I'll always stay with you."

"No, Vivienne." He slips his finger through my hair. "It's just that Salvatore is still on the loose. I can take anything that happens. I don't give a shit if I die, but I'll never forgive myself if I fail to keep you and our baby safe."

"You'll keep us safe; I trust you. I'll also keep you safe. We're in this together, remember?"

"No, you don't understand." His forehead creases with worry. "Vivienne, things could end up dangerous. Promise me you'll go back to your father if anything goes wrong."

Tears stream down my face. "No. Nothing will go wrong. I can't live without you, Antonio. Our child needs his father, and I need you. Instead, you have to promise me you'll always come back home to me."

"Vivienne—"

"Promise me!"

"Fine." He wipes my tears away with his thumb. "I promise you, I'll always come home to you."

"And you'll never ask me to leave, no matter what?"

"I'll never ask you to leave, Vivi." He brings his face dangerously close to mine, and the skin around my face tingles from the warmth of his breath. He smells like mint and citrus tonight.

"Promise?" I whisper back.

"Promise."

His lips claim mine, his hands exploring my body with a mixture of desperation and carefulness.

His lips are soft as they ravage mine with a primal need to devour them.

I kiss him back, moaning into his mouth as I wrap my arms around him. Kissing him feels so good, like an ecstasy I could only dream of.

It's hard to believe this is my life now—that this man who everyone thinks is brutal and cruel is mine now, and I get to see all the soft sides of him.

"Do you want me to take you somewhere you can watch the entire world from while I fuck you?"

I bite my lips. Shit! He always says the sexiest things at the right time. "Take me there."

He lifts me in bridal style and carries me to one of the balconies I haven't been to yet.

I take the place in when he puts me down. It offers an amazing view of the skyscrapers and bustling city life. From here, I can see the glow from streetlamps and cars racing down the road.

It's beautiful.

I can't believe I've lived here for months without knowing this place existed. The serenity I get just standing here for a couple of minutes is mind-blowing.

"Do you like it?" he asks, pressing his chest against my back. But it's the hardness of his erection pressing against my ass that makes my core start to throb.

I can already feel the wetness pooling between my legs.

"Like it?" I gasp when he grabs my ass and spanks me. "I love it."

His warm breath burns down my neck as he kisses his way up to my ear and licks my earlobe.

I shudder and moan as electric waves ripple through me. My entire body feels like it's on fire. I'm scorching with heat and desperation, needy for his touch and kisses. Good heavens, I want to feel him inside me.

Slowly, he grabs my breast from behind, fondling it gently while whispering dirty words in my ear. "How about I take you from behind while you watch the rest of the world from up here?"

My nipples harden, and I can feel my pussy clenching. I nod. "Yes."

He kisses my neck. "Yes, what?"

I lean into the hardness of his chest and start to grind against his erection. "Fuck me. Please."

I feel his grin behind me before he bends me over, raising my dress and pulling down the G-string panties I am wearing.

"*Cristo*," he whispers as he trails my ass with his fingers.

Goosebumps erupt on my skin. I swear I'll die from the anticipation of his cock inside me.

A mischievous smile plays on my lips when I feel his dick press against my entrance... and then, without any warning, he thrusts into me.

My head rolls back, and I let out a cry. I'm cocooned with pleasure.

He fucks me with slow, steady strokes, spanking me and

gripping my waist so hard that his fingers are digging into my flesh.

I grab onto the railing on the balcony for support as my legs become weaker with ecstasy. Every cell in my body is weeping, begging for him to go deeper. "Yes," I moan, biting my lips. "God, yes!"

He rips down my dress, catching my nipple between his fingers and teasing it hard. I feel pleasure and pain all at once, and I feel my orgasm build.

"Who owns this pussy?" he asks, his voice deep, husky and possessive. That's how he's fucking me, as if he's reminding me he owns me, that I am all his. And God, I love it.

"It's yours," I moan, moving my hips to match his rhythm as he completely devours me.

"I want to hear you say my name, *gattina*," he purrs. "Who owns you?"

"You..." My eyes roll in as my orgasm starts to reach its peak, threatening to rip through me. "I'm Antonio's. My pussy is his."

"Good girl."

He starts to fuck me faster and deeper until my orgasm rips through me. My legs begin to shake, and my body starts to tremble.

Antonio slams into me one more time before he shudders and comes with a powerful groan. His body collapses against mine, but he manages to hold his weight up from his grip on the railing.

He empties inside of me while kissing my back, and he whispers, "You're mine, *gattina*. Mine."

30

ANTONIO

"Salvatore snuck out of the city last night," Dario says, tapping the desk. "I have some of my men looking for him already."

I lean back in my seat and glance at him. "Snuck out of the city?"

I think for a moment. My men have been on guard for days, searching for him. There's no way he could have snuck out unless he had inside help or an ally.

"Do you have any idea where he could have gone?" I ask.

Dario shakes his head. "No idea, but Sicily seems to be the most likely. What do you think?"

Sicily is the least likely option. I have even more connections over there. The old bastard could have gone to Mexico. Even Russia would be more likely to welcome him with open arms than Sicily. "He's not stupid enough to set foot in Sicily."

There's a knock on the door before it creaks open, and Luca walks in.

From his expression, I can already tell what he's about to say. "I know already."

"About Salvatore sneaking out of the country?"

I nod. "Dario's men beat you to sharing the information."

Luca glances at Dario. "Damn! What do we do now, boss?" he asks. "We can track that animal down and kill him when we find him."

I disagree with a shake of my head. I might be quick to anger, but I don't make rash decisions. I only make a move after carefully considering all the options and deciding on the best course of action.

The problem, however, is that I don't have the time. With Vivienne and our unborn baby at risk, I need to get rid of anything that could hurt them. Salvatore is the biggest threat. No one knows what that sneaky bastard is up to.

"We can't hunt him yet."

Both Dario and Luca stare at me with stunned expressions.

"This might be a trap for all I can guess," I explain, pressing a finger to my temple. "Or a distraction. Lead us in another direction while he prepares to strike when we're most vulnerable. Something tells me that asshole hasn't left the city."

It's common sense. The entire city is heavily guarded by men who are on the watch for him. Some of my allies have their men looking for Salvatore as well. Leaving the city would be close to impossible in his situation.

By pretending to leave New York, he thinks we'll lower our guards, and he can escape or attack if he's stupid enough to try.

Dario nods in agreement. "We'll have to split then. I'll have my men find out where Salvatore is... if he's still in the city."

"That will do for now." I shift my attention to Luca. "Call

Lorenzo, have him check every flight and ship that has left the country in the last few days."

"Yes, boss. Is there anything else you'd like me to do?" Luca asks.

"No."

"I'll get to it then." He leaves the office.

Dario goes on about things I don't give a shit about; information about the drugs we supplied to Texas last week and all.

All I can think about is how to keep my family safe.

~

Vivienne's gaze is pinned on me when I look up from my phone. Her brows raise, and her forehead creases with worry. "You haven't touched your food."

I glance down at the grilled chicken breast and mashed potatoes on my plate. She's right; I've barely touched my food. I've been too busy making calls and replying to emails, anything to help me find Salvatore.

I've been that way since Dario told me the news of Salvatore's disappearance this morning. I need to find the bastard before he comes up with a plan that could hurt the people I love and fuck with my entire life.

"Sorry." I drop my phone on the table and grab my fork. "I was busy with work."

Vivienne exhales loudly before she eats a spoonful of her mashed potatoes. She lifts the glass of water to her lips but pauses just before taking a sip. "It's about Salvatore, isn't it?"

I don't try to hide it from her. It's better that she knows the truth so she can be more careful. "He left the city."

Her reaction is perfect for the situation. Her jaw falls

open, and her pupils dilate. "You said you had men looking for him. How could that happen?"

I shrug. "Beats me. I have a feeling he's still in New York, hiding around somewhere."

"What do we do?" she asks, finally sipping the glass of water.

"We?" My mind lights up as an idea forms. "You're all I care about. You'll leave for Sicily until all of this is over."

"Sicily?" She scoffs. "Why the hell do I need to go to Sicily?"

"Because it's the one place I know Salvatore can't reach you." The thought of Salvatore hurting her makes my fists clench. "I'll bring you home as soon as this is over."

She drops her fork. "And if I don't want to go?"

"This is not up for negotiation," I tell her. "You're leaving tonight."

She raises her hand. "Wait! What if I leave in two days? I need to see my father... and Harper. Please."

The way her bright eyes dull with worry makes my chest tighten. I don't want her to leave. Scratch that; I don't think I could function without her here, but I'd rather have her far away and safe than have her near and unsafe.

Still, I can't deny her the chance to see her father and her sister before she leaves. "Fine. I'll get everything ready for you. You leave in two days."

31

VIVIENNE

The diamond earrings in my hands catch my eye as I twist them slightly, tilting them toward the light. They shimmer, a cascade of colors bursting from their facets—fiery reds, electric blues, and glimmering golds dancing like tiny fireworks.

It's the day before I leave for Sicily, and goodness, I still hate the idea of being away from Antonio just as much as I did when he mentioned it at dinner last night.

I'd rather stay here with him—even die with him if I had to—but I know arguing is useless. He made it clear that it wasn't up for negotiation, and nothing I said would have changed his mind. He's just that kind of man who'll do anything to keep his family safe.

I rub a hand over my belly. I've been nauseous all night, and now I'm just anxious. What if he gets hurt while I'm away? Or worse—what if he loses?

No, he can't lose. Antonio just can't lose to anyone. He'll be safe. He has to be. I don't want to imagine a world where he isn't here with me.

I run my fingers over the diamonds on the earrings. "They're beautiful."

Antonio takes them from me and helps me put them on. "They look even more beautiful on you." He kisses the top of my head before pulling back. "They have trackers in them. Don't take them off for any reason."

I smile at how overprotective he's being. "Do you think my papa will hurt me?"

"I just want you safe. I am sure your father had something to do with Dante's death." He pauses and inches closer, wrapping his arm around my waist. "Call me the moment anything happens."

I disagree that my papa will try to hurt me. He's not the best dad in the world, but he'd never try to hurt me. I don't argue with Antonio because he has every right to be wary of my father.

Wrapping my arms around his neck, I peer into his eyes and tell him the words he wants to hear. "I won't take them off, I promise. And I'll call you if anything happens."

He presses a soft kiss to my lips, and then he cups my belly. "I hope you understand why I am doing all of this, Vivienne. You and our baby mean the world to me. I'll lose my mind and burn the world down if anything happens to you two."

Tears blur my vision. "I know. You have to stay safe, too, 'cause if anything happens to you, I'll do more than burn the world."

"I have our child's birth to look forward to, and we're yet to pick out baby names. I won't let myself get killed before I get to do that."

I narrow my eyes on him. "Don't tell me you plan to die after that."

He chuckles. "No, I don't. I'm not dying until I get to raise our kid and grow old with you."

I laugh, but tears stream down my face instead. I've been an emotional mess since I got pregnant. "That is enough for me."

He's about to say something when Luca and the new guy, Angelo, join us in front of the house, where the car I'll be leaving to see my father in is parked.

"We're ready to leave, boss," Luca says.

"Make sure nothing happens to her," Antonio orders sternly. "You know what to do if anything does."

He nods.

Antonio nods back at him, and then he pulls away from our embrace. "I have a meeting soon. I may not be back on time, but I'll have Agatha prepare some of the things you'll need before I leave."

I mouth *"Thank you"* to him.

He opens the back door for me and doesn't walk away until the car pulls out of the mansion.

It takes almost an hour before we get to the Cole mansion. There are guards everywhere as Angelo drives through the driveway, and there are new faces I haven't seen before. I can't tell if Papa is being extra careful, like Antonio, or if something's off.

Angelo and Luca tense in their seats as well. They feel that something's off, too. I can tell from the looks on their faces.

I texted my father last night to let him know I'd be coming this morning, and his reply was short and straightforward. Too short.

I'll be waiting.

That's all he said to me. I wasn't able to reach Harper, but it's Saturday. She's usually home on Saturdays.

Luca pulls up to the entrance, and Angelo hops out to help me out of the car.

I give him a polite, thankful smile. "Thank you. You don't need to come inside with me."

"The boss gave us instructions. We can't let you go in alone," Luca says. "You won't even notice we're here." His shoulder stiffens, and his expression grows colder.

I shake my head. He won't back down if that is Antonio's order, so it's no use arguing with him. "Fine."

The guards by the door inspect us for weapons. They take Luca and Angelo's guns and the knives they had strapped to several parts of their bodies. I find it very strange that my bodyguards need to be inspected in such a manner.

A shiver runs down my spine as we step into the manor. I can't find any of the housekeepers anywhere around the house. It feels like a ghost town.

I exchange glances with Luca and Angelo. "I need to speak with my father."

"Where's his study?" Angelo asks, speaking for the first time since our journey down here.

"Upstairs."

"We're coming with you," he says.

I lead the way to my father's study and knock once before pushing the door open. I'm stunned when I see my papa standing with his back to the door. He's staring at something outside the window.

"Papa?" My legs wobble as I step slowly into the study. Something's off. There's an unspoken tension in the air. "Are you okay?"

He turns around slowly enough to make my heart race. "Vivienne."

I turn around to my bodyguards. "Wait here."

Luca gives my father a suspicious glare and says, "Scream if something happens."

I frown at him. "I'm with my father, Luca. He's not a monster that will eat me alive." I close the door and step closer to my father. "Is something wrong? Where are the maids and Harper?"

He smiles, but it doesn't reach his eyes. His gaze flits to my belly. "You're carrying his child, aren't you?"

Air stalls in my lungs. I take a step back and cover my stomach. "How did you know?"

"Your sister told me." He walks to his desk and settles into the mesh chair. "It slipped out during an argument."

"Dad... It's... I came because I wanted to tell you about it." My scalp prickles, and my stomach won't stop churning. "I love him, Antonio, I mean. I'm in love with him and with your blessings—"

"You're an embarrassment, Vivienne," he says gruffly. "I am ashamed of you, and the bastard you're carrying is no grandchild of mine."

My throat burns, and it's suddenly too hard to say a word. I see how he sees it. I fell in love with my kidnapper and got pregnant. Father has every right to hate me, but my child has done nothing wrong. He doesn't deserve to be insulted just for existing.

"He is not a bastard. He has a father—"

"A father who kidnapped and violated you, Vivienne." He's raising his voice and clenching his fist now. "A father who is an enemy."

"He wouldn't be your enemy if you didn't kill the man who raised him. Don't ever speak about my husband and child like that." Bile creeps up my throat, and the only thing I can bring myself to feel is bitterness. Hatred for this man who is supposed to be my father, yet tried to sell me off for a connection.

All I feel is resentment for this man who has never looked at me with love but tries to bring me down every chance he gets.

He gives a bitter laugh, his eyes darkening with rage. "What will you do? Run off and report me to your darling husband?" He rises to his feet and starts to prowl toward me. "Kill me?"

A wave of unease crashes over me, but I don't step back or show fear. I straighten my spine and keep my gaze on him. "I will if I have to."

He gives me a smug smile. "You won't have to."

I flinch when two gunshots ring outside. I hear Luca groaning, followed by two thudding sounds. Tears gather in my eyes instantly because I know what that sounds like. I understand what is going on.

I whip my head around to face my father. "What the hell did you just do?"

He's standing in front of me now, his tall frame towering above mine. "Remember you betrayed me first, Vivienne."

Those are the last words I hear before everything goes black.

32

ANTONIO

I've called Vivienne's number exactly fifty times. It rang the first twenty times, then went unreachable. Neither Luca nor Angelo is answering.

Something's wrong.

Anger swells in my stomach, mixing with rising panic. This must be what fear feels like—the thought of losing Vivienne is enough to drive me insane.

Lorenzo strides into the living room. He looks frantic as hell as he holds out the tablet to me. "The CCTV in the area shows they arrived at Peter's place," he says. "Two hours later, it shows two of Peter's cars driving out of the same road."

My intestines twist into a knot as I play the video. I can see Vivienne in the backseat of the black Mercedes they left in, but I don't see a glimpse of her in her father's SUV.

Either she... No, it's not possible. Even an animal wouldn't harm its own offspring. There's no way Peter would hurt his daughter.

I pick up my phone from the coffee table and call Peter. It rings three times, but he doesn't answer.

"I think that's all the proof we need," Lorenzo says. "If he took her, then there's a chance he knows where Salvatore is—and that he had something to do with Dante's death."

I nod in agreement. "That's right." I quickly pull up the tracking app I have on my phone. It shows they're headed toward an abandoned port on the outskirts of the city. I put two and two together, and it all makes sense.

This is a trap to lure me out. Salvatore is definitely still in New York, and Peter—that son of a bitch—is willing to sacrifice his own daughter for whatever their mission is. I wonder what he gets out of whatever deal he has with Salvatore.

"We can't waste any more time. Get the cars and men ready. We're going hunting."

Lorenzo's brows furrow. "I can go, boss. It could be dangerous if you—"

"Those bastards have my wife, and they could harm her. I won't sit and wait like a fucking coward while my family is in danger," I growl, raging at the fact that he could suggest something so ridiculous to me. I don't care if I die, as long as I know Vivienne and our baby are safe. That is all that matters to me. "Get the car ready, we're leaving."

"Yes, boss."

Lorenzo starts to leave, and I call Dario.

Dario answers on the first ring. "Brother."

"Salvatore is still in New York. I'll forward the location to you, but I need you to do something first."

"Anything."

"Send some of your men to search Peter's house. Luca and Angelo are down—save them if you can."

I hear Dario shout orders at his men immediately to search Peter's property before he returns to the call. "What are you going to do now?"

"They have Vivienne. I have to go get her." I run up the stairs to the room where I keep my weapons and pack all I can. Knives, as many guns as I can strap to my holster, and bullets.

"Do you need me to do anything?" he asks, his voice heavy with concern.

"If you can, make sure no one leaves the city tonight. Especially not Salvatore or any of his allies."

"I'll do that, man. Be careful."

"Thank you." I hang up and pack a few more weapons for my men.

By the time Lorenzo comes upstairs again, I've packed a bag with everything we need. It'll take hours to get to the port, but I know Peter and Salvatore won't lay a finger on Vivienne before I arrive. She's bait to lure me in, after all. A weakness.

But they're wrong about that. To me, Vivienne is my strength. I'll walk through fire for my wife—and I'm not coming home without her.

33

VIVIENNE

The cold bites at my skin, waking me before I even open my eyes. My head pounds—an unrelenting drumbeat that sends a sharp ache through my skull as I try to sit up. The sharp scent of saltwater fills my nose, mingling with something acrid and metallic.

I blink into the darkness, disoriented. The low hum of engines and the distant crash of waves tell me where I am before my vision clears. The seaport.

Everything is blurry at first—shadows of towering shipping containers stacked like a maze around me. The night air is heavy with the stench of oil and fish, and the flickering orange glow of a distant floodlight makes the shadows dance in eerie patterns.

I shiver, rubbing my arms, and that's when it hits me—my wrists are sore.

I glance down, my pulse spiking as I see the faint red marks on my skin. Rope burns. The memory crashes into me like a wave—my father's voice, cold and sharp, his last words to me before I passed out.

The sting of betrayal bites into my heart like the edge of

a sharp knife. He betrayed me—my father killed my bodyguards and kidnapped me.

My throat burns, but I can't cry now. I need to find a way out of here. I need to save my child. And Antonio... God, I can't begin to imagine how scared he must be right now. He must be going crazy trying to find me.

Resting my hand against the wall behind me, I manage to stagger to my feet, though it's a struggle to stay upright because I'm still drowsy from whatever my father injected me with, and my vision remains blurry.

Still, I have to leave. I have to get back home to Antonio.

"I see you're awake," a voice says in front of me.

I flinch and back up against the wall. No matter how much I squint, I can't make out who the silhouette in front of me is. I can tell he's an older man from his voice and short, round frame.

He's not my father, and there's only one other name that comes to mind. "Salvatore?"

He chuckles. "Smart girl."

Ice trickles through my veins like water. It's truly him—Salvatore. My father really brought me to my husband's worst enemy. "What do you want?"

He shakes his head. "You're smart. I thought you would have figured it out already."

Right. It's Antonio he wants. I am just a bit of bait to get to him. My father set a trap, and I walked right into it like a fool. Now, my husband and unborn child are in danger because of me.

A shiver spirals down my spine. I know our relationship has never been good, but I still believed my father would never hurt me—at least not like this.

"I don't know what you're talking about." I inhale deeply, trying to stay calm. Being rash won't help me in any way.

"Oh, but I think you do," Salvatore drawls, closing the distance between us.

My stomach churns with disgust the closer he gets. He smells like cigarettes and rotten fish. Just how long has he been hiding in this place? "You'll never get Antonio," I spit out. "He'll kill you before you even get a chance to hurt him."

Salvatore presses a knife under my chin, and I stiffen as the cold metal pierces my skin. "Not if I kill you and his unborn child first. Pray that he cooperates, or you'll be dead before daybreak."

"That is enough!"

I look over Salvatore's shoulder to find my father standing several feet away from me. His eyes are bright under the moonlight, but his face is void of any emotions.

Salvatore snarls at me and moves away as my father approaches.

Tears I didn't realize I was holding back spill down my face. "Papa, why are you doing this?"

My father stops in front of me. He gives me a pitiful look and shakes his head. "I worked so hard to get here, Vivienne. I won't let anyone destroy everything I worked for, not even you."

"But..." More tears stream down my face. "I am your daughter. How could you choose material things over me, over your grandchild?"

"Antonio's spawn is not my grandchild, and you're a disappointment, Vivienne. I regret that you're my daughter. Your sister hates me because of you."

An alarm goes off in my head as I realize I haven't seen Harper. "What did you do to my sister?"

"Nothing... yet. You and Antonio will disappear tonight, and everything will go back to the way it should be." He lowers his voice to a whisper. "Your sister will forget you. The world will forget you ever existed."

The pain I feel is almost physical. I throw my hands forward, hitting my father's shoulder and screaming. "You bastard! You're insane. You should have been the one to die and not Mama."

"Your mother deserved everything she got. She wouldn't have died if she hadn't tried to save Antonio's family from me." He grips my shoulders and throws me to the floor.

My eyes widen with shock. "You killed Mama? You're responsible for everything that happened to Antonio's family?"

"His father should never have been Capo. Too bad Dante took the boy and raised him," Salvatore answers this time. "He should have died with the rest of his family."

My heart sinks to my stomach. I feel a lot of things at once—disgust, hatred, anger. I want to kill Salvatore and my father. God, I hate them so much.

I turn to my father, looking into his eyes and pleading, hoping all of this is just a façade.

He doesn't give me the answer I desperately want to hear, though.

"I killed them, Vivienne. Antonio's family, every last one of them. It had to be done. And I killed your mother, too."

My father's voice is calm, too calm, as if he's discussing a business deal rather than ending lives. The weight of his confession presses on my chest, and I can barely breathe.

"You're lying," I whisper, my voice trembling as my knees threaten to give out beneath me. The sea breeze chills the tears streaking my face, but I don't wipe them away. "Tell me you're lying."

He doesn't.

Instead, he turns, his back straight, his hands clasped

behind him like this is just another night at the office. Like he hasn't just shattered my world. "I won't kill you. You're my daughter, after all. I'll kill Antonio, and you'll get rid of that bastard in your stomach, and things will go back to the way it was."

"I'll never get rid of my baby, and I won't let you kill Antonio."

He spares me a glance, and then turns away again. He doesn't respond to anything I say after.

The silence is suffocating, broken only by the distant sound of water lapping against the docks. My head is spinning, my stomach twisting as I try to make sense of what he's just admitted.

Antonio's face flashes in my mind—his dark, piercing eyes, the quiet grief he carries like armor. And now I know why.

A sharp crack shatters the silence—a gunshot.

I flinch, my heart leaping into my throat as the sound echoes through the port, bouncing off the steel walls of the shipping containers.

My father doesn't flinch, but Salvatore does. His eyes bulge as if he's as surprised by the gunshot as I am.

"What the hell is that?"

"Check that," my father orders his men.

They nod and go out to check the source of the sound, but they don't make it out when more gunshots ring, and the men drop dead.

I hold my head, trying not to scream. It's Antonio, I can feel it's him.

My father, Salvatore, and what is left of their men pull their guns, ready to fight.

The chaos is deafening—gunfire cracks through the air, each shot a jolt to my already frayed nerves. I crouch behind a stack of crates, my body trembling as I watch the fight.

I catch a glimpse of Antonio through the haze of smoke and shadows. His men spread out behind him. There's a flash of relief in his eyes when they meet mine.

"Get her out of here!" my father shouts to one of his men.

Salvatore's sharp eyes dart in my direction, and a sick twist of fear churns my stomach. I don't want to go anywhere.

"No!" I scream, my voice drowned out by the sound of the shouts and bullets.

Antonio sees me. His dark eyes lock onto mine for a fraction of a second, his expression hardening with resolve.

"Vivienne!" he yells, his voice slicing through the noise.

"Antonio, no!" I cry out, desperate to keep him from running into the hail of bullets.

But he's already moving, weaving through the firefight like it's second nature, his men covering him as he advances. My heart races as I watch him, terror gripping me. I'm afraid he'll get hurt.

My father steps forward, his gun raised, and everything slows.

"Stay where you are, Mancini!" he growls. "Take one more step, and I'll kill her."

Antonio doesn't stop.

A shot rings out, loud and sharp, and I scream, clamping my hands over my ears as the sound reverberates through the night.

My father staggers back, his face contorts with rage and... pain. Our eyes move at the same time to the gunshot wound in his stomach. There's blood spurting out.

"P-papa."

His eyes go wide with shock as they lock on mine. He doesn't fall to the ground immediately. Instead, he raises his gun at me. "Bitch."

Before he can pull the trigger, Antonio fires at him one more time. He falls to the ground with a thud this time, and soon, he's in a pool of his own blood.

My mind goes blank. I don't know if I should be worried or relieved, but the image of my father lying lifelessly will haunt me forever.

"Fuck!" Salvatore yells. He's only a few steps away from me now, but before he can make a move, Antonio reaches me, grabbing my wrist and pulling me to my feet. His grip is firm but not painful, and the warmth of his touch sends a strange rush of relief through me.

"Come on," he says, his voice low but commanding.

I hesitate, glancing back at my father, who's bleeding out on the cold, concrete floor. His face has gone pale, his eyes almost rolling in.

The next bullet is from Lorenzo, and it goes right into Salvatore's head. The old man convulses for a few seconds before falling to the ground. His death rattle lasts a minute, then he goes still, his lifeless brown eyes peering at Antonio with so much hatred.

Antonio wraps his arms around me, kissing my forehead. "I'm so sorry I came so late."

I'm allowing myself to cry freely now as I wrap my arms around his neck. "No, you came right on time. I'm so sorry I put myself and our baby in danger."

He presses another kiss to my forehead. "What happened is not your fault," he says. "It's okay now. Everything is fine."

I pull back. "Angelo and Luca were shot."

His eyes grow cloudy. "Luca will be fine."

"And Angelo?" I ask, refusing to let myself breathe until I hear that he's fine, too.

"He died."

I collapse against Antonio. "Oh God, this is all my fault. I should have listened to you. I shouldn't have gone to see my papa."

"Shh," Antonio whispers. "You're safe now, and that is all that matters." He cups my face, and I tilt my head up to peer into his eyes. "I thought I would lose you. I was so afraid."

"I thought I would never see you again." I sniffle. "I'm so sorry."

"Don't be." He brings his lips to mine and whispers. "I love you, Viv. I love you so much."

"I love you, too, Antonio."

He claims my lips, kissing me amid the chaos as if our lives depend on it. And maybe it does. Maybe our lives and happiness depend on how much we love each other.

And there is nowhere else I would rather be than with Antonio.

EPILOGUE

It's been three months since the war with Salvatore, and things have finally calmed down. I've reclaimed the remnants of our territory.

Peter somehow survived getting shot twice. He's paralyzed from the neck down. I wouldn't call that living. I call it karma for what he did to his daughters and my family.

Vivienne's laughter draws my attention. She's standing across the field with Harper, Agatha, Ginny, and Mariana, laughing at something Ginny said.

My wife looks breathtaking in her white dress, with the wind ruffling her hair. She looks even more beautiful with her baby bump.

No matter how much time passes, my heart still flutters knowing she's carrying our child—a symbol of our love.

"I'll bet all the money I have that it'll be a boy," Luca says beside me. "I can't wait to teach him how to throw punches and shoot guns."

"My money's on it being a girl," Lorenzo argues. "A little Mancini princess. I'll protect her with my life."

Dario huffs a laugh. "You two are something." He looks at me. "What do you think?"

"I'm not thinking, man." It's impossible to think when my wife looks so goddamn beautiful in that white dress. The only thought on my mind is how to sneak her out of the gender reveal party, rip that dress off her, and make love to her like it's the first time.

Dario follows my line of vision, and a mischievous smile takes up his entire face. "Of course, you're not thinking." He slaps my shoulder gently. "You two are gonna make great parents."

I nod. "We will." And even if I am not such a great father, Vivienne will make a great mom.

Vivienne meets my gaze and waves me over.

I don't think twice as I abandon my friends and start toward her. She's been extra bubbly lately. All smiles and happiness. It's contagious, and I've found myself smiling more, too.

I snake my arms around her waist when I reach her and kiss her lips. "Hey, baby."

She pouts playfully. "Which baby? You have two now."

I smile at her. "How are my two babies doing?"

"Your babies are doing well." She giggles. God, I fall in love with this woman every single day. "It's time to pop the balloon."

"Oh." I'm anxious as fuck right now, but I don't let it show. I don't care whether our baby is a boy or a girl. All I care about is that they're born safely. I hold Vivienne's hand. "Let's do this."

We walk to the table where the oversized black balloon is tied down, floating gently in the breeze. The crowd gathers around us, buzzing with excitement. Vivienne's hand is warm in mine, her grip firm yet comforting.

"Are you ready?" she asks, glancing up at me, her emerald eyes sparkling with joy and mischief.

I nod, my heart racing. "I've never been more ready."

She smiles, squeezing my hand.

Our friends and family gather close—Harper bouncing on her toes, Luca grinning like a kid in a candy shop, and Lorenzo standing as protective as ever. Dario has his phone out, clearly recording every second, while Ginny clings to his side.

Mariana wears a bright smile, one I haven't seen since Dante's death. She looks more than excited about becoming a grandma.

"On the count of three!" Vivienne announces, her voice carrying over the cheerful chatter.

I take the pin, and she hands it to me. Together, we hold it against the taut surface of the balloon.

"One," she starts, her voice trembling with excitement.

"Two," I echo, my gaze fixed on hers instead of the balloon.

"Three!" we shout together, and I press the pin into the balloon.

POP!

Blue confetti bursts into the air, fluttering down like a thousand tiny snowflakes. Gasps and cheers erupt around us, but all I hear is Vivienne's delighted laugh as she throws her arms around me.

"It's a boy!" she squeals, her face lighting up with pure joy. "We're gonna have a boy."

A grin splits my face as I lift her off the ground, spinning her in a circle. "A boy," I repeat, the words tasting sweeter than I could've imagined. A son. I'm going to be a father to a little boy.

I swear I've never been happier than I am at this moment.

Luca pumps his fist in the air. "I knew it! Little Mancini warrior incoming!"

Lorenzo laughs, then looks over at me, sincerity in his voice. "He's going to have the best parents. You'll raise a king."

The rest of the group congratulates us, their excitement palpable, but my focus is only on Vivienne. She's beaming, her hands cradling her growing bump. I place my palm gently over hers, feeling the warmth beneath her skin.

"Our son," I whisper, leaning in to kiss her softly. "Our little prince."

She smiles against my lips, her voice trembling with emotion. "Our family."

In that moment, nothing else matters. The world may have been a battlefield before, but now, it feels like peace. And I'll protect this peace with all I have.

I will gladly lay my life down for my wife and son because they're all that matters to me. They'll be all that will ever matter to me now and forever.

THE END

If you enjoyed *Dark Mafia Heir,* then you'll also like *Dark Mafia Bride*.

(Click Here to get Dark Mafia Bride)

Mirabella is forced to marry the most ruthless mafia boss in the underworld to repay her debts in this gripping arranged marriage, secret baby romance that will leave you yearning for more. *Read Chapter One on the next page!*

34

SNEAK PEAK

Dark Mafia Bride SNEAK PEEK

ETTORE

It's the morning of my wedding.

I don't look like the ruthless mafia boss who rules the underworld.

No matter how fake this marriage might seem, by the end of the day, she'll be my wife.

Until... she's gone.

They call me the Reaper. Feared. Ruthless. Untouchable. I don't save people. I bury them.

. . .

Until she stumbled into my world. Fiery. Untamed. A mess I should've walked away from.

Instead, I rescued her and made her mine—for one night.

One taste of her, and I was addicted.

But danger follows her like a shadow. And I don't leave loose ends.

Marrying her was supposed to be a business deal. One year. No strings.

I didn't expect to crave her. I didn't expect to keep her.

And now that she's carrying my child... She's never getting away.

Yet in the shadows, someone else has set his eyes on her...

And I'll burn the whole world to protect what's mine—even if it means dragging her into my darkness.

MIRABELLA

It's the morning of my wedding.
One that ties me to a man I don't know
...and one I will not attend.
But the devil claimed my innocence...and now I'm pregnant.

It was only supposed to be one night.

A reckless mistake with the most dangerous man who saved me.

Ettore Greco—cold, controlling, and devastatingly irresistible.

A man who doesn't take no for an answer.

THE NEXT MORNING, I ran. But you don't escape a man like Ettore.

HE FOUND me before they could.

Now I'm wearing his ring and carrying his child.

Bound to him by a deal I couldn't refuse.

HE'S my savior and my nightmare. My protector and my captor.

I should hate him.

But when he touches me, I forget everything— Except how badly I want him.

BUT I SHOULD'VE KNOWN that a happy ending was nothing more than a dream for us...

Because someone else was after me...and I needed to protect at all costs the twins growing inside of me.

(CLICK HERE TO get Dark Mafia Bride)

CHAPTER ONE

Mirabella

THE RAIN POURS down in thick, relentless sheets, drenching me as I trudge along the cracked sidewalk. I yank my jacket collar higher, but it's pointless—I'm already soaked to the bone, down to my underwear.

My feet squish with each step inside my everyday shoes —my suede flats— which are slowly being ruined by the downpour. *Just great*, I think. The last thing I need right now is the extra expense of replacing them, even though they're long past their prime.

A shiver rips through me, and I mutter a bitter curse under my breath. I've been forced to smile all night at this awful new job. I can barely stomach it, serving drinks to drunken men, pretending to be polite even when their hands wander where they shouldn't. But I don't have the luxury of quitting. With a mountain of debt crushing me, I'll take any job no matter how degrading just to scrape together enough to pay everything off.

I tighten my grip on the strap of my bag as I approach the alley ahead. My knuckles throb from the pressure, and a flicker of unease crawls down my spine as I reach the entrance of the shortcut.

It's clearly a bad idea to do this. The alley is narrow and dark—dangerous at this hour—but I need to make it to the bus before it leaves, or I'll be stuck standing in the rain for another thirty minutes.

As I step into the alley, I glance over my shoulder, a strange prickle of anxiety gnawing at me. There's no one there—just the steady rhythm of raindrops splashing against the pavement. Still, something feels off.

I'm halfway through the narrow path when shadows shift ahead of me. My heart plummets as three figures step out of the darkness as if they've been lying in wait.

Abruzzi's men.

They move with a swagger that says they own this city, and in a way, they do. Abruzzi has eyes everywhere, and nothing happens without his knowing about it. I understand this because the few times I've met him, he always seems to be aware of even the most inconspicuous details about me—things I believe I hide very well. He knows the thoughts I'm about to voice, and at times he even articulates exactly what I'm thinking.

The three men close in on me, all clad in black, their leather coats slick with rainwater.

One of them flashes a cold, empty grin that doesn't reach his eyes. "Well, well. Look who we have here."

He's the leader of the three, tall and lanky, with a crooked grin that makes my skin crawl. I know him all too well. He's one of Abruzzi's personal righthand men and the person I'd met on the unfortunate day I foolishly stepped into their underground loan shark operation. Back then, I was naïve, clueless about the mess I was getting myself into. I had no idea that borrowing money would mean crossing paths with a dangerous, sketchy man like Abruzzi.

My body freezes, my heart pounding in my ears. But I don't show it. "I told Abruzzi I needed more time."

"Time's up, sweetheart." His voice is as slick as oil on water, and it takes everything in me not to visibly shudder.

My pulse races, the icy rain somehow feeling even colder against my skin. I square my shoulders, forcing steel into my voice. "I told him I'm working on it. He'll get his money. When have I ever backed out on a promise?"

The leader steps closer, his shadow looming over me.

"Yeah, see, that's the problem. Promises don't cut it with the boss anymore. He wants his cash. Now."

"I just need a little more time," I plead, stepping back instinctively, but the three of them fan out, blocking my exit, trapping me in the narrow alley.

"How many times does he have to tell you?" growls the second guy, a thick-necked brute. "The boss gave you a favor by extending the deadline, but that favor's worn thin."

I grit my teeth, anger mixing with fear, my heart beating louder than ever. "I wasn't talking to you."

I realize what a stupid move that is when the leader's grin widens. His sunken eyes gleaming with amusement. "Feisty. I like that."

"Bet she's a wild one in bed." The third guy speaks for the first time. He's bald, buff, and clearly a bonehead. He flexes his muscles like a predator ready to pounce, and the others snicker.

Morons.

"Look," the leader drawls, his tone oozing false sympathy. "We don't wanna make this ugly. But ugly's always an option, y'know? Boss man ain't exactly known for his patience, and you're late. $20,000 too late. You know what happens to people who keep Abruzzi waiting?"

I swallow hard, trying to keep my voice steady, though my hands are trembling.

"He gets mad."

Those words still haunt me—the same ones he said when I stood in front of his imposing mahogany desk in that dimly lit office.

"Pay up early, pretty girl. Don't let me get mad."

"Bingo," the second guy chimes in as if this is some sick game. "Give the lady a prize."

The leader steps closer, his eyes glinting with something

darker. "Maybe we don't gotta take it that far," he muses, his voice low and suggestive. "Maybe there's another way. Something...a little more in my favor."

I know exactly what he means, and my stomach churns. Bile rises in my throat as I instinctively back up, only for my foot to slip in a puddle. I stumble against the cold, wet brick wall of the alley. *Trapped.*

They close in on me, their laughter low and menacing. *This is bad. Really bad.*

"I-I'll get the money. I swear..."

"Of course you will," the second guy cuts in, smirking. "We just want a little payment for making us come all the way here to look for you."

My body shakes with fear, and I hate it. I hate how helpless I feel. How a desperate move to save my mother's life has led me straight into this nightmare.

The leader steps even closer, his cronies flanking him on either side, cutting off any escape. He reaches out, his fingers grazing my cheek. "Don't you worry, it'll be quick and painless," he whispers.

I clench my jaw, summoning whatever scraps of courage I can find. "You think I'm just going to let you?"

Their cruel laughter fills the narrow alley, echoing off the walls. "What're you gonna do, princess? Take us all on?" the leader taunts. "I'd love to see you try. May even make this a little more fun."

My hand tightens around the strap of my bag like it's some kind of shield, though it feels utterly useless. My mind races, searching for a plan, anything, but all I feel is the crushing weight of fear closing in.

And then, through the relentless pounding of the rain, I hear it—the low, unmistakable hum of an engine. The three men snap their heads toward the sound, and I know this is my only chance. My only way out.

Before they can react, I slam my knee into the leader's groin with every ounce of strength I have.

A groan escapes his lips as I tear myself from the wall, sprinting toward the alley's entrance. At least, I try to. Before I can take three steps, his large hand clamps down on my arm, yanking me back.

"You fucking bitch! Now you've gone and made a real big mistake," he snarls, slamming me hard against the wet brick wall.

The force knocks the wind out of me, and panic surges through my veins. I know in this moment there's no escape. He's mad now, and I'm completely trapped.

I bite back a sob as I feel his hand tighten around my arm as the other drifts downward, grazing my thigh. I want to scream, to fight back, but all that comes is a choked gasp. His hand creeps higher, brushing the hem of my dress just as the glare of headlights slices through the darkness.

"Who the fuck is that?" the leader snaps, his eyes narrowing.

I blink, focusing on the sleek black car now parked at the alley's mouth. The door swings open, and a man steps out. He's tall, broad-shouldered, and his perfectly tailored coat is immaculate despite the rain that has soaked through everything else.

There's something almost unnatural about how untouched he looks by the weather.

I can't properly make out his face as he steps in front of the car. All I can see is the silhouette of a tall man with long, curly hair that stops at his shoulders.

His face is hidden, swallowed by the light behind him. He moves with easy confidence, not caring about the rain soaking his pristine state. Every step deliberate and unhurried, as if he owns the very ground beneath his feet.

A chill slithers down my spine as I wait, unsure of what's coming next.

The second guy's face drains of color as soon as he spots him. And I don't know if that's a good or bad thing.

"Shit, Elia," he breathes. "It's The Reaper."

The Reaper? Who the hell is that?

The leader—Elia scowls, but even he can't hide the flicker of fear in his eyes. "What the fuck is he doin' here?"

I don't know who this man is, but the way they react tells me everything I need to know. This is no rescue, no guardian angel. He's here for something else, something darker.

The Reaper—or whatever ridiculous name they've given him—stalks toward us, his footsteps echoing on the wet pavement. His eyes, dark and unreadable, flick over me for the briefest of moments, but it's enough to make my skin prickle. His attention shifts to the men surrounding me, and the air in the alley thickens.

A sick silence falls. No one moves, no one speaks, but I can feel the weight of a decision hanging in the balance.

And then, without warning, he reaches inside his coat.

The tension snaps like a wire pulled too tight.

"You've got five seconds to walk away," he says to the men, his voice steady, almost bored. "Unless you want to end up dead."

He says it like he means it. The gravity of his words wraps around me like a shroud, and I exhale shakily as Elia's hand leaves my thigh. He squares up to The Reaper, his earlier bravado flickering back to life.

"We don't take no orders from you,"

The Reaper's lips curl into a slow, dangerous smile. "No? Pity."

Then everything unfolds in a heartbeat. A glint of metal catches the light, a swift slice cuts through the air, and in an instant, Elia clutches his neck, crimson gushing over his fingers.

"Fuck," One of the men screams, lunging toward The Reaper as the leader collapses to the ground.

I watch in a mix of horror and awe. This man embodies his nickname. He moves with the grace of a predator, lethal and precise. The sound of his knife carving through flesh blends with the relentless patter of rain.

The impact of fists on skin, the sickening crack of bones, the groans and curses—it's all brutal, efficient, and terrifyingly quick. Within moments, all three of Abruzzi's men lie sprawled across the wet pavement, lifeless, just as he had promised.

I stand frozen, my heart racing, staring at the lifeless bodies of the men who'd threatened to do unspeakable things to me just minutes ago. My chest heaves, the adrenaline coursing through my veins like wildfire.

The Reaper strides over the bodies as if they're nothing more than trash. He stops in front of me, his dark eyes gleaming under the streetlight. "You're welcome."

I feel a tumult of emotions—fear, relief, guilt—welling up inside me. Swallowing hard, I straighten my back, lifting my chin in defiance. "I didn't need your help."

Although his face remains partially obscured, I can make out the sharp angles of his jaw, the dark stubble that gives him an edge, and the subtle tilt of his lips as he smiles, a blend of arrogance and amusement.

"Is that right? Because from where I was standing, you were about five seconds from being raped."

Rape.

The word strikes me like a physical blow, stealing the breath from my lungs. I swallow hard, my heartbeat thundering in my ears as the reality of what could have happened sinks in.

I try to speak, but my voice fails me. He studies me in silence, inching closer with an air of casual confidence.

"I take it you were heading home from work," he drawls in a low voice.

I hate the sound of his voice—the way it makes my heart skip a beat. For some stupid reason, my brain stubbornly bypasses the fact that he just killed three men and focuses instead on the striking features of his face.

I glare up at him, trying to suppress the flutter in my stomach as I catch the dark glint in his eyes. "Why do you care? Why are you even here?"

His gaze sweeps over me, assessing every detail of my drenched skin as if he can see right through me. "I was bored."

A disbelieving chuckle escapes my lips. Of course, he was. Whoever this man is, he's infinitely more dangerous than Abruzzi.

Before I can muster a retort, he grabs my hand—not roughly, but with enough firmness that I don't even think about resisting—and pulls me toward his car. "Come on."

"I'm not going anywhere with you."

His smirk returns, dangerous and enticing. "You're shivering. At least let me get you out of this rain before you freeze to death."

I don't argue this time, mostly because my body betrays me with a violent shiver. I follow his lead, doing a bad job at ignoring the way his skin feels against mine.

When we reach his car, he opens the passenger door for me to slip inside.

The warmth envelops me immediately, the leather seats plush beneath me. He slides in beside me, his presence filling the small space with an intensity that makes it hard to breathe. The heavy rain drums against the roof, and our breaths mingle in the confined air.

"I'll take you somewhere to warm up," he says, starting the engine. His voice is still smooth, but there's an edge of something darker lurking beneath the surface.

He drives me to a small, intimate restaurant tucked away from the main streets—a hidden gem you only discover if you know where to look. The lights inside are dim, casting a golden glow over dark wood tables and plush leather booths. The air is rich with the aroma of spices and something mouthwatering sizzling in the kitchen.

We take a seat near the window. With him positioned opposite me, I take in his face fully for the first time. Damn. He's handsome. He resembles a fallen angel...or perhaps the devil himself. With hazel eyes narrowed into slits, sharp angles and contours defining his face, and long black curly hair cascading over his forehead, he looks almost unreal.

This entire situation feels surreal. Him arriving just in time to save me, him dispatching three men in less than a minute, and us seated here as if it's just another ordinary night.

"Are you in shock?" he asks casually.

I wrap my hands around the steaming bowl of soup the waitress sets down, allowing the heat to seep into my frozen fingers. Sitting across from me, he leans back in his seat, watching me with that same unreadable expression.

"I asked you a question."

"Do you always have to get your way in every situation?" I blurt out.

"Yes. And I think you're in shock."

I roll my eyes. "I'm not in shock. What's the big deal? I just witnessed three men get murdered right before my eyes—three men who would have raped me, as you generously pointed out. They could have killed me afterward, too. Now they're dead, and I don't know if I should feel relieved or guilty. But what can I say? I'm alive, so everything is just peachy!"

He stares at me for a beat before laughing. And god, it's such a beautiful sound. I hate it when he stops.

"What's your name?" he asks.

I sigh. "Mirabella."

"Mirabella," he repeats, testing my name on his lips. The way he says it sends a pleasant shiver down my spine.

"The men who took me were terrified when you showed up. That's before you killed them..."

I can't believe I'm talking about murder so casually.

Dark humor flickers in his eyes as he observes me carefully.

I swallow before asking, "Who exactly are you, Reaper?"

"A businessman."

"What's your real name?"

He eyes me for a few seconds, and I feel my breath hitch under his heated gaze.

"Ettore," he finally replies.

Ettore. I don't know why, but the name suits him.

"Your surname?"

He chuckles. "My first name is all you need to know, Bella."

Bella. A feeling I can't describe revels through me at the nickname.

"You're a little too vague for my liking," I muse. "I need to know more about the man who killed three men and saved my life."

His lips quirk. "And you're a little ungrateful for someone who needed saving," he counters.

I can't help the small huff that escapes me. "Touché. So do you do this often?"

"Do what often?"

"Save random girls in the rain and take them to restaurants afterward?"

His eyes glint with amusement and something else I can't quite decipher. "Just you."

"Do you flirt with them afterward?" I ask, deliberately sidestepping the fact that I'm fishing for information about whether this gorgeous man is involved with anyone.

What are you doing, Mirabella? This man is a murderer.

I shouldn't even be sitting here with him.

This man saved your life. Yes. You wouldn't be here without him.

"Just you, Mirabella," he drawls, this time putting more weight on my name, his eyes locking onto mine with a piercing intensity.

It's too intense, too deep. I look away, reaching for a spoon and scooping some of the chicken carrot soup into my mouth.

There's something about him that draws me in. Maybe it's the way he carries himself—so calm, so in control, even in the face of danger. Perhaps it's the way his gaze lingers on me—just a little too long, intense, and focused. He makes me feel things I've never experienced before, feelings I shouldn't be having at this moment.

But then I find myself wondering, *Why not?*

Why not take a risk for once? Why not do something for

myself instead of scraping by day after day struggling for everyone else? I could have died today. Hell, I almost did. And here I am, sitting across from a man who's likely the most dangerous person I've ever met, and yet I feel safe...and aroused.

I'll never see Ettore again. He seems like someone I could never stand a chance of bumping into on a normal day. After tonight, I'll return to my pathetic life moving from one dreadful work shift to the next.

Maybe it's the thrill of narrowly escaping death or the excitement of having the most gorgeous man I've ever seen staring at me in this way, but I lean forward, my voice soft as I blurt out, "I think I want to have sex with you."

(Click Here to get Dark Mafia Bride)

Printed in Great Britain
by Amazon